THE KINGDOM TRIALS

THE COMPLETE SERIES

ABIGAIL GRANT

FANTASY & PARANORMAL ROMANCE

Thank you to my amazingly supportive husband and my little human pups that keep me energized and always on the move.
I love you all.

Contents

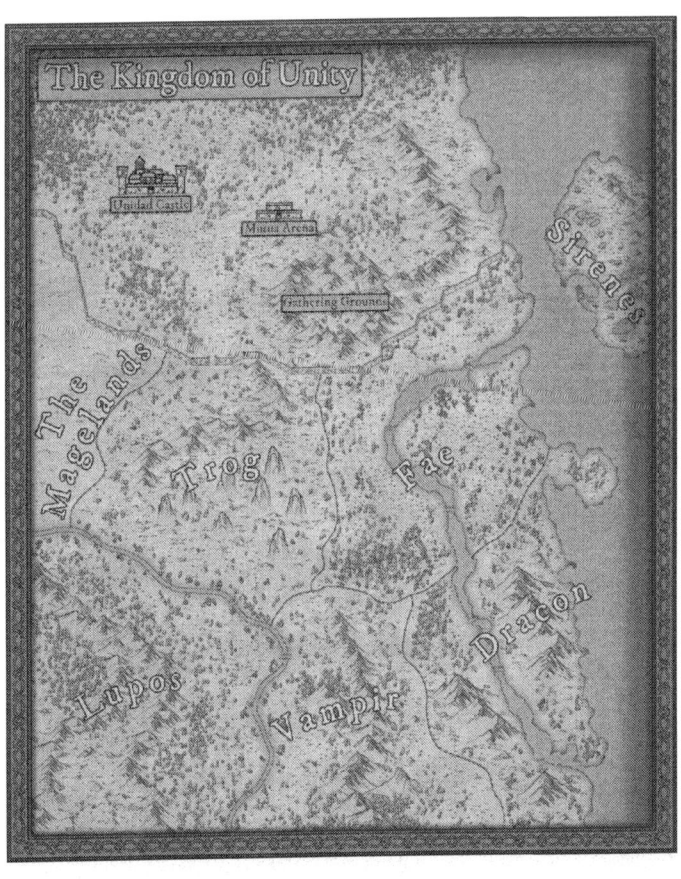

PART 1

A TRIAL OF RUIN

CHAPTER 1

✦←→✦

Nyomi

My knee-high laced boot lands like a feather against the soft dirt of the deserted Fae kingdom. I've never had much trouble sneaking through the forest, silent and invisible. Though, lately the animals seem to pick up my scent before I can get within range. Another soft step, and I spot the large hare. He's fast, but he hasn't caught onto me yet.

I knock the long hand-carved arrow, and draw the bow string to my cheek, steadying my excited breath. *Now I've got you, cute little sucker.*

The hare sits back with his ears high and alert, listening for the dangers that surround the dense wood. I hold my breath, ready to release the arrow with my exhale, when my stomach betrays my position with a loud rumble. It has been nearly three days since my last meal, and my body is done being fine with it.

The hare darts off as I let the arrow fly, and it hits the ground a good two feet behind the animal. "Dammit!"

I fall back against a thick oak tree and curse the universe for working tirelessly against me this week, but what's new? My whole life has been a struggle, so I can't expect any different just because it's my nineteenth birthday.

"Happy Birthday, Ny," I whisper to myself as I retrieve the arrow. If Dad were here, we'd be eating like royalty, or at least well-fed peasants. Now I'm going to have to venture into Trog, the kingdom of the trolls, but it's significantly better than the other alternative, which is the dragon shifter kingdom of Dracon. Those guys are ferocious, and love playing with fire a bit too much.

Dad was the best at making friends with the other lands, but he passed away two years ago. He was killed just days after the two of us got captured by King Duras' patrolmen. That's the thing about living off the desolate land of Fae. Thanks to the faerie's all being killed or banished to the mortal realm, the land is free for the taking, as long as the king's men aren't sweeping the area.

I was able to escape the king's dungeons the day after Dad died, but not without scars to constantly remind me of the time spent with the wolf guards. I have no love for the wolves, or the wolf king for that matter. He thinks wolves are the superior race, born and bred to rule over all six kingdoms for eternity. As a wolf shifter myself, I can't say I dislike the abilities it gives me, but feeling superior just isn't what Unity is about. At least, the Kingdom of Unity isn't *supposed* to be that way.

I stop through my camp as I journey on toward Trog, and I switch out the bow and arrow for my trusty sword, *Theo*. It's nearly as long as my leg, but it has always felt right against my hip. I named the weapon after my father, Theodore. He always had my back, and I know the sword does too.

It's an all evening hike before I reach the border between Trog and Fae. The sun is dropping behind the mountains and my black clothes and black hair help me to stay hidden. I scan the land boundaries for any patrols, but the coast is clear, so I dip into the untamed wilderness.

It's one of the things I love most about trolls. They don't give a damn about anything other than food and family. If a stranger encroaches on their land, they feed them and send them on their way, especially my good friend Bellona.

I spot Bellona's moss-covered cottage, resting aside from the main town, and my heart feels instantly lighter. The elderly woman has known my father since he was young, wandering through the six lands, and she has always taken me and him in when we needed it. I know she'll happily feed my grumbling belly, even though I hate to risk her by being here.

Of course, the woman's incredible nose catches my scent before I even reach her front porch and she dives out the creaky door to lift me into her burly arms. "Oh, my sweet Nyomi! It has been too long."

I grumble against her bosom where I can easily be suffocated, and she sets me back on my feet. "I have told you, Bellona. Please just call me Ny. My name is that of a fugitive, and if they find me, I'll surely be killed." I look up at her purple irises and dark gray curls. The woman is like any other, only she's thick and incredibly strong. I sigh. "As a matter of fact, they'd kill you for even associating with a tainted blood like me."

I turn to leave, thinking better of my decision to come here, but Bellona grabs my arm and drags me into her home. "You sit down, skinny baby, and eat or I'll force feed you myself."

She plops me into a large wooden kitchen chair and drops a plate of crumble bread in front of me. My mouth waters and it takes real concentration to breathe between mouthfuls as I shovel the bread in.

Bellona laughs boisterously and throws down a handful of dried deer meat beside the bread. *Oh, I'm in heaven!*

"You are an angel, Bellona," I say through mouthfuls, looking much like a chipmunk storing food in its cheeks. She sits her large frame beside me in a chair matching mine and her amused smile stares back at me while I drown in the nutrients my body needs.

I finally feel sated enough to catch up with my old friend and I grab her hands in my much smaller ones. "Hey, Bell. How have you been? The warm season is nearly over and I can help you with whatever you need to prepare for the cold."

Bellona shakes her head. "I have it all covered, dear. All I want for you is to remain safe and away from the nasty patrolmen." She scrunches up her nose as she strokes her thumb along the faded scars on my knuckles. "And maybe for you to find a man to keep your nights warmer."

I snort loudly. "Oh boy. A man is not in my near future, Bell. Or distant future either."

"Everyone has a soulmate, Nyomi. You are a wolf shifter, after all. You must have a *fated mate* out there."

I shake my head. "I love you, but you are wrong. I'm only half of a wolf on my mom's side. Dad was something different." *Something different.* If only Dad had told me *what* that something was. To him it didn't matter, though. I would still always be tainted with my mixed blood. An abomination. Unwanted by the kingdoms.

Bellona sees my face fall and she reaches her rough hands out to hold my cheeks. "Hey. Do not let your wild mind tell you whatever negativity it's spewing. Your dad *was* something different, but whatever it was, he was the best of the best, and you are just like him." She drops my face before continuing. "And I do believe there's a handsome man out there for you. A true soulmate who will accept you, no matter what *blood* is in your body."

I nod, trying to believe what she says, but I know better. My wolf hasn't even come out yet, because she knows the truth. I'm a lone wolf, and I will always stay that way.

⊷ ⊶

Cazimir

Clio side-steps to the right, her small feet impressive and quick as she circles me with a sharp glare darkening the green in her eyes. I flex the muscles in my biceps, gripping tightly to the hilt of my sword, showing her who is clearly the strongest in our ongoing battle.

Clio is unimpressed as usual, not missing a beat as she lunges forward and swings the long blade of her sword, slicing through the fabric of my white dress shirt.

"Ay, little sis," I shout at her, leaving my fighting stance to examine the hole now flashing my abdomen to the world. "This is my best shirt that you just ruined!"

My younger sister grins at me, happy with the mess she caused. "Oh, Caz. Mother is going to have an absolute fit when she sees that." She laughs, not concerned for my wellbeing in the slightest.

Honestly, I'm not worried either. Mom may have the mouth and temper of a pirate, but she is a saint. I'll just need to swing through the kitchens and grab her a blueberry muffin before I hand over the mangled cloth for her to fix.

I sheath my sword in my leather belt before reaching toward Clio and rubbing my knuckles in her dark blonde hair. She growls at me and swats my hand away, glaring again.

"Do you have to always do that? I can't have my hair a mess before going to the west wing. It's bad enough to be down in this dirty gym sparring with my rowdy brother. If anyone found out I wasn't a perfect lady, I'd be sent to Lupos to live with the packs."

I scoff. "Come on, Clio. I'd kill to be out of this castle and living off of the land out there with the wolves. A wolf shouldn't be caged in a place like this, ruled over by our father."

Clio lays her gold-hilted sword on the long wooden weapons table before unpinning her poofy dress skirt from her waist and fixing her messy hair. She comes down here to learn fighting techniques from me in the early mornings like this. It's a passion of hers to use weapons, and she's amazing at it, but she's only seventeen and princess to the king and queen of Unity. In Dad's eyes, it's not proper for the princess to fight when she can learn how to bolster our image instead.

As for me, being the prince of Unity, I am to focus on my strength and battle techniques for the upcoming Kingdom Trials. Every twenty years, two persons of royal blood from each of the six lands are meant to fight for the title of king or queen of all of the combined kingdoms. My father won the last trials, and he expects me to win this one. In fact, wolves have won the last two Kingdom Trials, so it's believed that our kind will continue to conquer.

If only I was interested in winning.

Clio punches me in the arm, getting my attention. "What are you stressing over, brother? You look tired."

I shake my head. "The Kingdom Trials are only two weeks from now. I'm hoping I won't be chosen."

"Caz, the mages' magic chooses the strongest royal blood holders from each land. Don't you think you're the strongest of the royal wolves? I know cousin Darius isn't going to be chosen."

We both laugh at that. Darius is a year younger than me and one of the worst fighters in Lupos, royal or not. The only other wolves with strength matching mine would be the Magnus Pack, but they're peasants. It's not fair in the slightest.

I pull my leather vest over my torn shirt and shrug. "Well, hopefully the second wolf chosen will be worthy of the throne. Then I can just help their sorry ass all the way to the win and return to our home land."

Clio shakes her head with a full-on eye roll. "You have so much potential, big brother. I hope someday you learn to live up to it."

Maybe, but not today.

CHAPTER 2

←—→

Nyomi

I slip out of my boots and dip my toes into the cold rushing water of the crystal clear creek. "Mmmm." I sigh and relax against the feel of the stream. I've always loved being in water, especially swimming in the clean rivers and streams that flow through Fae.

I tilt my head back against the morning sunshine and let the rays soak into my beige skin. I wish the warm season would last forever, but it's quickly coming to a close. It also means less animals will be out and about for me to hunt, and that thought scares me more than anything.

Thankfully, my visit with Bellona set me up with four days of food. That woman just can't send me away without packing a bag of goodies to fill my belly. Now, I've gone through all of Bellona's cooking and am back to eating off the land.

I've never been to this section of Fae as it's much farther south than my father liked to go. The wildlife is vibrant, a perfect place to try and secure a meal. Sadly, it's almost too close to the Kingdom of Vampir, and the bloodsuckers don't take trespassing lightly.

I take one last look at the area, knowing I can't stay, before slipping my boots back on and dusting my black pants off. A crunching noise has my head whipping to the left and I freeze completely.

The sound comes again, and whoever or *whatever* is walking toward me has no worries about being stealthy. That could be a good thing, or a terrible thing. I grab the hilt of my sword, ready to draw it out and fight if necessary.

Hard-hitting footsteps approach me and two tall figures immerse from the green trees. My heart launches to my throat, getting lodged there momentarily. *The king's patrolmen.*

The two burly men stand side by side, clearly wolves by the musky scent of them, along with their rugged appearance. I step back, drawing my long sword as I've done a hundred or more times since Dad bought it for me.

"I'm just passing through. I mean no harm to the land of Fae." I try to make excuses for myself, but it's clear that I don't belong to any of the kingdoms. I don't wear any defining colors or have any distinct features. I'm nobody.

The smaller man crosses his arms and his chocolate brown eyes scan my body from head to toe. "Are you Nyomi Mailon?" He's less than impressed.

I draw my chin back, shocked by the question. Nobody knows my last name. "Why are you looking for this woman? What has she done?"

The guard scoffs. "Well, if you're not Nyomi, then that's none of your damn business, is it?"

I take a step back, preparing to run. "You're absolutely right, sir. It's none of my business so I'll just be heading home now." I turn to leave but the guards are fast.

The taller guard grabs my scarred arm in one of his beefy hands, and he stares down at the long-healed gashes. "You are a fugitive, are you not? I have never heard of a royal fugitive."

I try to yank my arm free with little luck. "I'm not a royal." I spit at the ground by the man's boots and he winds back to strike me, but his partner stops him.

"Joff!" He yanks the tall guy's arm back, making him release me. "Whether she looks like a royal or not, she was chosen. Harming her would be an offense."

The gentler patrolman looks at me with his face much kinder than his buddy, Joff's. "My name is Bastian, and I am certain that you're Nyomi Mailon. There is not another soul for miles in all directions and we were told the woman we're looking for has black hair and would be at this location. You have to come with us immediately."

He sticks a gloved hand out to me and I scan his handsome face for any deceit. He seems genuine and I know he's not lying, but I can't be taken back to the dungeons. I refuse to be beaten and molested all over again. Just the thought of what could await me has my stomach turning and anger flaring in my chest.

I spin to run, but my whole body stills when Bastian calls out to me again. "You have been chosen to compete in the Kingdom Trials! Running will do you no good."

I slowly turn back around, not taking my hand off of the hilt of Theo. "What do you mean I've been chosen? The trials are for royal descendants only. I'm not royal, nor do I have any family who is. It's impossible."

The jerk, Joff, rolls his eyes. "Clearly it's possible if we were called by King Duras to come fetch one of the contestants in the land of Fae. The mages made the decision last night. They are never wrong."

I close my eyes in frustration. This has to be some kind of trick. They just want me to come without a fight and I'll surely be hanged by tomorrow morning. I groan and throw my head back. If it's true, and I have the chance to fight for the throne of Unity, I could make changes that will protect people like me.

I find Bastian's kind brown eyes and stare intently into them. "The mages called for Nyomi Mailon? To fight for the wolves for the Unity Kingdom throne? You are certain?"

The Kingdom Trials come around every twenty years. I wasn't alive during the last trial, so I don't know much about it. All I know is that royal blood must flow through the contestant's bodies. Could I have royal blood? Maybe distantly?

Bastian stares back into my eyes, unblinking. "I swear it with my life, madam. You are to fight for wolf-kind, to be our queen." He's telling the truth. I sigh and hold my hand out for Bastian to take. He grips my hand and nods. "Good. Well, Nyomi, prepare to meet your king. He won't know what to make of you."

♦← →♦

Cazimir

"Did you hear what I said, son?" Dad is standing on the front steps of the castle with me, a few places above myself as usual.

I nod because I did hear him correctly. I've been chosen by the mages to compete in the Kingdom Trials. The meeting was held last night in the gathering grounds. Only the twelve mages and the leaders from each land are able to attend such important events. I imagine the kings and queens of the six lands, minus Fae, are telling their sons, daughters, nieces, or nephews about their place in the trials.

Now's my turn. I've been training for this my entire life, and I still had hopes that the mage magic would pass me up.

"Yeah, Dad. I heard you. Who was the other wolf?"

He shrugs, a strange motion for him. "I honestly don't know the young lady, and I thought I knew all of the royal families." He pauses as he disappears into a silent thought. "Anyway, her name is Nyomi Mailon and she is nineteen. I sent Joff and Bastian to find her. Turns out she was located by the mages in Fae."

I'm taken aback by that. "A Lupos royal in the desolate land of Fae? Are we sure she wasn't chosen for the faeries? I've never heard of the wolves breaking your rule like this."

I can't help the intrigue that flares inside of me. Whoever this woman is, she's brave. Maybe she will be the one to win the trials and rule. I wouldn't mind that at all.

Dad shakes his head. "She is not Fae. She was chosen for the wolves, and the faeries will not be entered into the trials this year. Hopefully they all stay in the mortal realm, whatever's left of them anyways."

My father hates the faeries because of their attempt at attacking Unidad Castle and overthrowing him. According to the Fae queen, Dad wasn't worthy of the throne, and it caused a war between the wolves and the Fae when I was just a child. The wolves won, with the support of the other kingdoms, and many of the faeries were killed. The survivors were cast out to the mortal realm, not allowed back.

Still, I never imagined they wouldn't be participating in the Kingdom Trials when they came around again. Now, there will only be ten of us for the first time in history.

I run my hands through my hair, exhausted already at the thought of trying to be the perfect prince in front of the kingdoms. Dad pats me on the back with determination in his eyes that looks more like a blood lust.

"One week from today, son. You will show all of Unity what a true and worthy royal is capable of. Whoever this wolf girl is will have to fall in line, or she will be our enemy. Only you can rule Unity, Cazimir."

Only me.

I nod to my Dad as he turns to leave, heading back through the large steel doors of the castle I've called home my whole life. He thinks I'll be the next king, but I'm not about to follow in my cruel father's footsteps. To all of Unity, King Duras is powerful and just, but to those who really know him, he's nothing more than a power hungry monster.

I run down the rest of the castle steps and dive into the forest that snakes around the side of the building. I let my wild side take over as I shift into wolf form, reveling in the freedom of what I feel is my true self.

My four legs hit the earth hard, pushing me forward at speeds that make me feel like I'm flying. There's nothing else comparable to this feeling of connecting with the land, and the total peace it brings. The trials will try to take my freedoms from me, but I refuse to give in. I'll just have to do whatever it takes to make this Nyomi woman the future queen of Unity.

CHAPTER 3

✦← →✦

Nyomi

The wall surrounding the castle grounds towers over me. I can't believe I'm coming back to this place, and willingly. Every nerve in my body is screaming out to me to turn and flee back to my home, but there's no point. I have nowhere to go and nobody to watch my back. Bellona would be punished for associating with me, so I can't even run to her.

The last time I was brought to Unidad Castle, I was in chains, with my father chained by my side. And only for the fact that I'm a half-breed. It's said that a mixing of races to have children causes the bloodline to become tainted. It's a crime against the kingdom to go against nature, but that's me, a tainted blood, an abomination… and somehow also a royal? It doesn't make a lick of sense.

I remember my father's voice when we were dragged side by side through the large wall. *"I'll be beside you, Ny. Whatever happens, just remember that you're meant for greatness and this isn't the end."*

Could this be the greatness that Dad promised me? Maybe he knew that I would end up here. I release a long and heavy breath as the iron gates swing open with a loud creaking sound. My escorts, Joff and Bastian, told me that we'll need to enter the castle in the dark, hidden.

Apparently, my tight black outfit and unwashed hair isn't appropriate for when they announce me as one of the trial participants. I don't give a damn about starting some scandal. I only came here to find out where I came from, and if I really do have royal blood. And if I can win the trials, I'll do anything to ensure nobody gets treated as I have. Sneaking around in the dark isn't a new concept for me, but hiding the real me isn't something I'm used to. I can't step on anyone's toes just yet, though. I need solid answers.

It's black out, with barely a crescent moon to light our way up the long stone path toward the high castle walls. The dark red brick stretches high into the night sky, looking like a towering monster waiting to swallow me whole.

Flashbacks flutter in and out of focus in my mind, remembering seeing the castle from where the guards dragged me from the woods and down into the underground dungeons. I rub at the scars along my arms, feeling the ache of torture all over again.

Bastian and Joff stop in front of the steps leading up to the castle doors. Bastian turns to me and must see the panic in my eyes because he steps closer and grips my shoulders gently.

"Are you alright? Most first-time visitors to Unidad Castle have smiles on their faces. You look like you may be sick."

I shake my head. "This isn't my first time here. Though, the last time I only saw the darkness of the dungeons."

Bastian's brown eyes open wide and his eyebrows rise dramatically. "So, you really are a fugitive?" He looks at my marked-up arms. "And it's our people that did this to you? Patrolmen like Joff and I?"

I clench my jaw shut, trying to remain calm and strong. I can't let these men see me as weak and tortured. "It was nothing. They'll see the error of their ways soon enough."

Bastian steps back and looks like he wants to smile. "That's why you came willingly isn't it? For revenge on some asshole guards who were just following rules?"

I shrug and comb my fingers through my admittedly messy hair. Maybe I do need to freshen up. "I don't have revenge on my mind, Bastian. Don't worry about that, but I would like to know if I should go rest in a dungeon or if there is a particular place you'd like me to stay while I'm here."

Joff snorts behind Bastian and continues past the front steps toward the side of the building. "Come. You have a room to your very own, fit for a future queen."

I jog to catch up to his long strides. "So you think I'll win? What about the other wolf chosen? Are they any good?"

Joff laughs humorlessly. "The other wolf is the prince of Unity. He is the most likely candidate to win the throne and follow in his father's footsteps."

I want to be the one to laugh at that. "So, this prince also captures young women and tortures them before killing their father in front of their eyes?"

Bastian steps closer to me, looking angry now. "Watch it, Nyomi. Prince Cazimir is honorable and strong. He's not..." he trails off.

"He's not what? Not like his ruthless father?" The men both stay silent as we stop beside a wooden door on the side of the castle. "Right, can't talk trash about your king. You know, I may be an orphan living off the deserted land of Fae, but I still read and hear things about *your* king."

Joff doesn't respond, but he turns toward the door and knocks twice. The door is pushed open from the other side by a thinner guard with gray eyes. He looks me up and down, surprise lighting his handsome face. *Yikes, does the king only hire hot guys?*

The guard looks between me and the other two men without a word and he steps aside for us to enter. I rest my hand on my trusty sword, not a fan of new and unknown places. Bastian steps beside me and grips my elbow to lead me down a long hallway lit with flickering lanterns. Joff stays behind so I wiggle my fingers at him in a goodbye, and he only frowns as he watches me go. *I won't miss you either, ass.*

Bastian looks down at where I cling to my sword while we walk. "Are you planning on using that tonight?"

I shake my head. "I don't plan on it, but I can't say I wouldn't if the need arose."

He snorts. "Hey, I like the honesty. I think the royal family will enjoy having you here. I know you might not have the warmest feelings toward them, but they're not all what you'd expect. Try a little trust."

I raise my eyebrow at the kind patrolman. "You act as if you care for them."

We climb a winding staircase and the ceiling raises a long way to open up into a much nicer hall with ornate paintings along the walls and intricate gold mouldings wrapping around rows of doors and hanging chandeliers. I imagine I look a lot like a child staring up at a hall of candy as I stand in awe at the artistry.

Bastian opens one of the first doors and gestures for me to enter. Before I can obey, he grabs my arm again. "Nyomi, to answer your question, I do care for the family that lives in this castle." He locks eyes with me, his expression serious as he leans in close enough that I can smell sweetness on his breath. "I won't hesitate to protect them with my life. Do you understand?"

I nod, understanding completely. "I know what a threat is, Bastian, and in all honesty, I respect you for it."

He smiles wide as he leans back from me, letting go. "Great. Now, I hope we can be friends, as strange as it may seem. Get some rest, and for the love of Unity, take a bath." He scrunches up his nose for effect and I smack him in the arm before entering my bedroom.

Interesting... I've never had a bedroom before.

◂─ ─▸

Nyomi

I've been pacing this extremely fancy bedroom for over two hours. After entering the room, I immediately found the attached bathroom with a mammoth-sized bathtub in the center. The castle has running water pipes with scalding hot water and I lost myself in the warmth until it became cold.

The bathroom has all of the things I've never had access to. Sweet-smelling soaps and shampoos, fluffy towels and multiple styles of hairbrushes and pins to stick in my wild black locks. I braided my hair and found a dresser full of different underwear and dresses. I picked a simple nightgown that hangs loosely over my body, and though I need sleep, here I pace back and forth for absolutely no reason.

The large bed looks welcoming and plush, but my wild spirit just can't settle. How did I end up in this place? My father always told me that Mom came from a simple wolf family in Lupos. He never mentioned royal blood on either side, but I'm still here to represent the royal wolves. It makes no sense, and the only two people with the answers that I can trust are both gone.

I walk barefoot to the bedroom door and listen against it for any sounds. It's completely quiet, so I sneak a look out into the grand hallway. *Empty, yes!*

Who knows what my day holds tomorrow, so now is my chance to explore without anyone watching me. I can't pretend that I trust this place or the people living here, so I remind myself to stay alert. I tip-toe down the hallway to a staircase larger than the one

Bastian brought me up here on. The castle is lit by a soft orange glow from a few candles, but it's mostly dark.

I make my way down the staircase, admiring the decor and beautiful designs as I go. At the main floor, a large room opens up which looks to be the entrance hall to the castle. I don't know why the guys didn't bring me in this way, but I imagine it had something to do with my appearance. I hope being clean and barefoot in a nearly see-through nightgown is better than black clothes and dirty hair.

I turn a corner into a large kitchen and my stomach growls automatically as I stare at the wall of breads and fruit just sitting there for the taking. I haven't eaten in a couple of days, so I practically launch myself at the food like a wild animal.

I grab a roll of bread and take a large bite before loading my arms up with apples and oranges that I can take back to my room. I try to remain quiet so I won't get caught, but everything drops out of my arms when someone's arm snakes around my neck in a tight hold.

"What are you doing in here, thief?" The masculine voice speaks quietly against my ear as I'm held against a hard body.

I swallow my mouthful of bread, and my hands come up to grab the thick arm holding me. "I was just looking for some food. I'm not a thief."

The man scoffs and his hold tightens. "You are in *my* kitchen, and taking *my* food. Sounds like a sneaky thief to me, *fox*."

Anger fills me as I try to wiggle free. I don't like being held against my will. I've been in this situation before and vowed to *never* let it happen again. My heart thuds in my chest and I use my right foot to stomp my heel into the man's foot.

He grunts, but doesn't release me, so I use all of my strength to push my head forward even though it tightens his hold on me, and I toss it back into his face. That does the trick with a loud crack, and I'm released with only a slight headache. I don't waste any time as I spin around and throw my fist into the gut of my attacker, causing him to double over.

I hold my fists up, ready to keep fighting if I need to, but the man doesn't attack me again. He stands up straight and his light brown hair hangs messy over his pained turquoise eyes. He runs a hand through his hair, pushing it out of his face and my stomach clenches at the sight of him.

The guy is maybe a foot taller than me and his short beard covers a jaw that's sharp and strong as he rubs the red spot where my head hit him. He's built like a warrior with a broad chest and thick arms, though he's dressed more like a prince in black leather pants and a white long-sleeve button up shirt.

My eyes find his and he's scanning me from head to toe, assessing the thief in *his* kitchen. I try to stand tall, but not fully at rest.

"You're Prince Cazimir," I say, realizing who I'm dealing with.

He nods and his bright eyes glare back at me. "I am. And you are?"

His gaze drops to my nightgown again so I hurry to cross my arms over my chest. "I'm Ny, your guest, though I'm guessing you didn't know I'd be here since you just attacked me for no reason."

Prince Cazimir's eyebrows raise and he looks around at the food I dropped all over the kitchen. "I knew the other chosen wolf would be arriving, but I wasn't expecting to see you in the kitchen in the middle of the night, scavenging for a week's worth of food."

Heat floods my face and I drop my eyes to the floor, ashamed. Prince Cazimir has probably never known real hunger in his life, and here I am stealing his family's food for fear of going hungry, in a castle of all places. *I am a thief.*

"I just…" I shake my head, hating that I have to admit how pathetic I am.

Cazimir steps toward me, his hand stretching out with an apple in his palm. "I know nothing about you, *Ny*." My name falls off of his tongue so naturally, like he has said it a thousand times. "I don't know where you came from, or how you live day to day." He reaches his other hand out to grab one of mine. He presses my palm open and sticks the apple in my hand, making me close my fingers around the fruit. I raise my eyes to his again and he's staring down at where his hands still grip mine.

He meets my gaze and quickly drops his hands. "Just know that you don't have to be ashamed of being hungry. Hunger is a part of life, and you're living it just as I am."

My heart flips as he says the words, and a yearning fills my chest. *What the hell is that about?*

"Thank you, Prince Cazimir." My words are soft, and I don't recognize my own voice. "I should return to my bed."

He nods and I move to step around him, but he steps in my way so that I'm face to chest with him. "And please, when we meet again in the daylight, call me Caz."

I don't trust my eyes to look up at him so I quickly step around the prince and run upstairs to try and sleep in my borrowed bed. In only a few days, I will be thrown into the Kingdom Trials beside Caz, in a fight for the throne. Somehow, meeting the prince has made the upcoming fight so much more complicated.

CHAPTER 4

⊷ ⊶

Cazimir

I tossed and turned through the night, dreaming about a raven-haired angel with dark gray eyes. The wolf girl, Ny, caught me off guard last night. I was on my way to bed after training in the gym when I saw her in the kitchen, her arms piled high with food.

I could've guessed she was the woman Dad told me about, but I couldn't stop myself from pulling her into my arms and accusing her of thievery. I guess I'm a little screwed up, but it was so sexy how she wiggled free from my hold, even if it did give me a few bruises in the process. She's strong,there's no denying that.

I feel an extra urgency in my steps as I make my way to the dining hall for breakfast. I walk into the room where Mom and Dad sit alone, and their faces are grim when they look my way. *Crap.*

"What is it?" I ask, the lightness in my chest dropping to a heavy worry.

Mom calls me over and I place a kiss on her freckled cheek before taking the seat by her side. "Good morning, my boy. Your father was telling me that we have a new guest in the west wing."

I look toward Dad and he's frowning through his graying beard. "You're not happy with the girl? Have you met her?"

He crosses his large arms. "I visited with Joff in the night, after the girl was brought here. He says she is a fugitive and had mentioned spending some time in our dungeons."

My breath stops and I lean back in my seat. "A fugitive? What has she done?" *And I called her a thief.*

"She didn't say, but I awoke this morning and spoke with the dungeon guards. There are two of them that have been around for a long time, and they remember a young woman being brought in for having tainted blood two years ago." His upper lip curls in disgust at the thought of a tainted wolf in our home.

Ny can't be tainted, though. I've been told that tainted bloods are deformed and freakish. I have never seen a more beautiful woman than Ny.

Dad continues. "Her father was brought in with her, and he was killed for trying to escape. I guess the girl managed to free herself during a transport to the gathering grounds where she was to be on trial. Nobody has seen her since that day"

My mind reels. There has to be an explanation. It had to be a different woman. "Are you certain that the girl with royal blood in our home is that same girl? It's unheard of for a royal to be tainted."

Mom grabs my hand as Dad nods sharply. "There has been no other young woman in our dungeons in many years. Somehow, a fugitive tainted girl with some scattered trace of royal blood was chosen to participate in our Kingdom Trials. This is unacceptable."

Mom sits up straight. "There isn't much we can do about it now, dear. The mages don't make mistakes. We shall just let her fight and hope that she doesn't win."

Dad growls and stands abruptly, keeping his voice down, though the anger laces his words as he stares directly at me. "She *will not* win. Even if she has the power to do so, it will be *your* job to make sure she loses the trials *and* her life in the process."

An unexpected anger rolls through me, though not at Ny, but at my father. He wants me to kill the girl because she's tainted? It's against everything in me to end someone's life like that. I stay silent as he continues to stare at me, waiting for my obedience.

"I understand, Father," I say through gritted teeth. He accepts my words with a nod before stomping out of the room. I turn to Mom and her blue eyes are sad. "Do you agree with this, Mom?"

She shrugs. "I don't know. Tainted bloods have always been against our laws. They aren't allowed to live. In this case, though, I trust that the mages chose this girl for a reason, and that reason isn't to die."

That's what I love about my mother. Her level head and kind heart. How she ended up the mate to my father is beyond me. I wrap my mother in a warm hug and stand to leave without breakfast.

"Aren't you going to eat, Caz?"

I shake my head. "I need to speak with Bastian about the girl."

Mom nods and waves me on. "Go on then, but please be careful son. If you choose to let the girl live, it cannot be known to your father. He won't allow it."

She's right. He'd kill her himself if he had to.

Nyomi

I stretch out, the heat of the sun stroking my skin from the window above my head. I've never slept so well in my life, and I owe it all to the large, overstuffed mattress. I blink past the sleepy fog in my head and my eyes focus on a young woman standing beside my bed.

My instincts immediately take over as I swing my arm between the bed and headboard where I hid *Theo* last night. I grip the sword hilt and swing it in front of me, rising to my knees on the bed.

The girl's green eyes stretch wide and she backs away from me with her hands outstretched. "Woah, killer! I only wanted to say good morning and welcome you to my home."

Her lips lift in a slight smile but I don't drop the sword. "*Your* home? Who are you? Do you always welcome people by standing above their bed in silence while they sleep?"

She giggles as she flips her short blonde braid over her shoulder. "You're funny. Yes, this is my family's home. I am Clio Duras, Princess to the king and queen of Unity." She dips her head and my body finally relaxes.

I stick the sword back in its hiding place before climbing off the bed and bowing to the Princess. "Well, it's nice to meet you, your highness. My name is Ny."

Clio grabs my shoulders, causing me to freeze as she pulls me into a tight hug. I don't hug her back as I'm not used to this kind of affection, but I don't push her away either. *Why is this so nice?* She steps back from me again and turns around to show me a cart full of freshly cooked food. My mouth waters at the large array of pork and baked desserts beside a pitcher of milk.

"My brother asked me to bring you breakfast. I guess he thought you'd rather eat here than in the dining hall. I also don't know why he asked to bring you enough food for at least three people. He must think you're a large man or something." She laughs and shrugs.

Her words cause my heart to clench in a strange way. "Caz sent you with all of this food? Just for me?"

Clio's eyebrows climb her forehead and she nods with a curious look on her beautiful face. "Cazimir hates when people other than family call him Caz. Proceed with caution before saying that to his face, Ny."

Weird. I swore he asked me to call him Caz last night, but I'll have to be careful when I see him again. I don't want to end up on the bad side of the royal family. I step around Clio and grab a thick slice of ham, taking a needy bite of the savory meat.

"Oh wow," I say, closing my eyes in food ecstasy.

Clio giggles sweetly again and sits at the edge of my bed, shifting her heavy dress with a huff. "Ugh, I hate this dress."

I look her up and down, admiring the gorgeous blue embroidery that wraps around her thin waist. "I think it's gorgeous. I've never worn something like that."

"You should feel grateful. For a girl who knows how to handle a sword, I can tell you right now that you're not going to like it."

I look down at my long nightgown. "What do you mean I'm not going to like it? Am I going to have to wear dresses?"

Clio nods and walks over to the closet door that I have yet to explore the inside of. She steps inside, ruffling through some hanging clothes and pulls out a long red dress. *Red?*

I snort. "That is way too daring for me. I'm much more used to the subtle black or gray."

Clio clicks her tongue and shrugs. "You're the only tough warrior woman I've ever met. I'm not going to let you be hidden and unseen, girl."

"How do you know I'm tough or warrior material? The sword could just be all show."

Clio shakes her head. "Not a chance. I talked to my brother's guard, Bastian this morning and he said you're pretty badass. And anyone who sleeps with a sword above their head knows a thing or two about survival. I envy you."

That takes me aback. "You envy *me*? Being the sole princess of the six kingdoms, your life must be perfect, Clio."

She watches me tear into a frosted croissant. "I've never gone hungry, and by the way you attack your breakfast, I take it you have a time or two. I've been spoiled, looked up to, and protected my entire life. It should be perfect."

"But it's not?"

She shakes her head. "What is this life of luxury going to do for me when one of the initiates takes the Unity throne? I'll be back in Lupos with the other wolves, free to live a real life, with not a clue how to do it. I want to be strong and resourceful. I want to survive after this."

I try to understand where she's coming from, but our worlds are opposite of the other's. Still, I really like her, and I feel like we can learn so much from one another.

I take the dress from Clio's hands. "Okay, I'll wear the red dress. Maybe you can help me to act like a princess, and I'll help you learn a little about surviving in the lands."

Her green eyes light up and she hops up and down. "I love that idea! I already know a lot about fighting, thanks to my brother. Maybe we can spar later and I can see what it's like fighting a girl. Cazimir is three times my size, so it's not exactly fair."

I nod to her, trying to give her a kind smile. *Sheesh, this being friendly thing is exhausting.*

Clio steps around me as she surveys my body. "Alright, let's get you ready for the world of royalty, Ny."

Here goes nothing.

CHAPTER 5

++← →++

Cazimir

I find Bastian and Joff in their usual off duty spot, throwing axes near the back of the servant housing. I've spent many hours out here with these two, goofing off and trying to escape my father. They were both assigned to be my personal guards after the three of us came of age and shifted for the first time when we were eighteen.

We were friends in school together, so Mom invited them to work for us. She thought the castle should be full of friends and family. Without her, I'd likely have run off years ago, bored out of my mind without a friend in sight.

"Well, well, it's the chosen prince himself! Here to grace us with his company," Joff bows at the waist to me, but I smack the side of his head.

"Shut up, Joff. I just wanted to ask you guys a few questions."

Bastian tosses an axe at the wooden target and it sticks dead center. He turns to pat me on the back.

"What do ya need, Caz? Is this about the smokin' hot wolf girl in your guest wing?"

Something about him calling Ny *hot* rubs me the wrong way, but I try to ignore the itching feeling to punch his bearded face. Bastian is likely my best friend in all of Unity, and I'd do anything for him.

"Yeah, the girl, Nyomi Mailon. Dad says she's a fugitive, but I want to know your thoughts. You both found her in Fae, correct?"

Joff grunts. "Ay. She was on the south end, near Vampir, carrying a sword and looking like a wild animal. Smelled like one too." He scrunches up his nose and waves a hand in front of his face for effect.

Bastian shoves Joff before I get the chance. "She was on the run, and about ready to beat the hell out of us if we got too close. It's clear that she knows how to take care of herself for such a small thing." Bastian's brown eyes glow with a light of admiration for Ny's fighting spirit. My sore stomach where she punched me can attest to that spirit.

"I ran into her in the kitchen last night. She was loading her arms full of food, like she hadn't eaten in days. Was she not with anyone else when you found her?"

Bastian shakes his head. "She was alone, and I believe she has been that way for some time. Maybe her entire life."

The thought of Ny out in the woods alone for all of her nineteen years feels like a knife in my chest. It doesn't make any sense that a royal blood would be living that life, even if she is tainted. Someone had to know of her, or care for her. How will she survive the trials without any formal training?

"What about her fugitive status? Does she act like a criminal? Is she dangerous?"

Joff snorts derisively. "She's an itty bitty thing, Caz. I don't think she's capable of being dangerous. She probably stole a loaf of bread and was arrested for thievery. She's a fox, a sexy one sure, but not worthy of being a chosen wolf."

I can't stop my hands as they jut out toward Joff and wrap around his thick neck. Joff's eyes go wide as I squeeze his throat and a primal growl leaves my mouth. "Not another negative word about my guest, Joff, or I swear I'll rip your head off your body."

Bastian grabs my arms and pulls me back from our friend, leaving Joff choking past the tightness in his throat. Joff stares back at me as he yells through his quick breaths. "What the hell, Caz? Have you lost your damn mind?"

Bastian turns to Joff and shoves him back toward the servant hall. "Go have a nap, brother. Let me talk with Cazimir."

I glare at Joff as he stumbles away, and Bastian grabs my shoulder. "Hey, Caz. I get that Joff is an ass, but that's nothing new. We've handled his crap for years, so why the sudden mood change?"

I don't even feel like myself, so what can I say? Maybe I have lost my mind. I shrug and run a hand through my hair. "I don't know, Bastian. It's something about Ny. I feel somehow protective of her, but I know almost nothing of who she is."

My friend walks over to the target and yanks two axes from the wood. He returns to me with his hand out, handing me one of the weapons. "Well, I'll say this. I quite like the girl. Who knows what hold she has over you, but you'll have the next three months of the trials to figure it out... that is, if you both make it that far."

I take the axe from him and whip it at the target, enjoying the sound of steel slicing into wood. "If my father has his way, Ny won't make it past the first trial, but I can't betray her."

Bastian throws his own axe directly beside mine. "I'll help in whatever way I can, Caz. If you want to see Nyomi win the Kingdom Trials, we'll make sure she does. Though that means you'd have to lose."

I nod, already sure of my answer. "Then I'll lose."

Nyomi

I've circled the castle grounds with Clio three times today, exploring the gardens, the lush forest, and the architecture of the castle itself. The sun is nearly gone from the sky and I still haven't seen Caz since last night.

Not that I've been secretly looking for him.

Clio was right about these dresses. I'm burning up in the tight corset and I feel like I've been carrying unnecessary weight on my shoulders since putting the thing on. Even though I hate it, I also feel incredibly beautiful for the first time in my life. Somehow, feeling this way is almost worth the discomfort. *Almost.*

Clio is a joy to be around. Her twinkling laughter lifts my spirits every time I hear it, and I feel like I may have found an actual friend. I've learned that she is a couple years younger than me, but she is wonderfully smart.

"I have had so much fun with you today, Ny. Thank you for letting me be your tour guide." Clio grins happily as we ascend the castle stairs toward my bedroom.

"I've had fun as well. I never knew a day could feel as carefree as this one. I'm used to always being on the move."

"Well, you can't rest yet." Bastian's gravelly voice interrupts us as he meets us in the hallway. "Get dressed into something you can move around in. The initiates have been called to meet at the gathering grounds in one hour."

My eyes feel like they bulge out of my head. "We're meeting now? I don't have anything like that to wear, Bastian." I wave down at the red dress. "I can just go in this."

The bulky guard looks me up and down with a single eyebrow raised. "No can do, fugitive. I know my girl Clio has something you can wear." He winks at Clio and I don't miss the pink blush that stains her cheeks. "Just hurry up and meet me at the front doors in ten minutes."

I spin my head toward Clio and she practically hops in place. "Come with me!"

Clio drags me down the staircase again and past the kitchen toward the main entrance of the castle.

We climb a much more elaborate grand staircase to a wider hallway with just a few doors.

Clio points to the first door to our left. "Here's my room. I have some comfortable pants and a slip dress that slits up the side for maneuverability. It's a training outfit that I have yet to use, so it's yours now." She points to the door at the very end of the hall. "That's Caz's room down there. Just so you know."

Why would I care about Caz's bedroom?

Even as I have the thought, my eyes still stare at the prince's closed bedroom door for way too long as I wonder if he's in there right now. I shake my head and dip into Clio's room. She immediately rushes to the dresser against the far wall of the massive bedroom, and she pulls out the training outfit.

Luckily, the tight pants and simple light dress are a perfect fit. I'm able to bend and twist as needed, while still somehow looking professional. It amazes me what riches can buy.

Clio and I rush back to the front door where Bastian waits with my sword and belt in his hands. "Thought you might like your sword. Initiates are allowed to bring their own weapon to the trials, and I didn't want you to be the only one unarmed."

I smile up at Bastian, grateful to have another friend in this place where I was once tortured. "Thanks, Bastian. You might actually be nice... for a palace guard." I hook my belt around my waist and slide Theo into his sheath. Now I feel complete.

Bastian nods toward the door and rubs his hands together. "Alright. Are you ready to go meet your enemies?"

I scoff and shrug, looking from Clio to Bastian. "Hey, either I'm a fugitive, or a possible ruler of Unity. I'm ready to give this thing my all if it means never running away again."

CHAPTER 6

◂—⧫—▸

Nyomi

The walk to the gathering grounds is beautiful. It's not far from the castle. The area is a large valley surrounded by mountains and lush forest. I've heard that the gathering grounds have been used for forever, mainly when the kingdoms needed to come together for a meeting.

It's also the place where the Fae army attacked the king's army when I was just a baby. After a day and night of fighting, the faeries lost the war and were killed or banished from the lands altogether. Tonight is my first chance to see the iconic place, and I'm in awe.

There is one main road that leads through a canyon, ending at the open grounds. Fields stretch out toward the mountains, littered with trees and vegetation. Some covered pavilions rest at the center to protect from the elements, and a large crowd is gathered underneath the high ceilings.

I walk up to the edge of the group with Clio on my right, and Bastian on my left. A few eyes land on me with curiosity, but the majority are lost in their own conversations, causing a loud chattering of voices to blend together beneath the pavilion.

Clio grabs my hand and drags me through the crowd. "Let's find my mother and father. You still need to be introduced if they are supposed to announce you tonight."

We leave Bastian behind and push past so many different species of people. It's clear to me who the trolls are, as well as the sirens and vampires. Otherwise, the wolves and dragons don't have outstanding features as they all look human when they aren't shifted. Some are in their kingdom colors which helps determine their homeland as well. Red for Dracon, baby blue for Sirenes, green for Lupos, brown for Trog, silver for Vampir, and if any Fae were present, the color of gold would litter the crowd.

Clio and I break through to the center of the group where it opens up to show a nicely dressed man and woman standing together, and by their side is Caz. His button up shirt is dark green, representing the wolves, and it's tucked into leather pants. He wears a leather strap across his chest and a sword on his hip like me. He looks like a true warrior prince.

Clio runs up to the older man and woman. "Mom, Dad, I'd like you to meet the woman chosen to represent Lupos in the trials. Nyomi Mailon." She waves a hand at me "Ny, meet my parents, King Alix Duras and Queen Freya Duras of Unity."

I bow to them both, and Queen Freya smiles kindly to me. She reaches a hand out for me to shake, and I obey. "It's so nice to meet you, Nyomi. I'm sorry I was not able to welcome you to our home this morning."

"It's alright," I say, admiring the gorgeous woman. Her light brown hair curls all the way to her waist and her turquoise eyes match Caz's perfectly. "Clio has been very gracious and given me the grand tour."

King Alix snaps his head to his daughter, his hair and eyes dark brown unlike the light colors of his family. "You've given her the grand tour, Clio? Without telling me?"

"I... I thought she would..." Clio stutters through her explanation but Caz steps in.

"I told Clio to give Nyomi the tour, Father. I thought our *guest* should feel welcomed in our home." He turns to me, but not really seeing me. His expression is unreadable. "She is to be my alliance in the trials, is she not?"

I am?

King Alix nods and forces a small smile toward me. "Ay, that is true. Welcome, Nyomi. We are grateful to have you here with us."

I try not to cringe as the king speaks to me. My father died in his dungeons, under *his* rule. I've always hated everything about the Duras king, but I can't show him that. I just need to stay unnoticed as much as possible.

"Thank you, your highness. I'm glad I can participate." *Not really.*

The king grunts and turns his attention to the chatting crowd. "Everyone, please listen here!"

Everyone quits speaking immediately and all eyes turn to the center of the group. I look around at all of the staring eyes, and I forget how to move momentarily. A strong hand grabs onto my long sleeved arm and tugs me backward.

I glance up at Caz who is still not looking at me as he holds me at his side. "Is there something wrong, Prince Cazimir?"

His hooded eyes drop to mine and the blue in them seems to swirl with the green before he looks ahead again. He drops his hand and shakes his head. "Not at all."

Okaaay…

"Welcome, all representatives of Unity to our gathering grounds." The king's voice carries over the silent spectators. "Tonight, we are going to announce the ten initiates that will be battling in our Kingdom Trials for the coming months. This time will be tough, physically and mentally for our young people, but the royal blood that flows through their veins will see them through."

King Alix steps between Caz and I, grabbing our hands in his, and he raises our arms above our heads. "I, King Alix Duras of Unity, am presenting the Lupos initiates, Prince Cazimir Duras and Nyomi Mailon."

The crowd cheers loudly until the king releases us and steps back beside his wife. I notice him wipe his hand on his coat front, the same hand that held mine in the air. I'll try not to take that personally. I look at Caz again, and his jaw clenches tightly along with his fists at his sides.

My attention is brought to a tall pale man in an all black suit, with silver eyes and a shaved head. *Vampire.* He grabs the hands of the two younger men by his sides, just as King Alix had done.

"I, King Ciaran Ennui of Vampir, am presenting our Vampir initiates, my twin sons, Arnoux Ennui, and Azra Ennui, princes of Vampir." The twin princes both stand tall and thin like their father, and if it weren't for one of them having longer black hair and less muscles, they'd be completely identical. The Vampir king stares intently at Queen Freya for a moment before stepping back. The queen avoids his gaze, and I can't help but wonder what their problem is. Vampires and wolves have always been rivals unlike the other species, but there's something more there.

The crowd cheers for the Vampir initiates, and a slender woman steps into the circle. She's gorgeous and skinny with almost no breasts, long braided blonde hair, and a floor length blue gown. *Siren.* By her side are two younger women who are just as beautiful, but one has dark brown hair while the other has straight red hair that reaches her butt.

The older woman speaks. "I, Queen Astraea Laurier of Sirenes, present the Sirenes initiates, my daughter Princess Nyx Laurier, and my niece, Iris Laurier."

The crowd roars again, and I shift in my spot. The other initiates look confident and strong, all born royals. I feel out of place here, and real worry fills me. The next person steps forward, a muscular woman, tall and statuesque. Her dark brown eyes flash red momentarily as she looks toward the wolf king. *Dragon.*

"I, Queen Inara Driscoll of Dracon, am presenting our Dracon initiates, my son and daughter, Prince Dryden and Princess Juno Driscoll of Dracon." The prince and princess both bow at the waist, and they are every bit as robotic as their mother.

The last ones to make their announcement are the Trolls. The troll king grabs the hands of the two men beside him. All three of them are built wide with beards and pointed ears. The only troll I've ever befriended was Bellona, and it's clear that the entire breed is large and powerful.

The king's large belly shakes as he begins speaking. "I, King Eddard Barlowe of Trog, present the Trog initiates, my nephew, Echo Barlowe, and my cousin, Faxon Barlowe." He raises the men's hands and another round of applause breaks out.

King Alix raises his hands for silence and he shouts loudly for all to hear. "I welcome all ten of our Kingdom Trial initiates! As a special surprise for all, the trials are starting one day early. Let the Kingdom Trials begin *now*!"

My heart sinks at his words as the air erupts with more cheering. The trials start now? *Oh, dear Unity, I'm not ready.*

Nyomi

My mind reels as the noisy group shouts and cheers together. I've lived my entire life in near silence, surrounded by only the chirps and whistles of nature and my father's soothing voice. I feel overwhelmed, and I begin to sway on my shaking legs. Before I can make a show of my nerves, Cazimir's warm hand presses against the small of my back, keeping me upright.

"Just take a deep breath, fox. If you faint, the enemies will swarm." Caz's near whisper reaches my ear and I hate how easily it calms me.

I look up into his turquoise eyes and see worry there. "Do you care, Caz? It'd make your fight for the throne easier if I was taken out of the game."

He shakes his head. "I like a challenge, and I'm pretty sure you're the biggest challenge in this whole lot."

My eyebrows raise. "I think that was a compliment, your highness."

The corners of his lips lift slightly as he stares down at me only inches away. I feel drawn to him, like touching him could possibly make me feel whole. Caz opens his mouth, but his jaw snaps shut when he looks past me toward the suddenly quiet crowd. I follow his gaze and my stomach drops at the sight of four women in long white robes stepping through the throng.

"Ah, mesdames! Your presence is much appreciated." King Alix steps forward to bow to the four mage women.

There are very few mages of Unity, and like the sirens, they're all female. I don't know much about how they reproduce, but it doesn't require the use of men like the rest of the species. The mages are extremely powerful and are able to see things from the past, present, and future. They can also find anyone within the six kingdoms, just using their power. Being in their presence is stifling. I've never been near someone with so much power before.

The eldest mage with long gray hair and black eyes stops just before the king and turns to address the crowd. "All initiates for this year's Kingdom Trials, please stand before us."

She waves her arms in front of her, and the previously announced royals all line up in front of the mages. I almost don't move, until Caz bumps my shoulder. *Oh, right!* I hurry to stand beside Caz and the Vampir twins, realizing that I'm significantly shorter than the majority of the royals.

The four mages scan our lineup, eyeing each of us closely, and for some reason it feels like the eldest woman spends an extra few seconds trying to figure me out. It's probably my nerves, but I feel all too out of place under their gazes.

"My name is Mora, elder of the high mages. Welcome, initiates, to the day of your reckoning. Each of you was called by my sisters and I, chosen by your royal blood, and your potential to lead the Kingdom of Unity into the next generation."

I stand tall, feeling pride at Mora's praise, even though I'm not totally sure I fit into this elite group.

Mora continues. "Now, to kick off the trials, you have but one task." Her eyes fall on me momentarily before addressing us all again. "Each of you will show your capabilities based on your species. The initiates who give the largest show of power will be told the next step of the night as a sort of cheat code. This will be the head start, and will define the next several trials."

The crowd "oohs" and "aahs" as the initiates start to bounce excitedly. I don't bounce, and instead my brow begins to sweat. How will I show my power as a wolf shifter? I have yet to experience my first shift, which also means I have no official wolf capabilities.

I start to breathe heavily as the dragons take charge. The female dragon, Juno, leaps into the air, making several people around her gasp. She shifts mid-air, growing a long scaled neck and a heavy dragon body. Her wide wings flap toward the ground, picking up dust and blowing the hair back from everyone's faces.

Her brother throws his head back, not shifting, but he blows out a long red flame from within himself that heats up the entire covered pavilion. Thankfully, the ceiling is so high that his flame doesn't burn the whole thing down. The girl shifts back to her normal-looking self, still fully clothed in her tight red jumpsuit as she falls to the ground, only to be caught in her brother's thick arms. Being able to harness your shifting power and keep your clothing intact when you shift is a great skill.

The room bursts into applause at the incredible display, only making my heart sink further into my body. *Holy hell.*

"Very good," Mora shouts over the clapping hands. "Now, let us see what the sirens have in store for us."

The two gorgeous siren women smile at one another before their long locks of hair shift into octopus tentacles and stretch out to grab onto one of the Vampir twins. The twin, Azra I believe, smiles as he's lifted above the sirens' heads.

"I've always wanted to fly," he says, grinning from ear to ear as he enjoys the ride. A few members in the room laugh, and the sirens drop the vamp back in his spot beside his brother.

The girls' long tentacles retract and shift back to soft flowing locks of hair, and the crowd applauds the show. It doesn't beat the ferocity of the dragons, but I can't count out their abilities yet. I have a feeling they're holding back.

"Well then. I reckon it's our turn, brother," the vampire twin, Azra says with the same wicked grin. I think I like him.

The brothers crouch down together, taking the exact same stance, and then they leap off of the ground, jumping all the way to the pavilion ceiling. Both of them cling onto the cross beams, looking down at the staring crowd below them, and they each flash their sharp fangs as they hiss loudly. A few people flinch, not wanting to be touched by the vampire's poisonous fangs that can make a body go numb.

They both drop to the ground, landing gracefully, like a couple of leaves off of a tree, and applause erupts once more. I groan inwardly, not excited for my turn.

I look up at Cazimir, wanting to know what he plans to do. "Caz, I need to tell you something."

He turns to look at me, but a voice interrupts. "Brava, young princes! Now, we shall see from the trolls."

The trolls, Echo and Faxon, bump fists as they step forward, flexing their large muscles for the onlookers. "Please, step back," the larger troll says to the crowd, and they immediately make room.

Paxon and Echo step backwards from one another until they're at least twenty yards apart, and then they charge forward at full speed, hitting the ground hard with their heavy feet. They reach the middle again and slam their bodies together with so much force that it feels as if the air shakes and a loud crack fills the night. I can't imagine getting hit that hard by one of them, and it goes to show how useful brute strength can be.

"Impressive. Now, last but not least, our wolves." Mora points toward Caz and I, and my whole body stills.

Damn, damn, damn!

Caz smacks his hands together, flexing his biceps and raising his thick chest as he inhales deeply. He jumps into the air, spinning into a front flip, and his bones crack as he shifts into a massive wolf. I stare in awe at the beast in front of me, and he looks my way with glistening fangs and light brown fur along his body. The whole room waits for me to make my move, but I stay frozen in place, completely lost.

"Well, Nyomi Mailon," Mora says as she waves a hand at me. "This is when you are expected to show us your wolf side."

My palms are wet and clammy, and my heart feels like a brick inside of my chest. "No," I say, and I immediately want to punch myself in the face.

Surprised gasps sound out around me, and King Alix steps beside the mages, his eyes practically glowing with anger. "No? I don't believe you get a choice here, young wolf. You either shift, or you forfeit."

I grip the hilt of my sword, needing a lifeline as I fear for my life. If I forfeit the trials, I'll be killed. I won't make it out of this crowd alive. I make up my mind as I look around at all of the other initiates, their faces smug as if they've won already.

I call on my lifelong training with my dad, and slide Theo from his sheath. I whip my blade through the air with a satisfying whistle and leap as Caz had, into a forward flip. I land on my feet again and spin my sword in intricate ways, just for show. Dad would train with me for hours a day until I became better with a sword than even him.

The crowd seems satisfied with my show, and I decide to take it one step further, jumping over Caz's wolf back and slicing the blade just inches from the king's chest before slamming my weapon back into the sheath on my belt, dropping to my knee in a bow.

Applause fills the night again, and I take a steadying breath, trying to mask the true fear I feel. I glance up at Mora, and she is smiling down at me. "Clever girl. It is wise to be a capable fighter, even when you are not shifted. Very good."

I close my eyes in relief. *Oh, thank all that is holy.*

CHAPTER 7

←← →→

Cazimir

I draw energy to myself, calling on the shift and making sure to remain dressed. Even though my father can be a tyrant, I'm grateful that he taught me well. I slide my hair back from my eyes and look over at Ny.

She looks pleased with the mage, Mora's praise. Watching Ny struggle with the decision to shift or not made my heart pound in my wolf chest. I don't know why she didn't just shift and get it over with, but she's right about needing to have other abilities outside of the animal. Her fighting ability with her blade is incredible, and also way too sexy. I've never met another person like her, and I can already tell that she's going to cause my heart trouble.

"Alright, everyone settle down!" Mora shouts above the still cheering crowd. Everyone is excited for the trials this year, though they're probably just itching for my father to finally leave the throne.

Mora continues. "Now, the initiates with the greatest display of power are Dryden and Juno Driscoll of Dracon! Congratulations!" Cheering erupts again as the winning brother and sister jump up and down in excitement. "My sisters will give the two of you a hint, and you can be off to the next step."

The sister mages stare at the dragons with intense gazes, and it's clear that they are speaking into their minds, keeping the hint completely secret. Dryden and Juno smile at one another, and without another word, they take off at a full run into the tree line that surrounds the pavilion.

They're running north, in the direction of the Mutua Arena. I've been to the arena a handful of times in my life, when the kingdoms get together for big moon celebrations, or the yearly winter fights when the best of the best will show their strength. I've been asked a few times to compete in the fights, but I've Is turned it down.

The eight of us initiates are left standing in front of the mages, itching to run after the dragons. I glance over at Ny and she's looking ahead at the mages with her head held high. She has so much pride, but she also seems fragile in many other ways. I want to reach out and take her hand, but I turn my eyes ahead, clenching my fists instead.

Stay hands. No touching the competition.

"For the remaining initiates, your next trial begins now. You will head north to the Mutua Arena where you'll meet your trainers for the rest of the trials. Each pair of you will share a trainer, so be courteous to one another. The last one to arrive at the arena will miss the big dinner the trainers have prepared, and they will spend the night outside on the ground. The rest will have a room ready in the castle's east wing where you'll spend the next three months."

A missed meal and a night outside is the least of the punishments to come, but I'm not about to be the last either way. I ready myself to shift and run, and I notice the others crouching in preparation as well. Ny's head whips from side to side in worry, and I fear that she'll refuse to shift again. She won't make it to the arena before the others if she stays on two legs.

"Well, initiates… run!" Mora's words echo through the air and just like that, the race has begun.

⋆←→⋆

Nyomi

At Mora's command, I launch myself forward, running at my full speed. I've always been fast and strong, able to maneuver through the woods with ease, but running against the others with their magic abilities has me panting and falling well behind within minutes. My hair flies behind me as I leap over a downed tree in my way, and a thud lands beside me, keeping pace with my long strides.

I turn to see Caz sprinting along with me, still in his human form, but looking every bit the strong animal that he is. "What are you doing, Caz? You need to beat the others!"

What is wrong with this guy?

He shakes his head as he powers through the thick brush in his leather boots. "And leave my teammate behind? That wouldn't be very sportsmanly of me, would it?"

I growl. "Just stop it, Caz," I say through heavy breaths as I slow to a stop. Caz stops running and turns to me with a shocked expression.

"What? You *want* me to leave you out here to lose alone? Just shift and run, Ny!" He yells at me with his jaw ticking, and my anger builds to a flame. I don't even know why I'm mad at him. He's trying to be kind to me, and I hate it for reasons I can't explain.

I squeeze my eyes closed, trying to find words that won't start a fight. "I know you see me as beneath your kind, *your highness*." *Ooh, too much sarcasm.* "I have tainted blood, I'm an orphan born and raised in condemned land, and I'm the opposite of royal!"

Caz steps closer to me, his hot breath hitting my cheeks. "You were chosen for the trials, just like the rest of us, just like *me*! Clearly, you're more than what you see of yourself. I don't think you're beneath me." He grabs my hand, tugging me forward as he turns back to the north. "Now come on, Ny! Shift and let's show the assholes what you're capable of!"

I hold myself still, even though Caz's strength rivals my own. "No! I'm not shifting!"

He whirls on me, nostrils flaring... and angry Caz is *hot*. "Why are you so stubborn? You can't win the trials in this form! Use your damn wolf, Ny!"

I step to him, chest to chest, not okay with being bossed around even if his narrowed eyes and bulging muscles excite me a little too much. "Why are *you* so stubborn? Stop telling me what to do, and go make daddy proud! The *king* will be expecting your victory!"

"And what do you have against my father? You've been a nobody, living outside of his rule as you said. Quit acting like you have it worse than the rest of us!" His nose is practically touching mine, and my heart is pounding faster than it ever has. How can I be so incredibly pissed, and mesmerized in the same instance?

I push Caz's chest, shoving him a step back. "You know *nothing* about me, Cazimir Duras! It's because of your father, that *my* dad is dead!" I shove his chest a second time. "It was *your* dungeons that held my father and I for three damn weeks!" I hit him again and he doesn't stop me. "It was *your* father's loyal guards that cut me, bruised me, and made me wish I was dead right alongside the *only* person who ever cared for me!" My voice shakes and wetness fills my eyes, but I slam my fists against him once more.

Caz grabs my wrists in his hands before I can continue my assault on him. His piercing turquoise eyes bare down on me and his jaw is clenched so tightly that I worry it might snap. He doesn't say a word as he stares at me, but a low rumbling growl fills his chest.

"Ny," he says my name quietly, surprising me after all of the yelling. "Please tell me none of what you just said is the truth. Even if it's a lie, I need you to tell me that those things didn't happen to you while I was near enough to stop it."

I breathe in his musky scent as I shake my head, keeping eye contact with him so he understands. "I can't tell you that."

Caz growls again, and before I can blink, his lips crash into mine. I almost don't register the kiss, but my mind kicks into high gear as the reality of what is happening hits me. Caz grips my shoulders, lifting me higher as he deepens the rough kiss. His lips move hard against mine, almost desperate, and my body responds with a wave of heat.

I grab the front of his shirt, needing something to hold onto for dear life, and my lips open to invite Caz's tongue to taste mine. *Oh, holy Unity, is it always like this?* I can't stop the soft moan that leaves my opened mouth, but the sound brings me back to the reason we're here in this embrace in the first place.

No, this can't happen.

I pull away from Caz, my cheeks hot and my heart pounding. "You can't do that. *We* can't…"

His eyes look sad and he shakes his head. "Why not? It feels right, Ny."

It really does.

"We're initiates in the Kingdom Trials. We're not fated mates, even I'm aware that we'd know if we were. It doesn't matter what it feels like. We just can't." Caz steps closer to me again, reaching his hands toward mine, but I step back. "Run, Caz! I'll get to the arena in my own time. Please just go and find our trainer!"

"You'll miss dinner and you'll sleep outside. Why won't you shift and run alongside me? We could still beat the sirens!"

I shake my head. "I can't shift, okay! I never have, and who knows if I ever will?" I point toward the north. "Now, please go! I've slept outside for my entire life, and I've missed more meals than I can count. Don't feel sorry for me. Don't try to understand me. Just go!"

Caz closes his eyes momentarily and lets out a long breath before looking at me once more. He hesitates for only a second longer before shifting into his wolf form right in front of me. His large furry head nudges my hand, and then he takes off at full speed, pounding through the forest. I don't wait a moment longer before I run as well.

Just because I can't shift, doesn't mean I'm any less capable than the rest of them. I won't let this game control me, or put me down. Caz was right. I was chosen for a reason, and no matter what it takes, I plan to prove that to all of them.

PART 2

A TRIAL OF KINGDOMS

CHAPTER 8

❖← →❖

Nyomi

The Mutua Arena is a massive solid structure, built into a long hillside and made from gray stone. There are engravings along the entrance to the arena, artwork representing the six kingdoms. This is supposed to be a place where all creatures are welcomed and accepted. For someone with mixed blood like me though, nowhere is totally safe or inviting.

A tall rounded doorway leads into the center of the arena through a tunnel that empties out below the stone bleachers. I can see only one other entrance into the structure. A rocky path snakes around the stone wall and carves a trail into the hillside. The pathway stops somewhere above the arena, but I take the tunnel route instead, hoping it gets me inside faster.

It only takes me a few minutes to step out of the dark tunnel and into the moonlit circular field where the other nine trial initiates wait for me. *Well, crap.*

I knew I'd be the last one to arrive, but seeing all of the smug faces of my opponents only makes me want to crawl back into the woods and hide away like I have done my whole life. A man I don't know clears his throat and I realize it's coming from an older gentleman who stands with Cazimir.

The initiates stop staring at me to get back into their conversations with their new trainers. Each pair of us in the trials are assigned a trainer to help us navigate the next three months with ease. Or at least not extreme difficulty.

The man beside Caz holds a tan hand out to me. "I'm glad you finally made it, Nyomi. I am Everaux Wolfe, your trainer for the next three months."

I shake his hand. "It's nice to meet you. I'm sorry I didn't get here sooner." I could've gotten here a lot faster if my stupid wolf would make an appearance, but nothing comes all that easy for me, so what's new?

Everaux shakes his head with a kind smile. "That's quite alright. I'm here to make sure you win the rest of the trials and prove you have a right to the throne of Unity."

I glance up at Caz who has been too quiet since I arrived. He doesn't look my way, and I try not to let it hurt me. I remember his plump lips pressed firmly to mine less than an hour ago. His surprise kiss had me melting from the inside out, and just thinking about it makes a warm heat pool in my belly. *Stop it, Ny! Just forget about it.*

I listen to my inner voice and clear the memory from my mind, choosing to focus on Everaux instead.

He is tall with light caramel colored skin. His black hair falls just past his earlobes, fluffy and light, shaping his square jaw perfectly. He looks to be around the king's age, maybe mid-to-late-forties, with smile lines shaping his gray eyes. Everything about him is familiar to me, and I love that already.

"Okay," Everaux says, clapping his hands together. "Now that the initiates are all here, we'll be sending you back to the castle where you will find your rooms and a large meal waiting in the dining hall." He cringes at his words and looks at me with a sorry expression. "Sorry, Nyomi. I'm sure you already know that you will not be allowed to participate."

I shake my head. "Not a problem. I'm aware and it's nothing I can't handle." I try an unaffected smile, though it feels forced.

Caz grunts beside me but doesn't comment. Everaux ignores the grumble as he continues. "At sunrise, the two of you will be meeting me in the library that sits just below the east wing of the palace." He points to Caz. "I trust you know the place, your highness."

"It's just Cazimir, and yes, I have been to the library many times."

"Good," says Everaux with a wide smile. "Be on your way. Get some rest, and we will begin your training at sunrise."

I nod to Everaux and turn to see Caz has already begun stalking away with his fists swinging at his sides. *Moody, moody.*

I follow behind Caz, hating that I have to walk even more tonight. All of the other initiates are heading west toward Unidad Castle and I hope that they know where they're going because I've never walked through here before. I fall beside the crowd of people, listening to the chattering from some of the initiates.

The siren cousins walk hand in hand together, so light on their feet that they're practically floating. The princess, Nyx, hops with excitement as she speaks to whoever will listen. "I've never been to the castle before. I hear it's gorgeous."

The large troll, Faxon, grunts. "It's a damned paradise, but too clean for my liking. I prefer getting down and dirty in the wild."

"Nobody wants to hear about how you trolls get down and dirty, Faxon." It's Dryden, the dragon prince that responds.

His sister, Juno, gasps and shoves her brother in the arm. "Ew, brother! Don't be gross. He didn't mean it like that."

Faxon shrugs and winks at the young dragon princess. "Who says I didn't, eh?"

Juno's dark brown cheeks flush pink and she shakes her head. "You men are all beasts." She walks quickly ahead of the others, flipping her long braids over her shoulder.

I can't help but smile at the interaction. They may technically be my enemies, but they're entertaining, at least. The vampire prince, Azra, locks eyes with me while I smile and he grins back at me before slowing down to walk beside me. Azra is a foot taller than I am, with spiked black hair and silver eyes. He's muscular, and there's no denying that he's incredibly handsome.

"Hey, warrior girl. I saw what you did with your sword back on the grounds. It was really impressive." His toothy grin is contagious.

I place my hand on the hilt of my sword, *Theo*. "Thanks. I've had a lot of practice."

Azra nods. "I've never trained much with weapons. I've always been taught to use my fangs and strength against my opponents. I admire your skill."

My heart flutters slightly at the compliment and I can't help but glance toward Caz. Why do I feel guilty getting heart flutters from another man? I'm not even with Caz, nor will I ever be. Cazimir crosses his arms and shakes his head at something, but I try to ignore his weird mood.

I look up at Azra as he watches me like I'm something tasty. *Great. A bloodsucker thinks I'm yummy.* "Why are you looking at me like that? You're not going to suck my blood, are you?" I laugh awkwardly, though I'm mostly serious.

Azra laughs loudly and shoves his hands in his suit pants pockets. "I can promise you that I have no plans of drinking your blood, warrior girl." His smile falls slightly and he licks his lips as he whispers. "Biting on the other hand, could be arranged… if you allow it."

Oh boy. I gulp, not used to this kind of talk, and I nervously tuck my hair behind my ear. "You can just call me Ny. I'm not sure the loser of round one deserves the warrior girl title."

Subject change. Nice.

Azra chuckles. "Okay, Ny, though I don't consider you a loser… yet. We'll see where a few more trials get us."

I smile back at him, glad to possibly have a friend within my enemies. "Deal."

Cazimir

I'm an absolute idiot. I kissed someone who my father wants to see dead, and she shut me down, only to let a damn bloodsucker flirt with her. So, why am I sneaking out of my own flippin' palace to bring Nyomi some leftover food? *Yup, idiot.*

I hold the wrapped dish close to my body as I carefully maneuver through the shadows that are cast from the castle's east wall. Ny had to miss dinner because she doesn't have access to her wolf side, and now she's left sleeping out on the ground in the cold night. She told me clearly that she's used to this life, but I have no plans to let her stay used to it.

I check over my shoulder where I can see Nyomi, lying on her back with her ankles crossed and her head resting on her hands. She looks so content in the moonlight, and I feel like I could just stay here, watching her for hours. *Stalker alert.*

I carefully tiptoe closer to her, in case she's sleeping, and her rose scent reaches my nose. I almost sigh at the smell, but I stop myself before I completely freak the girl out. I've lost my mind since meeting Nyomi, and I hate how pathetic I am.

I take another step forward, thinking I should just set the food down and leave. Ny suddenly jumps from her laid back position and in the blink of an eye, her sword is in her hands and aiming for my throat.

"Who's there?" She whisper-shouts at me, but her eyes adjust in the dark and she lowers her sword. "Cazimir?"

I step into the light and try to look apologetic. "I'm sorry for surprising you. I just wanted to bring you some food."

Ny looks down at the foil wrapped dish in my hands and licks her perfect lips. "I can't take it, Cazimir. It's against the rules."

"You need to take it, Ny, and why are you calling me Cazimir?" Her formal tone irritates me in ways that I don't understand.

She shrugs, sheathing her sword again. "I thought you preferred when people called you Cazimir. Your sister said only the ones closest to you use your nickname."

I can't stop the large step that my leg takes to bring me within inches of Ny. Her scent is overwhelming at this closeness. "Sure, only my closest friends and family call me Caz, but I want *you* to as well."

Her eyelashes flutter as she peers up at me. "Me? Your enemy?"

She doesn't understand me at all.

I shake my head and push the food closer to her. "No, Ny. You're not my enemy. You're…" *what is she?*

Nyomi's hands lay on top of mine and she pushes the food away from her before taking her hands away. "I'm not your friend either, though. Right?"

I shake my head. That I can agree with. She is not my friend. I let my eyes memorize Ny's soft face and I sigh as I bend forward to put the food on the ground in the hopes she gives in and eats. She may have missed many meals in her life, but I won't let her do it here.

I take one last hungry look at my non-friend/non-enemy and turn to go back to my room. As I dip back into the shadows and round the corner to the front steps, a tall figure glares at me from the large wooden door.

"What do you think you're doing, son?" My father's narrowed eyes look me up and down like they're assessing my worth.

I shrug. *Play it cool, Caz.* "What do you mean?"

He growls low at me. "Don't act stupid, Cazimir. You're out here bringing food to the *tainted* girl. At least tell me it's poisoned."

I hold back my own growl. The way he talks about Ny has my claws threatening to break through my fingers. "Dad, it's just an act. I have to get close to her, right? Just poisoning her won't go over well with the other initiates and the mages."

Dad thinks over my words and smiles wickedly. "Brilliant. Make it look like an accident and keep the love of your people strong." He steps closer, menacingly slow. "But you *will not* allow her to win."

I let my sharp claws dig into my palm, likely drawing blood. "Of course, Dad."

CHAPTER 9

✦← →✦

Nyomi

Even the castle lawn was more comfortable to sleep on than many of the places I've spent my nights. I woke up just before morning and dug into the baked potato and buttered bread that Caz left behind for me. It was against everything in me to just let it sit there and be wasted.

I look out over the mountains that surround the forest and the sky begins to light up in blues and purples behind the mountain-top silhouette. The sun is rising, so I brush the dirt and grass off of my clothing as I stand and stretch my body out. I catch a few guards patrolling through the trees, and I immediately realize how unusual that is.

I've made sure to number the guards since arriving at Unidad Castle, just in case I need to make a break for it and fight my way out. There have only been two or three men guarding the wall that surrounds the northern land, and maybe four placed on the actual grounds. Just in the last minute, I've counted six guards in one large section of the trees and it makes my stomach a little queasy.

Something isn't right.

I make my way into the palace and through the main floor, choosing not to worry about the guards. I search for at least twenty minutes, but I have no idea where this library is. The sun has risen and I'm lost, late to my training with Everaux.

I groan as I end up in the same hallway for the third time. A sweet voice giggles behind me. "Are you lost, Ny?"

I spin around to see the smiling Princess Clio leaning against a stone wall. "Of course I'm lost. This place is like a giant maze of black and gray."

She giggles again and steps forward to lay a hand on my shoulder. "Come. I'll show you the way to the library."

"How did you know that's where I was going?" I walk arm in arm with her down the long hall.

"I saw Caz just before bed last night. He said you both were meeting Everaux in the library at sunrise. I figured you'd need help finding your way."

I scoff. "And Caz couldn't just tell me where to go? I guess the competition has truly begun." Clio doesn't respond, so I change the subject. "How do you know Everaux?"

"He is a royal from Lupos. He and my dad were friends when they were younger, and he was my tutor when I was really young. We don't see him much anymore, but I'm glad he's here." We round a sharp corner, somehow in a large sitting room that I completely missed. *So much for my grand tour.*

Clio leads me across the room where it empties out into *another* hallway, and she turns to me with excited eyes. "Oh! Did you hear about what happened last night just outside the wall?"

Her sudden switch to gossip-mode has me smiling. "I have no clue, but I'm guessing it's why guard duty has doubled."

"Well, one of the wall patrolmen was killed, and nobody knows what killed him!" She breathes out the words in a huff like she can't believe what she's telling me.

Clio and I stop outside a tall black door, and I tilt my head like a confused pup. "How? Murdering the king's men is unheard of. You'd think there would be enough clues to know what species attacked him at least."

She shrugs. "All I heard from Bastian is that the guard had twisted blue marks like lightning bolts across his body. Really weird, huh?"

I nod, but in the pit of my stomach, something clenches. I have a mark like that along my hip. I've had it my whole life. I don't mention it to Clio, though. Instead, I just look toward the black door, figuring we must've landed at the library.

Clio turns to me, her excitement fading. "We can talk more later, but I have to say something. Whatever you might think of my brother, he's a good man. I just hope you and I can stay friends, even if you choose not to like him."

I pause and give her a warm hug, hoping I'm doing it right and not being creepy. "I'm not sure the initiates can truly be allies, but I'll be your friend as long as you'll allow it."

"Thank you, Ny." Her happy smile returns and she pushes the door open. "Here you are. Good luck."

Clio hurries off to where we came from, and I make my way into the large round room. My jaw drops as I scan the two story high walls of books. There isn't even a window in sight, just books beside more books, making up every inch of the room. I'm so sucked into the grandness of the library that I don't realize the two pairs of eyes watching me.

"Ahem," Everaux clears his throat and I drop my eyes to he and Caz sitting around a small circular table. "The library *is* beautiful, Nyomi, but we have lessons to get to."

"Right," I say, cringing. Luckily, Everaux still smiles back at me, not angry in the least. Caz, on the other hand, has his arms crossed and looks everywhere except directly at me.

I hurry over and pull a seat out beside our trainer, not wanting to sit too close to Caz. "I'm sorry I'm late. I got lost in the halls."

Everaux's eyebrows raise in surprise. "Oh, I see you two aren't teaming up in the trials then?"

It's clear what he means by that. If Caz wanted us to be allies, he would've walked me here himself. I look toward the prince in question and there isn't a hint of emotion on his handsome face. *Okay, then.*

I shrug. "It's alright. It's not a requirement to work together, right? This is a competition after all. Only one can win."

Everaux nods. "I suppose. Either way, my job is to go over your mental knowledge of the kingdoms, as well as train you in combat, the powers you possess, and prepare you for each trial ahead." Caz and I both nod, and I lean forward in my seat, resting my chin in my hands while our trainer continues. "Today, I'd like to understand how well you both know the history of Unity. Raise your hand when you have a question or an answer to my questions."

Great, I finally get to experience school.

Everaux begins at the beginning, the *very* beginning, when the gods and goddesses who ruled over the mortal realm chose to create supernatural beings to live amongst humans. This was over three thousand years ago, and a story that my father taught me when I was young.

In the eyes of the gods, the humans were weak and they were known to go to war with one another over the most minuscule things. The gods thought that by creating and placing more powerful beings on the earth, it would keep the humans in line and give them something to fear. Instead, it only created a sense of comradery and a common enemy for the humans to war against.

A lot of the creatures were killed off and tortured, so the gods pitied them enough to create an entirely new realm for the supernatural kind to thrive. I've heard that the humans will occasionally still see shifters, vampires, or faeries in their realm. It's terrifying to think that some of them were left behind to have to hide their whole lives.

As for the faeries, thanks to King Alix, a lot of them were banished to the mortal realm to do just that. To hide and hope that the humans didn't find out what they are capable of. I already feel like an outcast, so who knows if being tossed in with a bunch of powerless beings would make a difference. I can't even shift.

Everaux's voice breaks me out of my wandering thoughts. "Is there anything I've said about the origin of our realm that's news to either of you? This stuff needs to be known if you wish to rule the kingdoms."

I raise my hand, and of course Caz doesn't. He probably knows everything. "Where are the gods and goddesses now? I don't think I've ever been told that before."

"Ah, yes. As far as anyone is aware, they still watch over the mortal realm. We were left to our own devices over here after the big move. I can't say I mind much, though."

I agree. One self-obsessed tyrant is enough.

"So, did we make our own rules with how to govern ourselves, or was that the gods?" I want to know who to blame for my lot in life.

Caz speaks first. "The gods didn't care how we lived, as long as we didn't start wars and destroy land. It came down to the decisions from the mages at that time, since they were the most powerful. They separated the species and drew the land barriers, as well as chose the first initiates to compete for the main throne."

Everaux claps his hands together once. "Good job, Cazimir. You're absolutely right. The mages put us on the path to have a thriving land of unity, hence the name."

I chew on my bottom lip, not wanting to ask my next question, but unable to stop my smart mouth.

"And who were the ones to decide that inter-species breeding was an abomination?"

The two men go completely still, and thick and silent tension begins to build between us. Everaux clicks his tongue. "Uh... that was the first chosen king of Unity. He was a wolf and his daughter fell in love with the faerie prince. The kingdoms all accepted the union at first. It was only when the king's daughter died during childbirth, birthing a faerie boy, that the king lost his mind."

"It was out of grief," Caz says softly, not looking at me. "The king blamed the faerie blood in his daughter. His belief was that if she had married a wolf, she'd still be alive."

I shake my head in disbelief. How did I not know this before? "It's ridiculous," I say with more spite than necessary. "One man's sadness starts a law that restricts free love forever."

Caz stands abruptly, startling me. "It's still the law, though, Ny. There's nothing we can do about it." With that, he walks off in a huff, leaving Everaux and I alone.

What the hell was that about?

Everaux looks as though he has the same question in his mind. "Well, I suppose that's the end of our lesson for this morning. You are expected to eat with the other initiates in the dining hall and then meet up at the Mutua Arena directly after for another trial." He stands, but doesn't turn to leave right away. "I won't see you or Prince Cazimir until tomorrow morning, so it's up to you to warn him of the trial at the arena. I guess, if you choose not to tell him, then it's his loss. The choice is yours."

He leaves me sitting alone and I ponder his last words. It's my choice to help Caz or forget about him. Why is it so damn hard to choose option two?

CHAPTER 10

← →

Cazimir

I find Bastian alone for once, not long after storming out of the library like a child. I couldn't control the anger that built in me when Ny got so upset about the law that forbids her kind from existing. I stupidly lashed out at her, though I really wanted to go back in time and talk some sense into that wolf king. *Or beat some sense into him if necessary.*

Bastian is working, circling the edge of the forest that surrounds the castle. He is in guard mode, focused and ready for a fight if necessary, and for the first time in a long time, he might actually get one. I couldn't imagine a better guard than him, and if I end up taking the throne, I'll keep him on as my official guard, with a large raise, though.

Voices and laughter carry across the yard from the side of the castle. I turn to see the sirens heading inside, giggling as they spin back around and wink at Bastian before stepping into the west entrance.

I stare wide-eyed at my burly friend. "You have some admirers, brother?"

He scoffs and crosses his arms. "Those sirens will flirt with anything that moves. I'm not about to be taken in by their tricks. Haven't you ever heard the stories about what happens to a man that goes to bed with them?"

I shrug, knowing very well the stories he's talking about, but what fun would it be to fess up? "What stories?"

Bastian shivers as he thinks about the possibility of becoming a siren victim. "They're beautiful on the outside, alluring. They can talk a man into going for a *dip* in the sea, and then they drag him to the bottom, drowning him and sucking the life from him as he dies."

"I don't really think it's true though, man. Do you know what the other kingdoms say about us? That when we transform, the wolf takes over and slaughters everything in its path."

Bastian nods. "I'm not about to test my luck with one of those girls, though. It's forbidden for my kind to mingle with the initiates anyway, especially with the other species."

I smack my hand on his shoulder. "Well, I may need you to get close to one of the initiates, Bastian."

One of his thick brown eyebrows lifts to halfway up his forehead. "Yeah? Who?"

"Nyomi."

"Ooh. So, you do like her, huh?" He grins.

I shake my head. "That's not it, Bastian. I fear that she's in danger, and she's at a disadvantage in the trials. Not to mention the threat that's looming outside the wall. I need you to keep an eye on her, because I can't."

He doesn't understand me completely, and I'm not sure I can really explain it. "Why can't you stay close to her, Caz? I mean, I'm more than happy to look after the girl, but I feel like you have the advantage since you're fighting alongside her everyday."

No sense in hiding the facts. "My father wants her dead," I say in a whisper so nobody overhears. "She's tainted, and the king is not okay with a tainted girl taking the throne of Unity."

Bastian's expression falls to anger. "Let me guess, he wants you to kill her?"

I nod. "I can't do it, brother. There's something about her that makes me want to keep her safe for as long as I'm able."

His eyebrows raise again. "Is it the mate bond? Could Nyomi be your fated mate?"

I think about it for a moment, and it's not the first time I've considered the possibility, but it can't be true. "I haven't seen any sure signs that she's the one. I've always been told that I'd know without a shadow of a doubt when I found my fated mate, and I just *don't*."

"But you do care for her, Caz, and that means something." He nods to me and straightens his shoulders. "Either way, I will do as you've asked. I'll stay close to Nyomi and make sure she's unharmed, alright?"

It feels like a weight lifts from my shoulders. "Thank you, Bastian. Just don't make yourself too obvious. I don't want my father knowing what's going on."

He nods and his eyes land on something behind me, causing his lips to lift on a playful smile. "Little sis looks like she's ready to murder you, Caz. You better go."

I spin around to see Clio glaring at me from the base of the castle steps, her skinny arms crossed over her sparkling dress. *Oh, dear gods.*

I hurry over to Clio with my hands up in surrender. "What did I do?" My little sister may be small and young, but she's feisty.

"I ran into Ny just outside the dining hall. She said she'd like me to give you a message because you're too much of an ass for her to confront face to face."

I almost smile, but stop myself. "Yeah, I'm an ass, but what's new?"

Clio rolls her eyes, which stops the angry glaring. "Ny says that the initiates are expected to appear at the arena just after lunch. She didn't think you deserved to know about it, because you're too moody to even stick around for your lesson to end properly this morning, but I guess she's too kind to screw you over."

I can't stop the smile this time, and Clio's mouth drops open. "Did my big bad brother just *smile* after getting insulted?"

I shake my head, trying not to think about how cute it is that Ny can be so angry with me, and still somehow care about my well-being. "I'm only smiling because it's adorable when you act like an angry little pup."

I reach forward and rustle up her curly hair, causing her to growl at me and shove my chest. "Just get to the trial, Caz, before you lose and end up getting whipped!" I grab my baby sister and pull her into a hug, making her gasp in surprise. "Are you dying, Caz?"

I laugh and shake my head. "Not yet, I'm just happy to have a sister like you. And, I was wondering if you'd be okay with keeping your eye on Ny. She needs a friend, and though it's against the rules to draw blood unless provoked, I worry that some of the others might want to hurt her, rules or not."

Clio leans back with her eyebrows pressed together in worry. "What do you mean? Who wants to hurt her?"

I look around for any eavesdroppers before whispering to Clio like I had with Bastian. "Our father."

Clio gasps and throws a hand over her mouth. "I shouldn't even be shocked. It's not a secret that Ny is only half wolf, but I guess I thought Dad didn't care since she's royal blood."

I shake my head. "He *does* care, and I'm worried that he'll get the other initiates to do his dirty work, since I won't."

Clio thinks about what I'm saying and the disappointment on her porcelain face is intelligible. She nods, looking me in the eye. "I'll help her in any way that I can, and I'll keep it quiet. She really is my friend, and I can't imagine letting her be harmed." She pauses as she notices the relief on my face. "And I won't tell Ny that you asked this of me. She can just continue thinking you're an ass."

*** ← →***

Nyomi

The trial at the Mutua Arena was almost too easy. The mages were waiting for us all, and they only pulled us aside one at a time to ask simple history questions. It seems that the mages are going to surprise us with these little "trials" just to see if we're really committed and can be held accountable. I don't know what they think I'll be doing with my time other than paying close attention. It's not like I have a social life.

After meeting with the mages and running laps, we all ate dinner together and were told to rest for physical training tomorrow. Nobody has said much to me, other than Azra. I can tell that they know I'm different, maybe they even know my blood isn't pure. Even Caz has ignored me all day, leaving dinner earlier than the rest of us.

I hurry ahead of the other initiates to the bedroom I was placed in on my first night here, needing to be alone and breathe. I step inside and shut the door before sliding the borrowed dress cape off of me and tossing it to the side. My arms are tired of being restricted in that dirty outfit.

I sink against the wood in my tight pants and sleeveless top, and I drop to the floor with my eyes closed, taking a slow and needy breath.

"Oh, gods have mercy on me," I whisper to myself, or maybe whatever gods and goddesses still give a crap about us. They have to be out there somewhere.

"Uhh… Ny?" Caz's liquid warm voice reaches my ears and my eyes fly open.

My mouth goes dry when I see the prince of Unity standing in the center of the room, wearing only his leather pants. His sculpted abs and pecs are on full display across his tan torso, daring me to reach out and feel if they're somehow fake.

It takes me a minute to force my eyes up to Caz's handsome face. His hair is wet and hangs wildly over his eyebrows. The look of confusion in his turquoise eyes brings me back to reality.

I leap from the floor and look around the room. It's definitely the same one that I was in two days ago. "What are you doing in here, Caz?"

He scoffs. "This is *my* room. I was assigned it after the meeting last night."

When I was asleep on the lawn?

"But, your room is across the palace. Clio showed me."

Caz steps closer to me, his eyebrows raising. "Why would my sister show you my bedroom?"

I roll my eyes. "No, it's not like that, Caz. She just pointed it out. Don't flatter yourself."

Caz takes another step forward and I take one back, but the door greets me, leaving no space to retreat further.

Caz's eyes search my face and roam south across my bare arms. He has never seen the scars on my upper arms before, and it's obvious when his eyes land on them. A darkness comes over him, erasing the teasing prince from seconds ago.

"What are those?" His voice holds one flat tone as he asks the question.

I cross my arms, covering the marks with my hands that have their own scars. "It doesn't matter. They're just scars. I'm sure you have your own battle wounds."

Caz locks eyes with me and his pupils dilate like those of a wolf's, leaving almost no color. "Battle wounds? Battle with *who*?" He growls the question this time.

I try to stand tall, but my body cringes at the feral sound in his tone. "Caz, I was a prisoner in your dungeons. I told you this already. Do you really think the king's guards just tickled me with feathers for two weeks?" My lip quivers, and I want to scream at myself for feeling so weak in front of him.

He closes his eyes tightly, only a breath away from me, and his hands reach out to rest against the door on either side of my head. His eyes open again, and he's staring down at the bare skin across my chest and shoulders, drinking me in.

He looks at my lips and then my eyes again. "Do you know their names?"

"Whose names?"

Caz growls again. "The guards! The ones that hurt you, Ny. Do you know their names?"

I shake my head. "I remember their faces, but they didn't let me know their names."

Caz's forehead falls softly against mine, surprising me, but I don't pull away. I'm lost in the tantalizing musky scent coming from him, and the heat of his breath against my face.

"Ny, I'm so sorry. I know you don't truly trust me, but I swear to you that I will find out who made those marks on you. And I will do whatever it takes to lay their broken bodies at your feet."

My heart hitches at his words, feeling like it's trying to free itself from my chest and cling onto the man in front of me. Even though his promise is deadly and absolutely criminal, everything about it excites me in a thousand different ways.

I don't respond to Caz's promise. I just stay frozen as his wild eyes continue to search my soul. I find myself lifting toward him, my lips inching closer to his, but before I can taste the warmth of his kiss, he draws back from me, running a hand awkwardly through his messy hair.

"Your room is right beside mine. That direction." He points to his left.

"Oh," I say, and I grab the dress cape that I tossed to the ground. "Right, thanks."

With that, I rush out of Caz's bedroom, feeling more empty than ever.

CHAPTER 11

+← →+

Nyomi

I thought I'd be a prisoner when I was brought to Unidad Castle less than two weeks ago, and I was absolutely right. I've been followed around like a dog on a leash by Bastian, barely able to escape into my room for sleep without his eyes on me. I don't know what his role is, but it feels a lot like he has gone from castle guard to prison warden, and he won't give me any damn answers.

The Kingdom Trials have merely been like school thus far, though I have never been to a real school. Each day consists of learning the history of the six kingdoms and doing physical training at the arena with the mages. I haven't made any friends with the other initiates, but I guess that's for the best considering we're opponents.

I sit down at a long table in the dining hall, the last one to eat like usual. I can't seem to catch up with the others, and I'm probably pissing Bastian off with my slow movements.

"Would you like to feed me that chicken leg, Bastian? Might as well make yourself useful." I glare at him from across the dinner table.

Bastian smiles and shakes his head. "Nah, I'll let you feed yourself."

I scoff and roll my eyes. At least he's kind to me, nothing like the prison guards from two years ago. I sink my teeth into the thick meat of the chicken leg and hold back a moan. The food here is amazing, and I don't know how I'll ever go back to living off the land after this.

Clio slides onto the bench seat beside me, snagging a bread roll from my plate. "Hey, Ny. How was training today?"

I smile at my best friend in this whole place and talk with my mouth full of food. "It was good. Your brother acts like I don't exist though."

The other initiates and I have been training in the afternoons together after the morning history lessons that Caz and I have with Everaux. Of course, *together* isn't the right word. All of the initiates ignore me while they show off their incredible fighting skills and supernatural abilities.

Caz ignores me too, always running out of the library as soon as Everaux dismisses us, and choosing to go through drills across the arena instead of beside me. I have tried not to let his attitude get to me, but it still hurts in ways that I can't explain.

Clio nudges my arm with her pink lips tilted downward in a frown. "I'm sorry about him, Ny. He has never been great with people. Don't take it personally."

I shake my head and feign boredom. "I don't really care. He's technically my rival anyway."

Bastian chortles from his seat and leans back with his thick arms crossed. "Sure, you don't care. I know when you're lying by now, Nyomi."

"Well, of course you know when I'm lying. You're my constant stalker, never giving me space to breathe. You likely know my sleeping and bathroom schedule too, though you won't tell me why!"

Bastian cringes and his eyes flick to Clio for a moment before finding me again. "Sorry. It's just protocol."

I push myself to my feet and flick my long braid over my shoulder a little too sassily. "Right. Protocol. I'm going to bed now."

I stalk away from Clio and Bastian, though I give Clio a softer look before leaving. I don't want her to feel bad for Bastian's part in everything.

I hurry up the stairs to the guest hall where my bedroom is, hoping to escape Bastian for just a moment. As I round the corner after the top step, my face slams into a hard chest, knocking me back onto the ground, and my sword makes a loud clash.

"Ow, dammit!" I shout, rubbing my sore nose.

I look up to see Azra blurring down to grab me and tug me to my feet so fast that I can hardly keep track. *Crazy vamp speed.* "I'm so sorry, Nyomi! Are you alright?"

I nod. "I think so. Don't be sorry. I was moving pretty quickly around that corner, so it's all my fault."

Azra smiles sweetly at me, his white teeth shining in the candlelight. "Good. I'd hate to hurt you in any way."

Azra runs a hand through his short black hair and my stomach gets little butterflies as I watch how sexy that small movement is. I can't deny how gorgeous he is, almost as handsome as Caz. *Don't think about him!*

I realize that Azra is still holding my shoulders after helping me up, so I hurry and step back from him. "I should be going to bed, Azra. Have a good night."

I try to move around the vampire, but he steps into my path, his silver eyes sparkling. "Wait! I wanted to ask you something, if that's alright."

I nod again as the butterflies in my belly continue fluttering wildly. "Yes, of course."

"Well, the official physical trials are starting next week, after the royals ball." *Right, the fancy dancy ball.* "Soon, all of us will be pitted against each other to fight. I was really hoping we could have one really great night together before we have to be real rivals."

I can feel my eyes go wide as I imagine what he could mean by 'really great night'. *Oh, dear goddess.* "I uh… I'm not sure we should…"

Azra laughs loudly, cutting me off with his hand in the air. "No, no! I didn't mean we should *spend* the night together. I'm just asking if you'd like to go to the ball with me. And then I'd drop you at your doorstep like the gentleman I am."

His half-smirk has me smiling back at him like an idiot and I laugh at my ridiculousness. "Oh, good.

I'd actually really like that, Azra. I don't know anything about royal balls, but I hope you don't mind if I step on your toes."

He grins. "I don't mind at all. The bruises will be well worth it." I blush and he strokes a cold thumb across my hot cheeks. "I'll pick you up at your room tomorrow night, then."

I tip my head in agreement and Azra steps around me with one last cute grin. I'm going to my first dance ever, with a vampire. What the hell has my life become?

←→

Cazimir

I've learned that I can easily avoid having to constantly lie to Ny, but something inside my chest hurts from not being near her. I can sometimes hear her in the night through the wall that separates our rooms. She practices with her sword before bed, slicing the air as she hops from foot to foot with skill.

I also occasionally wake to the sound of her crying as she sleeps through whatever nightmares haunt her. It's difficult to not sneak into her bedroom and try to calm her when she does that, but I imagine she'd probably slice my head off if I did.

Today is the day of the royals ball, and the trial trainings have been halted for two days. I don't look forward to spending my evening dancing for the royal families from the other kingdoms, just to show myself off as an initiate. Hopefully the other competitors will put on a good enough show that I can remain in the shadows.

I peek out of my door, looking for any sign of Ny in the early morning, and relief along with sadness floods me when I don't see her. I make my way into the hallway and stop beside Bastian where he's leaning against the wall with a tired smile.

"Your highness. I hope you slept well," Bastian says with a proper dip of his messy brown hair.

I scrunch up my nose, weirded out. "Don't be so formal, Bastian. It's kind of gross."

He chuckles and shrugs as he steps away from the wall. "I'm just practicing for tonight. I'll be on front door guard duty, welcoming the royal families to the castle."

I nod, remembering that my dad gave Bastian the assignment for this evening. I lower my voice. "Thanks for looking out for Ny, man. I was hoping you'd get a real break tonight, but I wasn't expecting Dad to get all paranoid about the ball."

Ever since the night that one of my father's men was murdered outside the wall, he has been extra cautious and doubled our patrolmen, as well as put more responsibility on the ones already employed.

Bastian's smile fades and he avoids my eyes. My alarm bells begin ringing in my head. "What is it, Bastian?"

He sighs. "I didn't want to have to tell you this, but that vampire prince, Azra, asked Nyomi to accompany him to the ball tonight…" My heart sinks and I can feel my wolf side roaring at the idea. Bastian answers my silent plea. "And she said yes."

An audible rumble escapes my throat and I clench my fists tightly by my sides. "She's going on a *date* with Azra?" *With that bloodsucker!*

Bastian nods. "Sounds like it." My breaths leave me in heavy spurts and I stomp down the hallway without a word. "Where are you going, man?"

I don't turn to look at Bastian as I grumble back at him. "I'm going to find something to kill."

CHAPTER 12

✦← →✦

Nyomi

I spin in the long purple gown, feeling like a true princess. The soft sleeves hang off of my shoulders, exposing my neck and collarbone, and they cover my scars along my upper arms. Clio beams at me while she hops up and down in her own maroon dress.

"You're a vision, Ny! All of the men at the ball are going to be struck dumb at the sight of you."

I slide my hands down the tight fabric around my thin waist. I have filled out since coming to Unidad Castle. Eating regularly has taken my bony frame and filled in subtle curves and strengthened my muscles. I feel truly beautiful for once.

I smile at Clio. "Thanks. I don't know about *all* of the men, but I hope Ca... Uh, *Azra* likes it." I hurry and look away from Clio before she can see the blush on my cheeks. I almost said Caz's name instead of Azra's.

Do I care if Caz thinks I look pretty? Apparently.

A soft knock comes from my bedroom door and I gasp as the reality of tonight hits me. I'm going on my first date ever, and I'm officially stressing out.

Clio steps in front of me with her eyebrows raised high. "You okay, Ny? You look like you're going to be sick."

I look around at my bedroom and spot my sword, Theo. "I should grab my sword. I'll feel better with it beside me."

Clio giggles and grabs my shaking hands. "Relax, Ny. It's a dance, not a battle." Her blue eyes are reassuring as she smiles back at me.

I nod and take a deep breath. "You're right. You're coming with me, right?"

She nods. "Of course I am. It's hilarious to me that you're brave enough to fight grown men, but when one of them wants to date you, all of that bravado goes away."

I shrug and chuckle at myself. "I've trained for survival, not royal balls."

Another knock comes and I move toward the door, pulling it open to reveal Azra and his twin brother, Arnoux. They're dressed in all black suits with silky silver bow ties that match their eyes, looking like fancy assassin twins.

"Good evening, Nyomi and Princess Clio," Azra says, and he gestures to his brother. "It's funny that I brought my brother, and Princess Clio doesn't have an escort for the night. It's a match made in Unity."

Clio laughs and sticks her hand out for the silent vampire to take. "I wouldn't say a match, but I'm happy to make a new friend."

Arnoux gives Clio a small smile and shakes her hand, but he says nothing. I haven't heard a word from him in the past two weeks, so I'm not sure he is actually capable of talking.

Azra pokes his elbow out for me to loop my arm in his and I oblige. Clio does the same with Arnoux and shuts my bedroom door behind us.

Before we head off toward the stairs, Azra dips his head to my ear and whispers to me. "You look ravishing tonight, Nyomi. I feel quite lucky to have you on my arm."

Before he pulls away, his cold lips brush my cheek with a small kiss and the butterflies in my stomach become an entire beehive of activity. I follow his silver eyes as he stands tall again and he leads us down the hallway.

The four of us descend the long staircase and make the short walk to the grand ballroom at the east end of the palace. I catch sight of Bastian standing at the front entrance and he rolls his eyes at me as I give him a smug look.

It's the first time he's not trailing me in two weeks and I feel a real sense of freedom, except that I'm hooked in a vampire's arm. Bastian looks behind me at Clio and Arnoux walking arm-in-arm and his brown eyes shift to nearly black with a look of envy. *Woah.*

I've never seen the gentle guard look so ferocious before. It's not a real surprise that he likes being around the Unity princess, but maybe he feels something more than friendship for sweet Clio. She's young, but she acts and looks like a goddess.

We step past the large arching entrance to the ballroom, and it's the first time I've seen this room in all of its glory. A lively melody floats through the air, mingling with the array of voices chattering around the room. Everyone is dressed in their best dresses and suits, making the event even grander.

Clio spins to Arnoux with a big grin. "Do you dance, vampire?" He nods once, silent. "Good. Show me what you're made of."

Arnoux smiles wide and drags Clio behind him to the center of the room. They dance an arms length apart from one another, hopping to the upbeat music and spinning elegantly. I smile as I watch their joy and wonder how I could look that graceful.

Azra bends toward me to talk over the noisy room. "Would you like to join them, little warrior?"

I chew on my bottom lip nervously. "I'm not sure I can do something like that. I've never danced before."

Azra chuckles warmly and grips my hand in his cold one. "Come. You will see how easy it is. If you must stomp on my feet, I'm okay with that."

I let Azra lead me toward the dancing crowd and I look at all of the happy faces as we pass through the room. I find King Alix and Queen Freya standing at the head of the room, greeting guests. The king spots me and his dark eyes narrow tightly as they follow me and Azra.

His glare disappears so fast that it could have been accidental, but the sickness in my stomach says otherwise. He despises me, but it's under his rule that my father has had to keep me hidden my whole life. I despise him too.

I smile at the king, an overtly fake grin, but he doesn't smile back. He just turns his head back to his other guests and his own fake smile finally appears for them. *What a fraud.*

Azra drags my attention back to him as he spins me into his arms and I gasp when our chests meet suddenly. He grabs my waist gently with both of his hands and the upbeat music slows to a more tolerable pace, but not achingly slow, thank goddess.

I'm not ready to slow dance with Azra. To feel his body move against mine to a sensual beat. Just stepping side to side at this pace has me feeling too warm with his bright eyes connecting to mine.

Azra spins me easily before pulling me back to his chest. "You're not as terrible as you expected. My toes are grateful."

I smile and shake my head. "That's all your leading skills, Azra. You're a great dancer."

"You flatter me. I like it." He laughs and I can't stop my own silly giggle.

A light tingling touches my neck, and I swipe at it, but nothing is touching me. I look around the room and my eyes fall on Caz as he watches Azra and I with his arms crossed.

He looks angry and also sort of sad, but the thing that has my heart fluttering is the turquoise in his eyes that flashes silver before he blinks it away quickly. I wonder if I actually saw the color change, or if it was some sort of reflection. Either way, I don't like the way Caz watches me and Azra dance.

I continue looking back at Caz as Azra spins me again a few times and his cool hands slide along my waist. Why do I care what Cazimir Duras thinks? He's an ass to me half the time. Actually most of the time. But still, my wandering eyes trail up and down the prince's large body, drinking in the sight of him with his deep blue suit on and his white neck tie.

Stop it, Ny. He isn't your date tonight. Just ignore... oh, goddess he's coming over here!

Cazimir

Holy hell, I can't stop watching Ny in that dress. All I want is to go to her and tell her how beautiful she is, but she's not mine. She can't be with Azra though, either. My father would kill them both if they mated. *Oh gods, please don't mate!*

I look over at my father where he commands the room, claiming his place in front of everyone else while they dance and mingle. His eyes keep landing on Ny and Azra, making him sneer in anger and disgust. I know he's not happy that the tainted girl is dancing with a vampire, but he doesn't even bat an eyelash at his own daughter doing the same. He trusts Clio, but he has no such feelings toward Ny.

I glance back at Nyomi and her wide gray eyes are watching me while she spins in Azra's arms. A hunger to just touch her washes through me as she keeps her eyes on mine. I watch Azra's hands wrap tighter around her waist and my feet begin to move.

I guess I'm going over there.

I stalk across the room, weaving through the crowd and I look back at my father's angry glare. He knows where I'm headed, so with quick thinking I wink back at the king, hoping he sees it as a sign. His thick brown eyebrow raises and I give him a small nod which appeases him.

I've told him that I plan to get close to Ny in order to end her life without any suspicion. He doesn't have to know that a carnal need is the thing dragging me across his ballroom. That can be my secret alone. I reach my hand up to tap on Azra's shoulder and he turns to me with his smile falling.

"May I cut in, friend?" I ask him, trying to unclench my teeth.

His eyebrows press together as he considers my question and then he steps away from Ny with a bow of his head. "Sure thing, your highness. If the lady doesn't mind."

We both look down at Nyomi and her pale cheeks blush crimson. She licks her lips and nods so subtly that it almost isn't intentional. "That's fine. Maybe just one dance."

Ny smiles at Azra and he leaves us alone in the center of the room without another word. I don't hesitate, since every part of me wants to be closer to her. I reach my hands toward her and let her step into them, not wanting to push her too much.

Ny doesn't speak to me as she sways from side to side in my hands, keeping rhythm with the medium tempo. I can feel her warmth through her dress, and my heart betrays me by pounding faster than the music.

"How have you been? Do you like staying in the castle?" I attempt small-talk, and I sound idiotic.

Nyomi scoffs in a frustrated way and avoids my gaze. "You're talking to me now? I'm surprised you know I exist at this point, your highness."

My heart sinks so fast that I worry it'll get lost inside of me. I've been horrible to her for two weeks now. How could I think a dance and some stupid words would be welcomed?

"I'm sorry, Ny. I haven't been trying to make you feel bad."

"You're a master at it, then. You don't even try and you accomplish it so well."

I hold tighter to her waist as the music slows down to a smooth, almost liquid rhythm. She's so mad at me, and all I've wanted is to keep her safe. Of course, she doesn't know that. Nyomi's heartbeat keeps pace with my own as she lets me pull her closer. Her small hands rest higher on my shoulders, nearly touching the skin of my neck.

"I understand why you feel like I don't care about you. To be honest, I'm not sure why I care quite as much as I do." I keep my voice low, hoping that the noise around us will stop my father from hearing my words. "And if I'm being even more honest, I don't see how anyone would *not* want to be around you all the time."

Ny's chest presses against mine as she sways with me, and my whole body feels like it's on fire. She looks into my eyes and her eyelids flutter slightly. "If that's how you feel, then why haven't I heard a word from you since that night in your bedroom? You saw my scars and you made a promise to avenge me or whatever, as if I'm some helpless princess. And then, what? You haven't said a word or even looked at me since then."

The mix of her anger and the feel of her body moving sensually against mine has my mind reeling. "Ny, please hear me out. Let's go somewhere and talk."

Her hands slide from my shoulders and rest against my chest, but she doesn't push me away. "I'm not sure we should be alone together, Caz."

She's right about that, but I don't even care right now. I slide my hand up Ny's back, needing to be closer to her, even though we're in a crowded room. Something sparks against my chest and I look down at Ny's hands. A blue light like lightning wraps around her fingers and crackles, threatening to burn through my shirt.

My hands leave her waist to cover the electric bolts, and they shock my skin. "Ny, what's that?"

Her round eyes stare at the blue light in shock. "I have no idea. I need to get out of here, *now*."

Her plea has me dragging her toward the back door of the ballroom, and I hope to the gods that nobody saw what I just saw. If I'm correct, Ny has faerie magic.

CHAPTER 13

←→

Nyomi

Why is this happening, and what does it mean? Caz pulls me into a dimly lit hallway behind the ballroom. The music bleeds through the walls, sounding muffled and dark. Caz doesn't flinch as he grips my blue hands tightly while we hurry away.

We stop once we're completely out of sight and sound of the others, and I pull my hands out of his. The blue electric light sparks and crackles before slowly fading away as I try to wipe it along my dress. It shouldn't work, but somehow it disappears just like that.

I look back at Caz in horror as he stares down at my hands. "What the hell was that? Was that magic?" I've never seen anything like it.

Caz reaches for me and grabs my hands again, inspecting them closely. His eyes roam over my body, looking for who-knows-what, and I feel just as hot under his gaze as I had swaying with him on the dance floor. Just as fast as it faded, the blue lightning appears again, starting at my hands and trailing up my arms.

Caz stares at the light and slides his hands along my arms. I can tell the lightning hurts him, because his eyes crinkle and he clenches his jaw tight with a hiss. Still, he keeps touching it and trying to figure the magic out.

"Ny, do you know what this is?" He releases my hands, and the blue fades away once more.

I shake my head. "Do I look like I'm in the loop here? This is new to me."

My hands are back to normal again, seeming to not spark up when Caz isn't touching me. He must realize it too as he says, "Touch me, Ny."

I laugh uncomfortably. "You want me to just touch you? Where?" He licks his lips and a darkness fills his turquoise eyes as his lips curl up at the corners. "Don't be gross, Caz! I'm just going to touch your cheek and stop that filthy mind from coming up with ideas."

He stands tall and ready, his smile still lingering as he nods for me to continue. I reach my hand up to stroke the stubble on his strong jaw. Caz's eyes lock onto mine and the same warmth as before fills me, causing my hands to send out blue lightning and shock his skin.

He hisses again but doesn't pull away. I snatch my hand back and gasp as the light fades for the third time. "Okay. I'm totally lost."

Caz steps closer to me, but quickly stops himself before trying to touch me. "Ny, this *is* magic. I've never seen it, but I've heard of it. It's unique to the Fae…"

My jaw drops and I look back down at my now shaking hands. "It's faerie magic? But how?"

"You're half wolf, right? What about the other half?"

I shake my head as I imagine my dad being a faerie. There's no way. I would've known, right? "My dad never told me what he was. I assumed he was either a dragon or just a human."

Caz shrugs. He tucks a strand of hair behind my ear and looks at the appendage. "Your ears aren't pointed. Were your dad's?"

"No, they weren't. He didn't have any qualities that stood out one way or another. He looked just like me. He had dark hair and gray eyes like mine. He never shifted or used magic in any way." *Why didn't I ask more questions?*

Caz eyes me for a few minutes. What could he be thinking? I probably seem so freakish to him. A tainted girl who doesn't even know what blood taints her. I don't belong in this place at all.

I turn to walk away from Caz's prying eyes, but he stops me with a hand on my arm. Somehow, he can grab me as the men did in those dungeons two years ago, and I feel safe, instead of trapped. I look up at him and his face is just inches from mine.

"What am I, Caz?" My words are a whisper. I don't even want to know the answer anymore.

He looks deep into my eyes and then at my parted lips. "I don't know where you came from, but I think I know what you are." His head dips closer and I can almost taste the warmth from his lips. "You're my mate."

Those are the last words I expected to hear from him, but every fiber of my being feels the truth in them anyway. I suck in a sharp breath and close my eyes, ready to kiss him again like I've dreamt of doing since the night of the first trial.

A voice interrupts our moment and I jerk back from Caz's grip. "You guys need to come back inside before Dad realizes you've gone." I snap my head toward Clio and she looks apologetic as she waves us to her. "I'm sorry."

Caz runs a hand through his thick hair and nods to his sister. "Don't worry, sis. Thanks for the heads up."

He looks back at me with a longing on his perfect face, and he leaves Clio and I alone in the hallway without another word. I take a steadying breath as Clio looks knowingly at me.

"What? We were just talking." *Lies.*

She shrugs and her smile is almost sad as she links our arms together. "Sure you were, Ny. Don't worry. I won't say a word to anyone about your naughty hall kisses with my brother."

And that is why she's my best friend.

Nyomi

I feel like I'll never get the chance to be alone with Caz again. The ball has dragged on well into the night, and it has been a struggle trying to stay present for my date. Azra didn't question where I disappeared to after dancing with Caz. I don't know if he just doesn't care or if he knows what's up and doesn't want to mention it. Either way, I really like the vampire, but not in the way any normal girl would.

Caz called me his mate, and I don't know how to feel about it. If we were true mates, we would've known two weeks ago. Though, it somehow feels more true than anything I've ever known.

I've watched as Caz has made his way around the room of people, mingling and smiling to his father's guests. He's perfect for the role of king, to follow in his father's footsteps. Occasionally, he will look over at me and let his eyes roam over me for a moment before returning to his rounds.

The guests and even the king and queen all retire to their beds or return home as the ball comes to a natural end, leaving us initiates alone. Clio warned me that the initiates in the past Kingdom Trials traditionally stay after the ball and have a sort of after party. If it wasn't for this so-called tradition, I would've escaped hours ago.

The trolls, Echo and Faxon, are flirting with the siren girls. They're causing a ruckus as they dip them and twirl them without any music playing. The rest of us watch and giggle at the scene, sitting on the ballroom floor. I keep finding Caz's eyes watching me from across the room where he sits with Arnoux and Clio.

Azra places his hand on mine. "I hope you've enjoyed this night. Tomorrow, we will be battling as competitors for the throne of Unity. I cannot see myself harming you in any manner, Nyomi."

I smile back at him. "I feel the same way." His longing look makes me squirm and I hurry to shut down whatever thoughts flood his mind. "I'm glad we've become such good friends, Azra. You'd make a great leader."

His eyes close as he chuckles and takes his hand off of mine. "Yes, friends. I see no reason why we can't be the best of friends after this mess is over and done with. You know, when I take the throne." He winks and I laugh.

"You mean, when I'm the next queen of Unity, right?"

He sighs and shakes his head. "We will have to see, little warrior."

Clio's laughter makes me look over at her. She's talking to Arnoux, who sits quietly listening with a sweet smile. I nudge Azra. "Does your brother ever speak?"

He shakes his head. "No. He hasn't spoken a word since he was seven years old. The old king of Vampir was a ruthless man, and brother to my father. He liked to teach his subjects the most cruel lessons, just for his own enjoyment." He pauses as a sadness covers him. "My mother was a kind woman, and she was incredibly brave. She stood up to the king and demanded that he change his ways. Arnoux was by her side when the king killed her in front of him and my father. I was off playing with my youngest sister and my cousins."

I gasp and my hand flies to my chest as I feel his sorrow. "I'm so sorry, Azra. Arnoux must have been terrified."

He nods. "It shook him to the point of silence. My father took his revenge on his brother and claimed the throne of Vampir not long after that day. Arnoux has never been the same."

I look over at the silent vampire brother and my heart aches for him. I know what it's like to lose a parent. I've lost both of mine, but I can't imagine seeing something like that at such a young age.

I find Caz's gaze again, and I sigh internally at how good it feels to have him looking at me that way. What do I have to do to make that look permanent? A loud shriek pierces through the chatter from the initiates, and all of us jump to our feet, suddenly alert.

A young wolf maid runs into the ballroom with her eyes dripping with tears and her voice panicked. "There's a fire! A fire in the kitchen!"

All of us look from one to another, and in less than a second we're running through the castle walls toward the kitchen. Smoke fills the hallways and red flames flicker out of the kitchen doors. A few of the castle guards and workers are dousing the fire with water buckets that hang along the walls for emergencies.

"Is anyone inside?" It's Caz who takes charge and yells the question.

"A young woman, your highness! She's passed out and we can't get to her!"

Before Caz can respond, the dragon prince Dryden begins shouting. "Where's Juno? Where's my sister?"

With no response, he shifts into a long red dragon with shining scales and large folded-in wings.

He dives through the kitchen doors and disappears inside the smoke.

"Dryden!" We all scream for him, with no answer.

After the longest minute of my life, Dryden steps out of the smoke with his passed out sister in his dragon arms and he lays her in the hallway, away from the smoke. He quickly shifts back to his human form with his nice suit torn and burnt all over.

"Juno! Wake up!"

All of us watch helplessly as Dryden cries for his sister. Her chest is still and it's clear that she's no longer with us. I step closer to her and reach my hand out to feel her pulse. There's not a single beat under my fingers and I look up at Dryden with pained eyes.

He knows the answer and doubles over, cradling Juno's body in his arms. As he pulls her higher, her long singed dress lifts up her legs, revealing dark jagged scars like lightning across her skin. I gasp along with the others that spot the markings.

Dryden looks down and his eyes go wide. "No, no, no. How is that possible?"

I turn toward Caz and his jaw is tight, along with the rest of his body. "It's just like the guard. Something has attacked Juno within our own castle walls."

"What is it, though? Who did this?" I feel like the only one who doesn't know what this means, and a sickness in my stomach makes me not want to know.

Caz swallows hard as he looks down at where I kneel beside the dragons. "The faeries are back."

PART 3

A TRIAL OF BONE

CHAPTER 14

←→

Nyomi

I stand beneath the crescent moon, my eyes closed as exhaustion wears on me. Floating all around me is thick smoke from the remaining ashes of the kitchen fire. The smoke mixes with new falling raindrops and I welcome the cold water against my face.

It was the siren girls that stepped in to finally douse the fire with their water magic and stop it from reaching the rest of the castle. Everyone was in a sort of shock after seeing the dragon princess die. Dracon is with the king and queen now, discussing the events of the night, and the others have all gone to bed.

There's no way the fire killed Juno. A dragon is impervious to fire, but the lightning-like markings along her body are something unexplainable. I think about my own jagged markings that snake across my lower back that match Juno's perfectly. My father told me I was born with them, but I'm beginning to fear that was another lie. *Was I harmed by a faerie too?*

"Are you alright?" Caz stops beside me, joining me in staring at the moon.

I shrug. "I don't understand. Even if the faeries are back in Unity, why would they want to hurt Juno? She was kind."

We stand alone in the dark while Caz contemplates my question. I glance over at him. His profile is so handsome. Just hours ago, I found out that he and I are sort of fated mates. News that both excites me and fills me with overwhelming anxiety. It feels real, but something is holding back the feeling that should tell us without a doubt that we're meant for one another.

He doesn't look at me, his turquoise eyes remaining fixed on the sky. "I think Juno's death wasn't planned. Nobody would target her above my parents or myself. She must've been in the kitchen when the attackers ran into her. I wouldn't be surprised if she started the fire trying to fight back."

I nod. "That makes sense. But what about the faeries? They were exiled nearly seventeen years ago. Why come back now?"

Caz shrugs and he turns toward me. His eyes explore me with so much thought and feeling that my heart aches just from his gaze. "Ny, about what I said earlier… that you're my mate…"

I shake my head. "We don't need to talk about that. We'd know for sure if it were true, right? Do you know, like without a single doubt?"

It feels like eternity between my question and his long sigh. "Honestly, I can't imagine it not being the truth, but there is a small unexplainable doubt." He groans. "What the hell is happening? Please tell me you feel what I'm feeling and that I'm not just an idiot."

I smirk and nudge his arm. "Well, you're definitely an idiot…" he glares at me with his own little grin. "But, you're not wrong about the feelings between us."

Silence fills the air as he continues watching me like I'm some indecipherable puzzle. "What does this mean for the trials tomorrow? We'll have to fight one another."

I nod. "Right. Well, for now, maybe just pretend like this connection between us isn't there. We have a role to play in these trials, Caz. You should know that better than anyone."

It hurts to say the words, but they're true. Caz and I can't be together, at least not now. Even if it weren't for the Kingdom Trials, he's still a prince, and I'm still a tainted blood.

Caz contemplates my words. "Okay. I'll pretend, then. If it'll keep you safe, I'll do anything." He reaches toward me and his hand strokes along my warm cheek, stopping just below my ear for a moment as his voice lowers to a whisper. "I'll be thinking about you though, Nyomi Mailon. Every single minute."

I close my eyes tightly, having to hold myself back from doing something stupid. A coldness touches my cheek from Caz's absence and I open my eyes to see him gone.

I'll be thinking about you too.

❦ ❦

Cazimir

The trials started just two weeks ago, but today is when we are to be really put to the test. It's time for the initiates to fight, and it's not going to end well. Growing up, when I have been told about the Kingdom Trials and their layout, it has always seemed so wrong to let the initiates spend time bonding before they have to beat the crap out of each other. Just another thing to thank the first king for.

We were called to Mutua Arena first thing this morning and told to pick our sparring partners upon arrival. Everyone stands around, unsure who they want to fight with first, so I do a quick eeny-meeny-miny-moe in my head and land on the siren princess, Nyx.

I try to ignore Ny as I walk past her, but I still pick up her scent and my eyes turn of their own free will. She looks at me with a small smile, looking like a warrior with her sword on her hip, hanging over the tight leather pants that hug her perfectly. She watches me watch her for a moment, but then she turns toward the vampire twins.

Her soft voice floats to me. "Hey, Arnoux. Will you be my partner?"

The silent vamp nods with a kind smile, but I can't help being angry with him already. He could hurt Ny, and I'm not sure I'll be able to handle that. *Gods, this will be torture.*

Nyx notices me approaching her and she flips her incredibly long red hair over her shoulder. "By the look in your handsome eyes, I guess I'm the lucky one who'll fight the honorable Prince Cazimir."

She smiles evilly, and I try not to cringe. Sirens are wicked and smart, and they don't care who knows it. I nod to her. "You up for it?"

"Big time, although..." she glances at her cousin, Iris. "After what happened with Juno, you'll have to fight the both of us."

I swallow hard. She's right. The pairs would be uneven now after losing Juno. I look between the two smiling sirens and shrug.

"Well, damn. I guess I'm fighting two sirens then. Go easy on me?"

They both laugh, and Iris shakes her head. "Not a chance, your highness."

I'm really sick of people calling me that.

"Good morning, initiates!" My father's voice breaks the chatter in the air and we all stand at attention, everyone paired up now.

The king continues, "I hope you all found worthy opponents for your first fight. I'll personally be overseeing these next trials. The rules are simple. Each pair that was chosen by you will spar for the others to observe. We ask for no bloodshed, and no broken bones. You are expected to show each one of your abilities in today's fights."

My father's eyes scan the matched up initiates and land on the sirens beside me. "Nyx, Iris, and Cazimir. Your match is acceptable for today only. Based on your performances today, I will assign the pairs for the next four days."

What?

I step forward and dip my head to my father. "After today, what are the rules for the next fights?"

The corners of his mouth lift slightly and one of his thick eyebrows raises high. It's a look that I know well. Clio and I call it his evil-plan-look. "Good question, Prince Cazimir. After today, the fights have but three rules. One, you *must* draw blood on your opponent in order to move on to the next trial. Two, there will be *no* fighting to the death." He pauses and his eyes scan over each of us. "And three, the losers of each fight will be penalized in a form of *my* choosing."

I suck in a sharp breath, my stomach aching at my father's words. If Ny loses a fight, my father will be the one to choose her punishment. He claims that killing and fighting to the death isn't an option, but there is no such rule that the king can't kill who he pleases. I thought watching Nyomi be beaten in a fight would be torture, but this could mean war with the king of Unity himself.

CHAPTER 15

← →

Nyomi

The king's speech has everyone on edge as we are pushed to the sidelines of the grand arena. I knew the trials would be brutal, but I never imagined I could be beaten and then re-beaten by the king of Unity if he so chooses. As for today's so-called "sparring" matches, we are expected to show *all* of our unique abilities. What will happen if my new blue Fae magic makes an appearance?

I never thought I could even have abilities, except maybe the ability to shift into a wolf. But faerie magic? Not even in my wildest nightmares could I have imagined that.

I look over at King Alix where he stands smug at the center of the large field. Every so often his dark eyes land on me and I can see the disgust that flashes across them. My hatred for him is not just a simple feeling, but there's no doubt in my mind that he feels equal animosity toward me.

"Now," the king says with his loud voice. "Let us begin with my son, Cazimir, and his two lovely opponents."

He waves a hand at Caz and my stomach lurches. I don't want to see Caz fight the siren women by himself. They're strong and cunning. Come to think of it, though, I've never seen Caz actually fight. *Oh, goddess, I hope he doesn't suck.*

Caz's muscles shift beneath his tight white shirt as he folds the long sleeves up to his forearms. He steps out to the center of the arena, taking his father's place, and the sirens follow him to stand a few yards away.

Caz glances over at me like I've seen him do a few times today. His turquoise eyes meet mine and he quickly turns his head forward to face the threat in front of him. He's so gorgeous and exudes so much power that I can't imagine him being overpowered. Still, everything in me wants to protect the man that may or may not be my eternal mate.

"Begin!"

The one word from the king has Nyx stretching her arms wide to create long tentacles like an octopus. Her teeth flash in the sunlight and shift into razor-sharp rows of fangs. Caz doesn't flinch at the terrifying sight. He only watches on with what looks like boredom.

"Come on, pretty prince. We're waiting," Iris taunts as she stays in human form beside her cousin.

Caz chuckles softly, and then he runs full speed at Nyx. One of the siren's long tentacles snaps toward Caz, and I flinch, but he jumps over the thing like a jump-rope and lands easily on his feet. Iris opens her mouth to spew out a jet of water that hits Caz's feet and knocks him on his back.

He recovers quickly as he rolls to his side, avoiding a tentacle hit, and he jumps back to his feet, dripping wet with his hair hanging over his eyes. *Damn, he's sexy when he's all wet.*

"Thanks, Iris. I needed a little cool off," Caz says with a grin before grabbing onto the next tentacle that flies at his face.

He grips the slimy appendage and pulls it so hard that Nyx falls forward and hits the earth hard. She throws another tentacle at him and it wraps around his waist, squeezing tightly. Iris laughs at Caz trapped in her cousin's grip and she dives at Caz, clinging onto his back while her arm wraps around his throat.

I gulp and my hands start to sweat as I watch Caz locked in both of the siren's clutches. He wiggles and grunts as he tries to free himself with no use. Then, his eyes flick to me and I watch as the blue and green fades away to complete black. He releases a deafening howl before his body sprouts long dark fur and he bursts from the siren's hold as a large wolf.

Nyx and Iris stumble backward and Caz growls menacingly at them both. His black nose scrunches in anger and he licks his massive jaws. Excitement ripples through me at the sight of Caz in his animal form. He's incredible and I wish so badly that I could feel that feeling of freedom and strength.

He growls once more at the girls as he circles them on all four legs, and then he leaps toward Iris with his teeth reflecting rays of sunshine. Iris shoots another wave of water at Caz, but he pushes right through it with ease, like a light drizzle hitting him. He pounces on Iris, knocking her to the ground with a loud thunk and she elbows him in the face without any luck.

"Okay, I'm down," Iris yields with her hands up, and Caz climbs off of her.

Iris scrambles away, but Nyx isn't ready to concede just yet. Her two long tentacle arms stretch farther than I've seen yet, and she slams one of them into Caz's side. The hit makes him stumble, but he doesn't go down. A whistle pierces the air as her other arm whips at Caz.

He ducks his large wolf head, narrowly avoiding the hit, and then he leaps at Nyx's unprotected torso. His head rams into her, knocking the breath from her, but she recovers by jumping over Caz and landing on his furry back. She does the same thing Iris had, and she wraps her arms around Caz's much bigger neck.

She squeezes tightly as Caz tries to buck her off of him, so he changes his tactics and rolls onto his back, crushing her beneath his heavy weight. Caz just lays on top of the siren princess until she screams and sticks a human arm out in surrender.

"I'm done! Let me up!"

Caz obliges and moves off her, shifting back into human form once he's a few feet away. His clothing remains on him, and I'm slightly disappointed by that fact. I try not to visibly pout in front of everyone, and I cheer for him with the other initiates.

"And we have a winner of our first spar!" King Alix cheers loudly and waves Caz over to the rest of us. "Alright, now for our winner, who do you choose to follow this victory of yours?"

Caz looks at the other three pairings of initiates and his eyes land on Arnoux and I. "Them. Nyomi and Arnoux will fight next."

My mouth drops open as I stare back at Caz's pointed finger. *Stupid handsome idiot.*

+←→+

Nyomi

I walk out onto the field with Arnoux by my side. We stop in the spot that the others just vacated, and he turns quietly to me with a dip of his head before backing away a few yards. The vamp's silence usually makes him seem shy and sweet, but in this moment it feels much like the calm before the deadly storm.

This is the moment that the others will see the truth about me. I can't possibly get away with hiding my inability to shift after this. We have to show *all* of our abilities, and I have none.

I raise my hand and turn to the king. "What about weapons? Can I use my sword?"

King Alix crosses his arms and looks down at Theo hanging from my hip. "Your body should be a weapon, young wolf. I need to see that you can be victorious without the crutch."

My stomach feels sick as I think about fighting a vampire with my bare hands. My dad taught me how to fight well, but I don't have Arnoux's strength. I unhook Theo and lay it on the dirt by my feet.

My eyes find Caz and the worry creasing his brow makes my heart hurt. His muscles are tense and he looks ready to jump in at a moment's notice. I know exactly what he's feeling because I felt it for him while he fought. I shake my head barely, hoping he can see what I'm trying to tell him. He can't try to be my hero.

King Alix shouts for us all to hear. "Begin!"

I crouch and spin back to Arnoux who is already charging me head on. *Dammit!* His black ponytail blows in the breeze and his silver eyes narrow as he slams into me, grabbing me around the waist.

All of the air leaves my body, and I gasp at the force of his hit. Arnoux drops me to the ground, releasing my waist and I think back to the many sparring matches with my dad. The energy from those fights comes back to me, and I quickly swing my leg out from my horizontal position, kicking Arnoux in the ankle.

The vampire stumbles with a grunt and I swing my other leg up into his handsome face with a crack. *Yes!* He steps backward, reaching for his broken nose.

"Sorry about the nose," I say, climbing to my feet. Though, after his first hit, I'm not *that* sorry.

Arnoux growls and spins on me again. His speed catches me off guard as he circles me so fast that a whirlwind of dirt begins swirling around me, blocking my view of everything. I turn in circles, trying to pinpoint where Arnoux actually is in the small tornado.

I catch a glimpse of his ponytail and reach my hand out to grab hold of the hair with all of my strength. My grip stops Arnoux from his speed-running, and I take the chance to leap onto his back, locking my ankles around him.

"Do you like giving piggyback rides, vampire prince?" I tease in his ear.

Arnoux shakes his head and takes off running with me clinging onto him. I try to get my arm secured around his neck to choke him out, but the speed of the wind hitting me makes it hard to move at all.

Arnoux slows down and does a flip with me hanging on for dear life like a baby monkey. Unable to shake me off, he drops onto his back, landing on top of me with another powerful hit to my body.

I groan but don't let go, despite the pain in all of my muscles. I take his stillness as an opportunity, and I climb up his back to secure my legs around his neck like I've seen my father do before.

Arnoux throws his head back into my stomach, making me let him go, and he jumps to his feet. His sharp fangs extend with a small snap, wet and shining in the daylight. If he could speak, I imagine he'd be letting me have it at this moment.

I push myself up as well, crouching in a fighting stance as I pant heavily. Arnoux shows off another one of his abilities by leaping high into the air and rocketing back down to me. This should be my moment to shift into a wolf, but nothing comes when I call for it in my mind.

Instead of shifting, I dive to my right, barrel rolling away from the oncoming Arnoux. He lands amazingly gracefully on the ground, inches from myself and whirls on me, his hands tightening around my neck.

There's no wiggling free of him this time as his grip strengthens and I gasp for air. The fighter in me refuses to yield, and I curse myself in my mind for being so stubborn. I try to throw my knee into Arnoux, but he moves out of my reach every time.

No, no, no!

I pull at his forearms with all of my strength, but it's no use. I'm finished. A burning feeling fills my lungs and I notice the beginning sparks of my unexplainable faerie magic light my fingertips. I can't let King Alix see the magic.

I raise my hand in surrender and let my body go limp. "I yield," I rasp out, barely loud enough to be heard.

Arnoux releases a heavy breath as he lets me go, but he catches me before I drop to the dirt. He hoists me to my feet, making sure I'm steady enough to walk before stepping away with a smile of victory.

"Another winner! Congratulations, Prince Arnoux of Vampir." The king claps along with the others as Arnoux and I walk back to them. King Alix looks at me with his eyes narrowed. "Nyomi, you did not shift. That goes against the rules I set for today. Can you explain?"

I avoid everyone's judging eyes as I rub my sore neck. I try to stand tall and proud as I address the king. "Yes, your highness. I'm sorry to say that I haven't yet connected with my wolf side... I am unable to shift."

A few of the others gasp behind me, but I keep my eyes on the monster in front of me. His eyebrows raise in surprise as he looks me up and down. "Okay. You have not broken my rule, then."

That's all he says before turning to the initiates and having Arnoux point to the next fighters. I can't tell if I'm in trouble or not, but at least I have a minute to breathe before I find out.

CHAPTER 16

◂← →▸

Cazimir

Yesterday's sparring matches ended with four winners. Arnoux, Azra, Echo and myself. The vampire twins have proven to be strong and skilled fighters, though the real competition is Nyomi. She had the upper hand in her fight with Arnoux, and she did so without any abilities. If she was free to use her faerie magic, nobody would stand a chance.

It's barbaric of me, but watching her fight like a warrior was incredibly sexy. I only wish she could harness her wolf. Without it, I fear she'll be hurt in the coming trials.

It's another day of fighting, but the real battles begin today. It's time to break bones and draw blood, but I feel underprepared. I don't know what my father has up his sleeve for the losers of these challenges and he's not known to go easy on anyone, even his own children.

"It's time to show what you are all made of," my father says above the sound of the falling rain hitting the trees above our heads.

A storm is coming, and the fights are supposed to happen in the forest surrounding Mutua Arena. We are free to fight all along the trees, only to be monitored by the mages. Their gifts help them to track our movements, though they can't see every move we make. Anything goes in these woods.

My dad continues, "Yesterday, you all put on a good show for your competition. Now that we have all seen what each of you is capable of, everyone should be prepared. As for pairings, we will begin with a match that I thought would do well to start us off." He points to Dryden, and then to Ny.

You've got to be kidding me.

"Nyomi Mailon and Prince Dryden. You both lost yesterday's fights, so I have been itching to see how you'd both do in a real battle."

I trail my eyes along Nyomi and can tell she's nervous for this fight. Dryden has been distracted of course, because of Juno's death, but he's still one of the most powerful of us all. This fight could go horribly wrong for my Ny.

My ny? Damn, I've lost my mind.

"But," my father says, drawing all of our eyes to him. "We have a bit of a number problem here." He looks at the sirens. "You two will not be fighting in a pair like yesterday. This leaves me to bring in a volunteer."

Out of the trees steps a man shorter than myself, though just as broad. I've seen him before, but I don't know him well. He's a wolf shifter guard in the dungeons, around my father's age. His shaved head getting pelted with raindrops makes him look mean.

"This is a good friend of mine, Zaros Darmain. He will step in to fight as one of you."

A small whimper brings my attention back to Nyomi. Her wide gray eyes are staring at Zaros like he has three heads and matching horns. I can hear her fluttering heartbeat and smell the fear coming from her. It makes my wolf side stir uncomfortably, needing to save her from whatever it is she fears.

Zaros steps beside my father with a smug grin on his wrinkled face. "It's good to be here with you initiates. I wish you all good fights to come." His eyes narrow on Nyomi in the same way that my father's eyes do regularly, and something twists in my gut as she shivers under his gaze.

No, no, no. This isn't right.

The king continues telling us about his little game. "So, Nyomi and Dryden will not be fighting one another today. Instead, Zaros and Nyomi Mailon are our first match." *Shit!* "You have five minutes to prepare yourselves, and we will meet you both at the castle grounds. Let the fights begin!"

I hold back the growl in my throat as the reality of what just happened sinks into me. Nyomi was just targeted by my father, and his weapon is one of the guards that tortured her before killing her father in the castle dungeons. I can't let this happen.

Nyomi

It's him, the man that haunts my dreams. His dark eyes and the small scar just below his left eyebrow are a vision that hasn't left my head for two years. I spent weeks enduring this man's torture, and this is when I learn his name? *Zaros Darmain.* Even his name makes bile rise in my throat.

The other initiates begin to leave, making their ways back to the castle where my fight with Zaros will come to an end. They're leaving the two of us alone, and I already know that no eyes will be watching when he gets his hands on me again. This is King Alix's plan, to get rid of the tainted girl in his Kingdom Trials.

I peel my eyes away from the haunting ones of my devil, to find the calming ones of my potential mate. Caz is frozen as his father and the others disappear into the trees, his fists clenched at his sides as he looks between Zaros and I. It's clear that he knows what this fight means, but there's nothing he can do to stop it.

Zaros waves a hand at Caz. "You should go, Prince Cazimir. Get out of the rain. Your fight will come."

Caz growls so deep that it vibrates the earth beneath our feet. The sound makes all of my nerves go wild, and I want to gravitate towards it. "Zaros Darmain," Caz says with disgust in his voice. "How long have you been a guard in my father's prison?"

Zaros smiles like it's another day in paradise. "All of your life, young prince. Every prisoner that crossed those doors in the past twenty years got a good look at my ugly mug."

His voice makes my skin crawl. I watch Caz take a step forward and I step in front of him. "This isn't your fight, Cazimir. Go home so I can kick the guard's ass." I hate having my back to Zaros, but I need Caz to leave. If he gets involved, his father would know.

Caz's turquoise eyes connect with mine and the anger in them subsides. "Is he one of the ones that you told me about?" His eyes fall to my covered arms where the scars of my past hide. "Did he do that to you, Nyomi?"

I try to steady my breathing. I can't let him see my fear. I need to be strong. I nod to Caz, answering his questions, and it makes another rumble rise in his chest. He tries to step around me but I don't let him.

"Caz, please," I whisper, but I know Zaros can still hear my words. "This. Isn't. Your. Fight." I force each word out separate from the other so he will hear the seriousness in my tone.

Zaros clears his throat behind me, but neither of us looks back at him. Caz shakes his head. "I made you a promise."

I don't have to ask what promise he's talking about. I remember him telling me that he'd lay my enemy's broken bodies at my feet. But he can't keep that promise while we're in the middle of these trials.

"Go," I say again, pulling my sword from its sheath and raising it between us. "I made my own promise to myself, and I intend to keep it."

Caz hesitates momentarily before nodding once and running off without another word. Now it's just Zaros and I, alone once again. I turn to the wolf shifter with the gentle raindrops hitting Theo's metal.

"I'm not the same little girl you once knew. I need you to know that before I kill you."

Zaros laughs, his shoulders shaking from the movement. "You'll always be that little tainted girl. The same one that cried for her daddy day and night."

My heart twists, but the anger rising up my neck outweighs the sorrow I feel for my younger self. "You want a fight? Come get me."

I spin and take off at a full sprint through the wet woods, needing to get somewhere out of the open where I can kill the nasty guard without repercussions. Killing isn't allowed in the trials, but it's well-known that it happens out in the trees where no eyes can see.

I stop when I realize that I can't hear any footsteps behind me, and I turn in a circle. Zaros is nowhere to be seen in the dense forest. The only sound is my own heavy breathing and the pelting rain on the leaves above my head.

"Where are you, asshole?" I call out.

I wait as I try to hear anything that would give away Zaros' position. Something like a heavy footfall on the wet earth has me spinning to my right. Crouched in the overgrowth is a large black wolf. His black eyes watch me with an evil stare and I swing my sword toward him.

The wolf growls and leaps at me, narrowly missing the swipe of my blade. His teeth scrape my arm as I try to side-step him, slicing along where my scars sit, and I cry out in pain. I don't hesitate as I turn and swing at him again. This time I make contact with his back leg, cutting into his flesh. The wolf roars as he limps away from me. I crouch, ready to fight off his next attack, but he doesn't come at me. He just stares at me in anger, his hind leg bleeding into the wet earth.

I scoff. "Done already, Zaros? That's no fun. You used to have more stamina."

Something hard hits me in my back, knocking me onto my face as I drop Theo in the mud. I gasp as something crushes me from behind, taking my breath away from the force. I struggle against whoever has me pinned on the ground, but they're strong.

"I still have plenty of stamina, little girl. I'm just getting started." Zaros' voice comes from my back, but the black wolf still snarls in front of me.

I reach for my sword, but a boot stomps down on my hand, crunching my fingers beneath the weight. I try not to scream from the pain. "This is how you fight, Zaros? You invite a friend and attack from behind? You're the same piece of crap you were in those dungeons. Scared of a little tainted girl."

A knee slams into my back, making me choke on air as Zaros speaks again. "Shut up! You have never been worth anything. Your father kept you hidden because he knew you were an abomination." He presses harder again and the black wolf makes an almost laughing sound as he watches on. "You even made it all the way to the Kingdom Trials, disgracing our entire kingdom with your presence, and here you lay. In the mud where you belong. I should've killed you when I had you in my grip the first time. Thanks to the king, I get to watch you bleed for the last time."

A claw scrapes across my shoulder blade, making me whimper from the pain, just like it did when I was sixteen. I try as hard as I can to free myself, with no luck. I can see the wolf in front of me begin to shift into a man slightly older than Zaros with dark skin and a bleeding leg from where I cut him. It's the other guard that held me captive with Zaros, and the one that killed my dad.

Fierce anger makes me shake and I scream out at the other guard. "I'll kill you!"

He only laughs, but his laughter is cut off as he's hit from the side by a large gray wolf. The wolf pushes the man to the ground and sinks his teeth into his neck, killing the guard in one bite. The weight of Zaros on my back leaves me in an instant, and I feel like I can breathe again. The gray wolf turns to me with fierce black eyes and a blood-stained snout. *Caz*.

CHAPTER 17

◂← →▸

Cazimir

My wolf side loves the hunt, but even more than that, it loves the kill. I tried to leave Nyomi, well sort of. Okay, I didn't try all that hard. I had faith that she could hold her own against the old guard, especially with her sword. Still, I couldn't imagine that my father would leave it up to Zaros to get rid of her. I know my father, and he doesn't leave things to chance.

I run through the trees on two legs, tracking Ny's mesmerizing scent that I couldn't forget even if I tried. She had to have run a long way, because it's no easy feat to find her. When I come around a large boulder with wet moss along the side of it, the scent of blood hits my nose, and within seconds I'm on all fours as a wolf.

Muffled words reach my wolf ears, and I can barely tell that Zaros is speaking. As I come closer, I can hear Ny grunt and shout with pain in her voice. "I'll kill you!"

I see another one of my father's guards who I recognize, but can't name. He laughs and I follow his dark gaze to Nyomi lying face down in the mud with her arm bleeding and Zaros kneeling on her back. Rage boils inside of me and the next thing I know, I'm tearing into the man's throat, loving the taste of his blood.

I turn to my beautiful Ny and I can almost feel her pain as a wet tear slides down her dirty cheek. I shake with anger, my wolf eyes finding Zaros crouched a few feet back from Ny now. I have never felt so wild in my life, but Ny's protection is all that I know at this moment. I stalk toward Zaros slowly and I can feel my lips rising to bare my fangs at the threat.

Ny stays on the ground, completely still as I move past her. I know she had her own revenge in mind, but I want nothing more than to fulfill the promise I made to her when she stood in my bedroom. She said this isn't my fight, but Ny *is* my reason for fighting.

"Get out of here, young prince. Your father won't allow this." Zaros tries to talk me out of killing him, but in my mind he has been dead since I saw the scars on my mate.

I growl, and Zaros shifts into a mangy-looking light gray wolf. He snarls at me, and I don't hesitate to attack. I leap at him, knocking him into the mud. I sink my teeth into his side, making him howl into the pouring rain. His blood mixes with rain as it pours from his side. He snaps his jaws at me, trying to return the bite, but I'm not allowing it.

I bite down again, this time on his neck like I did with his buddy. I bite until I hear a snap, and then I release him, backing away from his limp body. I stare at my kill while I listen for Ny's pounding heartbeat behind me. If I were in human form, I wouldn't be so literal, but I bite down on Zaros' body and drag it over to Ny, dropping it at her feet where she now stands. Then I do the same with the other guard, backing away so she can admire my kills.

I bow my head to her as I look into her wide gray eyes. She holds one of her hands against her chest, but she reaches the other one out to pet my head. If I were a cat, I'd pur at the feel of her touch. She steps around the dead wolf bodies to kneel in front of me, grabbing her fallen sword along the way and tucking it back against her hip.

"Thank you, Caz. You saved me."

I call on the shift, slowly pulling the wolf back inside of myself. Ny watches me as my body changes and I'm standing before her in human form again. "I'm so sorry I wasn't here sooner, Ny."

She scoffs and shakes her head. "I'm sorry I thought I was tough enough to push you away and fight on my own."

Does she really think she's not a total badass? I touch her cheek, wishing I could feel it against my own. "You are the toughest woman I have ever met. You can't help that some idiots don't know how to fight with honor."

She nods, but her lip trembles and her eyes fill with tears. My heart aches as she falls against me, resting her head on my chest while she cries softly. I wrap my arms around her back, pulling her tighter against me, but it makes her flinch and gasp in pain.

I quickly release her and step back with wide eyes. "Dear gods, did I hurt you, Ny?"

She shakes her head and actually laughs. She doesn't say a word as she looks up at me with a sigh. "I know a thing or two about pain, Caz. I'm used to it, and I hate that I am. Do you want to know what I'm not used to though, that I would really like right now?"

I know I look like a confused little pup as I tilt my head in question. Instead of answering me, she steps up on her toes and presses her warm lips to mine. If I didn't feel like a wild animal just minutes ago, I do now.

Nyomi

Kissing Caz is like a dream, and one I never want to wake up from. He fulfilled his promise to me, literally laying my enemies at my feet, and I should not have liked it as much as I did. All I wanted at that moment was to fall into his arms and stay in them for as long as possible. Thanks to Zaros, I'm pretty sure at least a couple of my ribs are broken, as well as the fingers on my right hand, but just one kiss from Caz makes it all disappear.

I press myself against him, wrapping my good hand around his neck while I let the other stay at my side. Caz groans against my lips as he explores my mouth with his, pressing urgently for more of me. He doesn't move to hold me again, but I crave his touch.

I pull away just enough to speak. "I know you're worried about hurting me, but I want to feel your hands on my body, Caz. I don't feel any pain right now." It's not the full truth, but the pain is worth it if his touch causes it.

His turquoise eyes are darker than usual as he watches me. "Don't say you want to feel my hands on your body if you don't mean it, Nyomi. I feel like you're giving me permission to make all of my dreams come true."

I smile and shrug, ignoring the pain in my cut shoulder as I do so. "Permission given."

His eyes narrow into a deadly look as he gently slides his large hands over my hips and grips my thighs. "Hold onto me if you can." I wrap my one arm around his neck as he lifts me by my thighs into his arms.

My legs wrap around him and it surprisingly doesn't hurt my back or ribs more for him to carry me. He walks away from the carnage behind us, carrying me through the trees as the rain begins to pour harder, accompanied by distant thunder. His steps are sure and so smooth that I could nap in his arms if I wanted to.

"Where are you taking me?"

"Somewhere that I can live out my dreams." He rubs his rough face against my wet neck, making my whole body tingle. We are both drenched from the downpour and it somehow makes being this close to him even more exciting.

The trees open up to reveal a small grassy knoll risen above a steep cliff edge. Caz steps over the knoll and sits with me on his lap on a mossy rock just on the other side. He pulls me against him until our bodies are as close as two bodies can get while both being fully clothed.

His wet warmth seeps into me and I lose myself in his eyes as water cleans the dirt from our faces. "Aren't you going to relive your dream with me Cazimir Duras?" My lips want to explore his so badly, but he seems perfectly content to just hold me here on his lap.

Caz smiles and his hands slide across my bruised back, soothing my pain. "I am living my dream, Nyomi Mailon. I never said which of my dreams I wanted to live out with you."

"Oh," I say. "So they aren't all nefarious and risqué? I'm shocked."

He chuckles and the vibration from his chest makes me want to press harder against him. "Don't give me credit just yet. Most of my dreams are very indecent, especially the ones that involve you." He leans in to press a soft kiss against my neck and I shiver. He looks into my eyes. "But, sometimes the dreams I never want to leave are just like this. Holding you in my arms with the world in front of us. Just you and I."

I close my eyes briefly, wanting nothing more than that dream. "Sounds perfect."

"Just like you," Caz says against my ear.

I open my eyes to see him leaning in again and pressing his lips to mine. I let him explore my body with his hands as I memorize every taste of his mouth. Our tongues connect and my body feels like a fire, roaring to life in the midst of a hurricane. I let out a moan as Caz's fingers dig into my hips and he moves me against him.

Caz pulls back from me and I can see pure hunger in his wild eyes. "Nyomi, we have to go back to the castle. You need to finish your trial today and announce your win over Zaros."

I lick my lips and look up at the cloudy sky. The mages will come looking for me if I don't return soon. "Do you think they'll know that you helped me? That you killed the guards?"

I find his eyes again and he shakes his head. "You'll need to tell the others, including my father, that you were ambushed by both guards and you shifted for the first time, losing control and killing them. You'll be in the right, and my dad won't be able to argue it."

I scoff. "He orchestrated it, Caz."

He nods. "I know."

Silence falls between us and I push myself to my feet. I try to brush mud off of my pants but it's no use. Hopefully Clio has extras. Caz stands in front of me and touches my chin.

"My father won't get away with what he has done, Ny. We're going to win the trials, and then the kingdom will be under our rule."

I look up at him and can see the truth in his gaze. Well, what he thinks is the truth. I worry that King Alix will never get what he deserves, and in my eyes, all he deserves is a slow death.

CHAPTER 18

+←→+

Cazimir

I sit on the front steps of the castle with the other initiates and my father. The rain has stopped and thankfully I was able to show up long before Ny without a trace of blood left on me. Who knows where I'd be without the torrential downpour. Nobody asked questions when I joined them separately. I'm known to wander and keep to myself. Though it doesn't make for a good ruler, it makes for getting away with a few things.

Leaving Ny in the woods to find her way back to the castle wasn't easy. It helped knowing that we were able to prevent her assassination for another day, but I can't stop worrying about her out there. As for the feelings I have for my father, they have become something rotten. I can never see him in the same light, even though I always knew he had a dark side.

I keep my eyes trained on the trees that surround the castle, waiting for my mate while the others talk with each other about meaningless things.

"There she is!" Faxon jumps up, blocking my view of the trees to our left with his giant body.

All of us watch Ny exit the tree line, cradling her hurt hand and walking with a grimace on her beautiful face. She's in pain and it's torture not running to her and carrying her the rest of the way. Azra and Arnoux don't stay behind. They run to her and help her walk the last few yards to my father.

It's so hard to hate those damn vamps.

I step to the side so I can see the surprise on my father's face when Ny drops to a knee in front of him, broken and cut from her fight. Just her look is convincing enough that she battled the others well.

Ny bows her head, looking at the ground by her king's feet. "King Alix. I apologize, but I was forced to kill your guard, Zaros. He and his friend chose to ambush me and threatened to end my life. The fear triggered my wolf and I lost control. They are both dead."

Everyone is silent as we wait for the punishment my father will give Ny for her actions. Killing a fellow initiate in battle isn't unheard of, but killing two of the king's guards could mean Ny's execution.

My father stares at the back of Ny's head for too long before clearing his throat. "Well, it looks like Nyomi has won this battle. Let us go inside for some dinner and celebrate her victory."

"That's it?" Ny blurts the question out before covering her mouth.

My father raises an eyebrow. "Would you prefer some sort of punishment? The rules were to draw blood. It seems you accomplished that well enough. It was foolish of Zaros to trick us and betray his kingdom by attempting murder of one of our beloved initiates. You did what was necessary."

Ny dips her head again. "Thank you."

She glances in my direction and I can see the relief in her eyes, but she is thinking the same thing as me. That was a pile of bull shit. The king of Unity isn't done with Ny yet.

⟫← →⟫

Nyomi

I can't sleep. Clio snores on the floor beside my bed, her messy blonde hair sprawled across her open mouth. It amazes me that the girl can still look gorgeous in that position, and I can't help but smile at the scene.

I skipped dinner with the others, desperately needing a long hot bath to wash today's events away and heal my aching muscles. If I really had shifted for the first time today, my broken bones would be healed on their own by now, but I can still hardly take a deep breath because of the broken rib pressing against my lung.

By morning, the king will wonder why I haven't healed yet, and I don't know if I can pretend well enough that every part of me doesn't hurt.

Clio was kind enough to bring me a warm meal after finishing her own dinner, and we had what she calls a "slumber party". I never had friends growing up, other than a few of Bellona's little troll nieces and nephews, but we never had slumber parties. We'd only play together if Dad let me stay in Trog for more than a single night, which only happened if he had to go do whatever it was that he did without me. After getting no answers from him, I chalked it up to Dad being lonely and meeting up with women, but I'll never know for sure.

I sit up in bed and stretch my back out, nearly screaming from the aching all over my body. I curse under my breath so as not to wake Clio, and I shuffle quietly out of the bedroom in my stupidly girly borrowed nightgown. I comb fingers through my messy black hair before turning toward Caz's bedroom.

I know it's foolish, but I haven't been alone with him since our time on the cliff side. My body craves being near to him in a way that overpowers the pain. I reach my hand out to turn the handle on Caz's door but something tugs on my mind, telling me to stop.

I turn around, feeling like eyes are watching me, but I see no one. "Hello?" I whisper the single word once, but get no answer.

The tugging on my mind makes me gravitate to the end of the long hallway where the small dark staircase leads down to the back entrance of the castle. The "servant entrance" as I've heard it called.

Only a few burning candles light my path into the dark hall that Bastian brought me through when I first arrived at Unidad Castle. I couldn't explain the nagging feeling in my head that's dragging me through the dark alone without my sword on my hip, but it doesn't feel dangerous to me. If I run into King Alix or one of his loyal goons then I'll likely be killed on the spot. I scoff at that, knowing that I'd fight til my last breath, even in this ridiculous nightgown.

The hallway ends at a door that exits out onto the castle grounds. I slowly open the door, hoping that no guards are around to surprise me. With the recent attacks, the yard should be swarming with the king's men, but I stand alone, shadowed by the tall building that blocks my view of whatever moon lights the sky tonight.

I don't hear the sound of another person's breath until it's in my ear and I'm being held against a warm body. Someone's arm is around my aching ribs and my mouth is covered so I can't call out for help. *Not that I'd get any help if I tried.*

"Don't make a sound. I'm here to rescue you, *fatis*." The familiar voice makes the nagging feeling in my mind intensify, like I've heard this man speak every day of my life. The problem is, I have no clue who it is.

I try to mumble a response under the man's hand that is clamped over my mouth. He slowly takes his hands off of me, and I take the opportunity to spin around and throw my fist at what I hope is something breakable on my attacker.

My hit is blocked by the stranger standing before me with wide eyes. He isn't tall for a man, but still taller than me. His tan jaw has sharp edges that make him seem statuesque and incredibly handsome, framing his plump lips and bright green eyes. *Why are all the men here so hot?* The thing that stands out to me most, though, are the points at the tops of his ears.

"You're a faerie!" I whisper-shout the accusation, shocked by what I'm seeing.

The faerie smiles at me, flashing his perfectly white smile and the deep dimples in his cheeks. "Well, yeah. So are you, *fatis*."

His hand still holds my fist and I quickly pull it back. "But I'm a wolf shifter. I'm not one of the Fae." He raises an eyebrow at me like I'm an idiot, so I scoff angrily. "Your kind were exiled years ago. You have no right to be here." I don't agree with the banishment of the Fae, but something about this one has me flustered and moody.

He sighs, seemingly exasperated and steps closer to me, invading my personal space. "Come, my fatis. We need to leave now before the war begins. I can keep you safe."

I shake my head. "Why do you keep calling me that? My name is Nyomi, not fatis. And what war? Your war ended when I was just a baby."

The faerie man growls and rolls his eyes. "The old war wasn't even a true war. The wolf king sent us away, too afraid that he'd lose if we gave him a real fight. I know your name is not *fatis*, Nyomi. I am Alston, and I am saying that you are *my* fatis... My fated mate."

I take a step back, feeling like I was just struck dumb. This faerie man can't be my fated mate. Caz is my mate, right? I know it in my soul that Caz and I were made for one another, but looking at Alston, I feel almost the same as when Caz told me we were fated. It has to be true.

Alston and I stare at one another for a minute as I try to figure out what it is that I'm feeling. I can't have two fated mates, can I? It's unheard of. Alston's green eyes scan my face and then roam south to the rest of my body. He looks me up and down so intently that I feel hot under his gaze, and I wrap my arms around myself.

"Stop looking at me like that!"

IIc doesn't stop though, and instead his eyes turn dark, but not from desire. He looks angry and I can see from the rigidness of his lean body that he's pissed. "You have been beaten, fatis. Your ribs are broken, as well as part of your clavicle and many bones in your right hand. How did this happen?"

The concern pouring off of him, as well as the accuracy of his assessment has me in shock. I look at my bruised hand and touch my clavicle. I hadn't even noticed the pain there until he pointed it out.

"How did you know about my injuries? Can you see through me somehow?" *Oh, goddess.* The idea that he can see through my clothing makes me stupidly cover my vital parts.

Surprisingly, Alston chuckles and shakes his head, making his black hair shift with the movement. "Do not cover yourself on my account, fatis. I can't see through your gown, only the injuries you have. I'm a healer, so each of your pains glows like a marker for me to spot and fix."

"So, you can heal me… with magic?" Just the thought of him healing me sooths my pains a little bit. If I could be healed, the king would never know that I didn't actually kill those wolves in the woods. Caz would be safe from punishment.

"I can. Will you let me?" Alston steps closer to me again. I don't move away this time, hopeful that my pain will go away if he just touches me.

I nod to him and he reaches a hand out to grab my broken one. He holds my smaller hand between both of his and a small glow fills his hands. The feeling almost burns, but not in a bad way, and I gasp when something snaps back into place in my middle finger. Another few snaps come from my hand and then Alston releases me.

I hold my hand up, wiggling each of my fingers with ease and no pain. I smile, grateful for the relief of having my good hand back to me, and I look up into Alston's eyes. "Thank you, Alston. That was incredible."

His eyes connect with mine and his eyelids become hooded, making my heart race beneath my chest. "I would do anything for you, my fatis."

He reaches both of his hands out again to place them against my ribs. His touch is more than soothing, and I curse myself for enjoying it so much. Do I like his touch as much as Caz's? I gasp again as my ribs snap back together under Alston's glowing hands and it feels like breathing for the first time as my lungs fill with the cool night air.

He doesn't hesitate as he moves a hand to my right clavicle. He gently touches the bare skin just below my neck, pressing his hand to me once again. It glows and the healing is much faster as the small fracture melds together again. Alston takes a moment to step back from me, even after the glow from his magic fades.

I feel too warm under his gaze, and guilty, so I back away from him as I clear my throat. "Uh... Thank you, Alston. I can't tell you how grateful I am for your help."

"You must come with me, fatis. You aren't safe in this place, with the wolf king and his family."

"I know I'm not safe with the king, but his family is different. I can't just leave in the middle of the trials. I have a chance to change all of Unity if I win."

Alston shakes his head. "You will not win. Don't you see that? I know you think you are just a wolf, but you are Fae too. When your king realizes what you truly are, you will be killed."

I growl. "Alix Duras is not *my* king. I don't care what you think I am. My mother was a wolf shifter, and my father raised me to be like her. If he never told me that I was part Fae, it was for a good reason. I'm not going with you."

"If you choose to stay, I cannot stop you. But, the Kingdom Trials will not end as you hope. My queen and king have a plan for the wolf king, and there's no stopping it." He pauses, his face softening. "You don't look like a faerie, Nyomi, but you are one. I know in my heart that we are fatis. Just be safe, and remember who your people are."

I nod, knowing that what he says is true. Somehow, my father was a faerie, but he hid it from me and the world. Now, I have a fatis and a wolf fated mate... but as for who my people are, I have no idea.

CHAPTER 19

✦←→✦

Cazimir

None of us has been told who will fight today. I can't help feeling a sense of relief that Ny's fight is finished and she is still alive and well. I don't even care if I end up in a life or death battle again today, as long as she's okay.

I follow Ny out into the gardens after breakfast. She hasn't spoken to anyone, and hasn't even looked at me this morning. We are supposed to be at the Mutua Arena in an hour, but she escapes into the tall walls of the garden maze. I follow her scent, weaving left and right as she does, and I find her sitting alone on a wooden bench.

"Ny? Is everything alright?" I sound desperate to even my own ears.

She looks up at me with a start, as if surprised to see me here. "Oh, I'm sorry, Caz. I didn't sleep much last night and I wanted a moment of peace before having to face… you-know-who."

I know exactly who. My father isn't someone that *I* want to see daily, so I understand why she is hesitant to go. I sit beside her, reaching my hand out to grab hers, and thankfully she lets me. It hits me that she doesn't have a single bruise on the fingers that were broken just yesterday.

"How did you heal, Ny? Is this part of your…" I lower my voice to a whisper as I look around for eavesdroppers. "Your *new* magic?"

"No, I had help." She plays with my palm, circling her fingers around my skin. I hold back the shiver that threatens to come over me from such a simple touch.

"Who healed you? Only a few people can heal others so quickly, and I don't think we have any on the castle grounds." Her calmness has me worried and I want to drag whatever she's hiding out of her.

She looks around us in the same way I had moments ago, and then into my eyes. The perfect peak of her top lip calls to me as she speaks. "Caz, I hope you know how much you mean to me."

My heart leaps in my chest, but I can tell she's still keeping something hidden. "I hope it's half as much as what you mean to me. I can't imagine not knowing you, Nyomi."

I can hear the flutter of her breath as I say the words, and I raise my hand to touch her soft cheek. She closes her eyes against my touch. "I couldn't sleep last night, so I decided to come to your bedroom."

Holy Unity.

"You came into my room?"

She shakes her head. "I was about to, but I had this feeling like something was calling me downstairs.

I went out through the servant entrance and a faerie man stopped me."

My eyes go wide as I assess Ny's body for any new injury from a faerie attack, but she is perfectly unharmed. "What did he do? Did he say anything to you?"

"He… Well, he said the Fae rulers are planning some attack. He told me I can't possibly win the trials… and he told me that I'm half faerie."

I nod. I had already figured that was the truth. "The blue lightning magic sorta gave that one away."

"I guess I still expected it to be something else. My dad didn't look like a faerie, and how did he raise me instead of getting exiled like the rest of them? It's all so confusing."

"Why did this faerie man seek you out? Is he the one that healed you?" She nods. "Well, then I'm grateful to him." She scoffs and I tilt my head at her in confusion. "Should I not be grateful for this guy? Did he do something wrong? I know he must be a part of the attacks that have been happening, but I can't say I blame him for wanting to rise up against my father."

I have never thought the Fae deserved to be exiled for fighting my father. He has always been a tyrant and I see that more now every day. Ny sighs and her warm gray eyes scan my face in the way that I love so much.

"Caz, the faerie man from last night… He isn't just a healer or a soldier for the Fae… He's my fated mate." My heart sinks at her words, but she rushes out the next ones before I can die right on the spot. "But I believe you're my fated mate also. I think because I'm half of two things, fate chose two people for me."

Well, shit.

Nyomi

Caz stares at me like I've broken his heart and I hate that I did that to him. "Caz, I'm so sorry. I never thought this could be possible, but I hope you know that it doesn't change anything."

He nods slowly. "I mean, it does change things though. I've taken your time, and I've stolen kisses from you greedily. I never thought your fate could be with someone else."

I turn my body so that I'm facing him on the extremely uncomfortable wooden bench. "You never stole kisses from me. I wanted every moment we've spent together. Everything with you feels right and wonderful. How could my fate be promised to someone else when you make me feel like we're the only two people in the world when we're together."

Caz's eyes fall to my lips and he licks his own. *Holy Unity, he's so gorgeous.* "Ny, as idiotic as this is, and I am going to hate myself for saying it... I believe with my whole being that fate doesn't make mistakes."

I cringe at his words. "What does that mean? I can't be with two people, Caz. I'm not someone to be tossed around from man to man."

His eyebrows drop and he growls at me. His hands grip the sides of my head, surprisingly gently. "Dammit, Nyomi. That's not what I'm trying to say.

You are incredible, smart, beautiful and deadly. You know why fate gave you options? Because you are someone who chooses her destiny, without letting the crap that this world has thrown at you get in your way. Do you understand? You are the only being that can choose who she wants to spend her life with."

He kisses my lips once, tender and lingering. "Fate dropped you in my life, Ny, and I don't want another choice. You're it for me, okay? But maybe you need to find out more about what's-his-name. I imagine you're the only one for him as well, and he's a damn lucky guy who likely deserves a chance."

The pain in Caz's voice brings a tear to my eye. I couldn't imagine sending him to another woman after he has infiltrated my heart, but he's letting me choose my destiny. I nod between his hands and he nods back before releasing my head.

The air between us is silent until someone makes a grunting sound behind Caz. "I'm sorry to interrupt, but may I have a word with Nyomi?"

Both of us jump apart and look up at our third wheel. Queen Freya is smiling down at us, and my stomach clenches at the realization that she caught Caz and I in a much too familiar position. Caz stands and turns to his mother.

"Mom, I'm sorry I didn't hear you coming." His voice is a lot less panicked than mine would be, I'm sure.

She raises a single eyebrow and the look is actually flattering on her pretty face. "I can't imagine you could hear much with how focused you were on your mate, son."

I swallow hard, my heart pounding. "Queen Freya, I'm so sorry…"

She holds a hand up to shush me. "Oh, stop that. I'm not my husband. I'm glad my son has found such a strong woman to love, regardless of your blood, but that's not what I'm here for. I'd like to talk with you." Her eyes are on me only and I stand from the bench.

Did she say love?

Caz turns to me with wide eyes. "I'll head to the arena. Please be safe on your way over." He embraces the queen. "Thanks, Mom."

With Caz gone, I stand nervous and sweaty in front of the queen of Unity. Her smile sits perfectly on her face and she sits on the bench in the spot that Caz just vacated. I join her and twiddle my fingers in my lap, waiting for chastisement from my queen.

"Nyomi Mailon. That's your birth name?" *Weird.*

I nod. "It's the name my mother gave me before she died."

"How did she die, if you don't mind me asking?"

"My dad told me that she was killed not long after I was born. I don't know how, but I always thought it had to be because their relationship was against the law." Maybe there was more to it.

Queen Freya nods. "Well, to be honest, I have a theory that your father was someone I once knew. Someone who fought in the Kingdom Trials with my husband and then disappeared along with a woman who also fought in those trials. A very brave woman."

She looks long and hard at me. "You look just like them."

My heart races at her words. My parents fought in the last trials together? How could I not have known this? "What were their names? The two that you believe to be my parents."

She thinks for a minute, as if unsure if she should tell me what I'm dying to know. "The woman was a wolf princess, princess to the last king of Unity actually. She was strong with long black hair and eyes as gray as the hair on a wolf itself. Her name was Rhae Wolfe."

My heart feels as if it stutters. My dad told me that my mom's name was Rhae, but he never gave me a last name. I thought she was just a wolf girl, casted out from her people because she fell in love with someone from another kingdom. That's why I am in the trials, because I do have royal blood after all.

My voice is breathy as I lean closer to the queen. "Wolfe, as in the trainer Everaux Wolfe? Were they related? What about the man? What was his name?"

Queen Freya holds a hand up to stop my incessant questioning. "Yes, Everaux is the brother of Rhae. If she is your mother, Everaux would be your uncle." *Holy crap!* "And as for the man that disappeared after the trials, he was prince to the Fae queen and king at the time. His name was Theon Keene."

I freeze. The queen knows that I'm half Fae, a death sentence. I think about the name she gave me... Theon. The pieces click together in my mind and I gasp loud enough to make Queen Freya jump. My father called himself Theodore… *Theon.* I'm royal on both sides of my family. I'm a faerie. My parents fell in love during the kingdom trials. And now the queen of Unity knows it all.

I look into the queen's blue eyes and swallow a lump in my throat. "Your highness, I had no idea who my parents were. Please don't…"

"Stop. I'm not going to harm you, Nyomi. You may think that because I married the ruthless king of Unity that I loved him and agree with his laws, but you are mistaken. Alix is not my fated mate, and I despise everything about him other than the daughter we share."

I'm at a loss for words, but I attempt to form actual sentences. "What about your son?"

She stiffens at my question before slouching for the first time since I met her. "Cazimir is not Alix's son, Nyomi."

I open my mouth to ask who Caz's father is but an explosion shakes the ground beneath us. Queen Freya and I jump up and grab onto each other, both of us looking up at the cloud of dust that billows above our heads.

A voice screams from far off. "Someone has blown up the king's wall!"

I look at the queen and she watches me with fear in her eyes. "I've always hated that stupid wall."

.

PART 4

A TRIAL OF DECEPTION

CHAPTER 20

≫

Nyomi

The path to the tall stone wall that surrounds the northern king's land of Unity is fogged in a brownish-gray dust. Queen Freya and I run side-by-side along the small dirt road, looking for who is to blame for blowing up the thing that keeps Unidad Castle from the other six kingdoms.

From what I've heard, a wall didn't exist until King Alix took the throne. His paranoia led him to create something that would protect the elite from the "lower" creatures. I never imagined that his paranoia would be justified, but here we are. Somehow, the wall has been taken down, and it's an act of war.

"Over here! Somebody help!" The panicked voice of a man comes from within the dust that floats above rubble and debris.

Queen Freya runs ahead of me, her wolf speed helping her move faster than myself. I follow her mirage as I make my way over mounds of dirt. When I reach the queen, she is kneeling over the body of a fallen guard, likely someone working to protect the wall that was just destroyed.

"He's dead," another guard says a few feet away with a tightness in his deep voice.

I move around the queen to look at the face of the fallen man and my heart clenches. It's Joff, the guard who brought me to the castle weeks ago with his partner, Bastian. I had no love for Joff. He was rude and didn't care for me in the slightest, but just knowing him and seeing him like this hurts.

The queen nods her head, confirming Joff's death for the few of us standing around to see. Queen Freya looks past me and her body slouches forward as a new sadness fills her eyes.

"I'm so sorry, son. Joff was killed in the explosion."

I spin around and find Caz's drooping eyes and turned-down lips. He cared for Joff in a way I can't understand. I move to embrace my mate, but I stop myself when I see King Alix enter the cloud of dust. His eyes are furious as he scans the destroyed wall in front of him.

The once tall and strong structure is broken down to nothing but piles of bricks and powder as long as fifty yards wide. I have a suspicion about who did this, but I'm not about to give that information to the king and give him more reason to hate my people.

My people? What am I thinking?

Do I really feel like I belong with the faeries even though it has been less than a day since I discovered I'm one of them? It feels more real than the idea that I'm a wolf shifter. King Alix and his abusive guards have made me see the wolves in a sort of darkness, though the friends I've made here change that view.

Caz scans the area surrounding our gathered group. "Where are the attackers?"

The same guard who found Joff dead stands at attention. "When we arrived, whoever did this was long gone. It had to have been planned for a while, sir."

Caz looks at his father, or not his father if the queen was telling me the truth about him. "Do you want to continue the trials today, father?"

King Alix shakes his head, fury causing his face to look red beneath his prickly beard. "We will continue with the fights this evening instead. All surviving guards will go into the forest to patrol for whoever thinks it wise to break what belongs to me."

The scattered men all gather as Queen Freya loops her arm in mine and drags me back toward the castle. I look back at where Caz stands over his lost friend, his eyes closed in grief. It hurts to walk away from him, but I can't put him in harm's way. If the king knows that Caz isn't biologically his, maybe he is more capable of hurting him than I thought.

I shuffle my feet quickly, trying to keep pace with the queen. She releases me once we reach the green lawn in front of the castle.

She leans in to whisper. "Nyomi, whatever you do, don't let my husband see you and Cazimir together. He will never approve of a relationship between the two of you."

I nod, already knowing she's right. "I figured he wouldn't. I'll keep my distance."

Queen Freya sighs and touches my arm gently. "Don't stop fighting, okay?"

"Never."

Cazimir

Darkness descends over Unity as the sun drops over the west, out past the endless waters that surround the island of Sirenes. It's impossible to see over the mountains around the castle lands, but I've always wondered what it looks like toward the water. I've never been west, only south through Trog and over the long river to Lupos. How can I imagine being a king when I don't even know my own kingdom?

The night isn't an issue for my wolf-vision, so I easily maneuver through the rocky hillside trail that leads over the back of Mutua Arena, my feet padding roughly against the dirt as I go. I'm not particularly in the mood for night fighting after seeing my lifelong friend dead on the ground, but my father doesn't care about that.

Joff has always been an ass, but I cared for him like a brother. He didn't deserve to die in the mess that my father and the faeries have caused. I don't know who I'm more angry at honestly. The Fae army may have been the ones to bomb the wall, but my father brought this war upon himself.

"Gather around, young royals! Tonight's fight will begin shortly." The same high mage that started us off in the first trial stands before the group of initiates, wearing a long white robe.

I find Ny standing beside the two beefy trolls, looking so small and frail at their sides. Her black hair is braided behind her back, hanging just past her shoulder blades. Her fresh scent reaches my nose and I want to gravitate toward her, but I hold my ground. *Now's not the time, Cazimir!*

The mage continues. "King Alix cannot be here this evening due to the events at the wall earlier, so I will be monitoring this fight. The two who will battle tonight will be Prince Cazimir and Prince Azra. A strong match."

I whip my head to the right, eyeing my opponent. Azra grins back at me, straightening his shoulders as he stares me down. He may not realize that he took my mate on a date, but I'll make sure he gets the point. The mage gives the orders to begin and I look at Ny again as the initiates all disperse.

She looks between Azra and I, and she frowns. I don't want to hurt her by beating the crap out of the vamp, but I can't help the deep urge to do just that. Even though Ny can't be my fated mate right now, I still feel a need to claim her as mine by beating anybody who has eyes for her, no matter how barbaric that sounds.

I am an animal after all.

Everyone scatters, leaving to the castle to await the end of our fight, and I turn back to Azra who just stands with that stupid smile. "Well, are we going to fight or what?"

He shrugs, raising one of his hands. "I haven't decided yet. On the one hand, I'd love to see which of us is the better fighter. I'm not so cocky that I just assume it's me." He raises the other hand. "But, on the other hand, I don't think a certain woman would appreciate it if I beat her mate near to death."

My jaw drops open and I step back. "Mate? What makes you assume that?"

Azra laughs like that was the funniest thing he ever heard. "Come on, man! You guys are *not* that subtle with the moony-eyed looks and whispers in the halls."

I groan. "Just shut up, Azra. It's not what you think, and if you go around saying crap like that, you're going to…"

He holds both hands up between us to stop me. "Woah, seriously? You think I'm about to spread rumors that could get the girl of my dreams killed? I know very well what your father thinks of Nyomi's kind. He'd never approve of you two."

He's right, and it's exactly what I already knew. "You won't tell anybody about your suspicions then? Not even if it wins you the trials?"

"Hey, I may be a vampire but the rumors aren't true. We aren't all soul-sucking demons. We have hearts, and we have family. I won't just stab someone in the back unfairly. If I'm going to win, it's because I kick your ass fair and square."

I scoff and shake my head. "You can try, vamp, but you're not going to win."

He shrugs and crouches into a fighting stance. "Suck it." Azra dives at me, narrowly missing the head ram into my stomach as I move to the side.

I spin around and kick him in the knee at half strength, not wanting to break his leg. He turns to me, glaring angrily as he throws his hands in the air. "We have to draw blood, wolf prince. Don't go easy on me. If you can break something, do it. I know I will."

He proves his point by using his vampire speed to kick me in the knee, the same way I had done to him. The force of it makes my leg snap backward. "Dammit!" I yell in pain and take off at an awkward and painful sprint so I can give myself a moment to heal before retaliation.

I duck behind a tree wider than the troll royals put together, and I call my wolf side forward a little so the healing speeds up. A rustling sound comes from the tree branches above me and I look up to see Azra preparing to drop down on my head.

I move out of the way as he jumps, and I quickly throw a fist into his right side, cracking something of his in the process. Azra grunts and doubles over in pain, but it's not enough to stop him from attacking again. His fangs emerge and he hisses at me before lunging for my neck. One vampire bite can paralyze me, if only for a few seconds. Of course, a few seconds is all he'd need to break my neck.

I punch Azra in the face, knocking him back a step and I immediately follow up with a second hit, making him fall back onto the ground. I take his moment of weakness to call my wolf side forward and I shift into the beast right in front of Azra.

His eyes stretch wide, just enough for me to notice, and it makes me smile on the inside. *That's right, be afraid!* I growl at him as I step closer, looking for a place I can bite him enough to wound him but not kill him. It's not that easy to kill a vampire, but a wolf bite into the neck, cutting off his blood flow would do the trick.

I avoid his neck and snap my jaws at his leg instead, but he's too quick. He shoots to his feet and takes off running east toward the castle. My wolf instincts rocket as I watch him speed off and I leap into a sprint after him, loving the thrill of the chase. I never lose sight of Azra as he zig-zags through the trees in the dark of the moonless night.

I am a lot faster in this form, so catching up to him isn't too difficult. I follow him onto a boulder and then jump off of it close enough to tackle him to the ground. I land hard on his back, hearing something snap inside of his arm. *Yes!*

Azra growls at me as he struggles beneath my weight. "Just bite me already you furry animal! Blood hasn't been drawn yet."

I look down at Azra's struggling body and I have no urge to make him bleed. As crazy as it sounds in my own mind, I am grateful to him for being willing to keep mine and Ny's secret. He really cares about her and I completely understand that feeling. I ease up on his back, distracted by my own thoughts, and that gives him the chance to spin around on the ground and sink his fangs into my front leg.

The venom from Azra's bite spreads quickly throughout my body and I drop to the ground, completely paralyzed. He jumps up, brushing the dirt off of his black clothes and he looks down at me with a victorious grin.

"Well, I know I only have a second, so I'm going to quickly say sorry for the bite." He takes a small knife out from his boot and cuts it across my paralyzed wolf cheek. "And sorry for the cut, but you know the rules. See ya back at the castle!"

With that, he takes off running and I'm left to just watch him leave with my blood on his knife. *Well, damn. That didn't go as I planned.*

CHAPTER 21

⇤ ⇥

Nyomi

All of us stand silent, wondering if what King Alix just said was a mistake. I'm pretty sure I didn't just hear the king tell his son that he was to be whipped for losing his fight against Azra. I look over at the victorious vampire, but the look on his handsome face is one of sadness and regret.

"Your highness," Azra says to the king. "It was a fair fight and Cazimir did nothing to be punished for."

King Alix narrows his dark eyes at Azra. "It is either you or him, Vampir prince. The penalties are of my choosing and will not be changing." *Does he know about Caz and I?* I can't stop the thought from wiggling into my brain. It would make sense for him to lash out if he knew.

Azra looks like he might argue on Caz's behalf again, though I can't imagine what brought upon this new loyalty that wasn't there days ago. Caz steps in front of Azra, his hair a mess from the fight that finished only minutes before.

"I accept my punishment."

I open my mouth to talk but my mind stops me before I can make a mistake. *Don't show weakness. Don't stand out.* Queen Freya asked me to stay away, but I never thought it could be this difficult.

I glance around at the other initiates and each of them has a similar look on their faces, except for the sirens. If I'm not mistaken, the girls are more than happy to watch Caz get sliced up by his father. Nyx grins as she watches the drama unfold and I have to fight a new urge to pounce on the siren and rip her long auburn-colored hair out. Or maybe just a tentacle or two.

"Alright," the king says loudly, clapping his hands together. "Bastian!"

My head spins to the right where Bastian steps around the corner leading toward the back of the castle. His face is grim and an invisible weight presses down on his shoulders. Bastian raises the weapon in his hands, a whip made for causing torture. King Alix has planned this. Whoever lost was getting beaten... no matter what.

Caz looks over at Bastian, his lifelong friend. The two men share an unreadable look as Caz steps past him to stand against the castle doors. In a swift motion, Caz tugs his button-down shirt over his head, revealing the most sculpted back I have ever seen, like hills and canyons of muscle. He places both of his palms against the thick wood and glances over his shoulder at me momentarily.

His turquoise eyes meet mine and I can feel his resolve from where I stand with the others. He's okay with this, and I know that he's only allowing it so that the king doesn't go after someone else. He blinks, breaking our eye contact, and he turns back around to face the door in silence.

King Alix stands tall and uncaring. "Bastian, we shall have a strike for each of our six kingdoms. You may begin."

Bastian turns to the king with wide eyes. "Are you not doing the… honors, sir?"

King Alix scoffs and shakes his head. "You want me to strike my own son? Of course not! Now hear my words. You. May. Begin." He says each word with more malice than the last.

My stomach turns as I watch Bastian's tortured eyes. He loves Caz like a brother but he has no choice. He must obey his king, his alpha. Bastian's hands shake as he turns back to Caz with the leather whip in his palm. He pauses, just staring at Caz's bare skin, untouched and perfect.

Caz looks over his shoulder at Bastian, no anger in his eyes. "Come on now. You heard your king, Bast."

Bastian nods and raises the handle of the weapon over his head, tossing the long braided cord behind him. With a grunt and a speedy flick of his wrist, the whip snaps through the air and slices into Caz's back. I gasp at the sight and sound of the hit, but I'm not the only one. The other onlookers can't control the disgust on their faces at the red blood pooling out of Caz's wounds.

They'll heal. They will heal!

I repeat the words in my head, needing hope to hold me back. My whole body feels like a roaring fire, hot and angry. I want to burn the king to the ground, slow and torturous. I want him to experience every pain he has ever caused another, a thousand fold.

"Again," King Alix yells in the night air.

Bastian obeys with a tick of his jaw, administering five more slow and painful lashes across my mate's back. The lines make a painting of red along Caz's skin and I fight the urge to vomit, though my stomach feels like it's sitting in my throat. Caz stays still through it all, not making a sound of pain but I can almost feel the excruciating shame that radiates from him.

King Alix clears his throat and from the corner of my eye, as I keep my gaze on Caz, I can see the king step up to Bastian's side. "Everyone return to your rooms and rest for tomorrow's fight. Let this be a lesson to battle at your best, or suffer the consequences."

Anger claws beneath my skin, needing to be released and I whip my head toward the retreating king's back. I clench my sweating fists and take a step toward him, one of my hands reaching for the blade on my hip. Before I can get close to my enemy, a hand grabs my shoulder, holding me back.

I whirl on the person restraining me and find Azra with his brother behind him. The two vampires look at me with tender emotion on their handsome faces, and Azra shakes his head.

He whispers to me, "Nyomi, you cannot."

I growl back at them. "I can't just let him…"

"You have to." Azra cuts me off with a sharpness in his tone. "Look around, little warrior."

I let my eyes scan the dark castle yard and there are multiple guards standing off toward the trees, watching us. All of them are the king's men, and they would protect him no matter what.

Azra grabs my wrist and begins dragging me toward the palace with Arnoux following close behind. I look back at Caz to see Bastian speaking quickly and desperate to him, though I can't make out the words. They both lost a dear friend this morning, and now this. Caz shakes his head and pats his friend on the arm, even though the movement looks painful as he does so. His eyes flick to where I am dragged away by the vampire twins, and he just nods once before turning back to Bastian.

⤛ ⤜

Nyomi

The castle is quiet after the night's events. The sun will rise in just two more hours, but I don't look forward to another day in this kingdom under King Alix's rule. Since Azra and Arnoux dropped me off at my bedroom, I have been sitting against the wall that holds strong between Caz's room and mine.

I've been listening and wishing I could go over there and be with him, but he wanted me to explore whatever potential I have with Alston, my Fae fatis. If there really is any potential future with Alston, then why can I only think about Caz and comforting him.

All I see is Caz. Maybe I'm the one in need of comfort.

I push myself up and off the floor, wrapping my body in the warm fur throw blanket that I have grown to love. I walk quietly across the floor as I exit my room and quickly glance around the silent hallway before dipping into Caz's dark bedroom. I push my back against the closed door, trying to force my eyes to adjust in the dark as my heart pounds in anticipation of seeing Caz in bed.

"Caz, are you in here?" My voice is a whisper, but I get no response.

I tip toe along the floor, barely able to make out the shadows of what I know to be a dresser and the end of the large bed. My bare foot brushes across an item of clothing and the thought that Caz could be naked in bed has my mind reeling and my heart pounding. *Oh, dear goddess save me.*

I can see a bit of blue moonlight behind the closed curtain that hangs in front of the window, so I reach my hand up and pull the curtain open enough to be able to see a few details of the bedroom. The soft light falls over Caz's bed and I see him lying face down, shirtless and fast asleep. My breath catches in my throat when I see the lines across his back, healing but not yet gone... Just raised mountains of torn skin.

I drop my blanket softly on the floor, suddenly very warm as I watch my sleeping mate, and I gently sit beside his long body. I can see his back rising and falling with his breaths, and unable to stop myself, I reach a finger out to stroke the healing scar that trails from his right shoulder blade to his left hip. His skin is hot and the scar is jagged.

I let out a long frustrated sigh at the sight of his wounds, and then Caz suddenly spins around to grab my wrist hard with a low growl in his throat. His fiery eyes meet mine and the anger of having someone sneak up on him in the night fades just as quickly it came.

He lessens his grip on me as he sits up with wide eyes. "Ny? Is everything alright?"

My face flushes with a hot red blush and I nod, suddenly feeling ridiculous for crawling into Caz's bed in the middle of the night. "Yes, I'm sorry. I... I guess I was just... I don't know. Worried or something. I'll go." I try to stand, but he pulls me back down.

I find his eyes again and the sleepy hunger in them makes my heart ache. *Goddess, he is so sexy.* He reaches a large hand up to rest against the side of my neck, his touch like electricity on my skin. His turquoise eyes are fast as he looks back and forth between my eyes, my cheeks, my lips, studying me in the moonlight.

"Ny, you are the most exquisite creature I have ever seen." His eyebrows press together at the center as if he can't possibly comprehend what he sees when he looks at me. "I wish you could tell me that you will always be mine." I open my mouth to tell him just that, but he shakes his head, stopping the words. "Someday maybe. Not now. I can't let your words fill me with that kind of hope. It will only kill me when that hope is crushed."

My heart crumbles at his words. Caz thinks I'll crush his hope, that I'll crush the feelings we have between us. Is that really who I am because of what fate has dealt me? I raise my hand to lay it above his and I lean in to his touch. I don't know what to say that can mean anything to him. Nothing is promised.

I choose not to say anything, so instead I climb farther onto his bed and wrap my arms around his neck. I allow my fingers to graze the wounds at the top of his back, and I settle myself onto his lap, straddling him. Caz allows me to invade his personal space, grabbing my waist and pulling me against his bare chest.

His eyes darken to the color of a calm pond reflecting the trees that surround it, and he doesn't wait another second to lower his lips to mine. Every inch of my body trembles against Caz's, desperate for more of him. More than I can't fairly take.

I let my hands slip into his messy bed-hair and I breathe in his warmth as our mouths move feverishly with one another's. I open my lips and Caz's tongue slips through the gap, tangling with mine. The heat of it has me moaning and pressing harder against him, needy and wild. Caz's hands move to the bottom of my gown, dipping below the fabric that is bunched around my thighs.

His hands slide up my bare legs and over my moving hips. They slip higher, gripping the skin of my waist and tugging me harder against his chest. My mouth leaves his as I gasp for air, but Caz growls at the distance and one of his hands leaves my waist to grip the back of my neck, drawing my lips back to his roughly. I can't even complain about losing the oxygen that my lungs need. My body seems more than happy to asphyxiate on Cazimir.

Caz's lips leave mine again and they wander along my jaw and down the sensitive skin of my neck. I cling to his thick arms as he traverses my collarbone with his mouth, leaving a trail of hot kisses. He pauses on his way back up my neck to gently bite down on my flesh and then lap at the spot with his tongue.

I'm gasping again, perfectly lost in the feel of Caz's hands grabbing at my body and his mouth tasting my feverish skin. "Caz," I whisper his name.

His attention leaves my neck and he looks deep into my eyes. His eyes are now black like the wolf's and it makes me feel even more wild. He releases my waist and both of his hands rest on the sides of my head as he breathes heavily and lets the color return to his irises.

"I need to let you go back to bed, Ny." I can hear the strain in his words, but I know it's the truth. I can't let Caz and I complete our bond when there's so much uncertainty ahead of us.

I nod and swallow past the lump in my throat. "I know. I'm sorry for waking you."

Caz's slow smile is sad as he shakes his head and he stands easily with me in his arms before setting me on my feet. "I'm not sorry, Ny. I'll never be sorry for that."

CHAPTER 22

❖←→❖

Cazimir

Trying to sleep after having Nyomi in my bed was absolutely pointless. I feel like I might never be able to sleep in that bed again with her scent on my sheets and the memory of her skin against mine. Call it masochistic or idiotic, but I couldn't just save myself from this torture of wanting her. I took what she was willing to give me and now I'm in hell without Ny.

She has done an incredible job ignoring me all day. My father called for a new fight this morning, between Faxon and Iris, which left the large troll the victor. It felt almost like retribution watching the siren tremble before my father while he dulled out his new choice of penalty for her loss. She was left to spend the rest of the day in the dungeons without food or water. I'd have preferred that over the lashings from my best friend. Fatherly love, right?

It's dinner finally, after the hours of laps we were forced to run through the surrounding forest. My father is pushing patrols, and has included us initiates in this task. He calls it conditioning and labor for our kingdom, but so far the Kingdom Trials are looking more and more like my father's own private show. Things are being done differently this year, and I'm wondering how involved the mages really are anymore.

"How are you doing, Dryden? You've been really quiet since... well, since Juno." My head picks up at Nyomi's voice.

I look across the dining room to where Ny slides gracefully into a chair beside Dryden, the dragon shifter. Since his sister's death, he has been a loner, such a contrast to the outgoing show-off that first arrived at Unidad Castle. Even though Ny's voice is low, I can still pick it up with my wolf hearing. I listen in and watch them out of the corner of my eye while I pretend to be focused on my pork ribs and salad.

Dryden clears his throat. "I'm doing okay, thanks. It has been hard to do the trials without her support, but we knew that coming into this could be dangerous. I always hoped that I could protect her, though."

"I think you could've protected her if you were there. None of us expected an attack within the castle, or anywhere for that matter. I'm still sorry it happened though, if that means anything." *She's a damn angel.*

I catch Dryden's sad smile as he looks at Ny, seeing the kind heart that I see in her every day.

"Thank you, Nyomi. I really hope we can keep being friends."

Ny smiles and nods. "Of course we can, Dryden. I don't see any reason why we couldn't." She takes a bite of a carrot from her plate.

Dryden continues to eat his food as well, but pauses after a minute. "Hey, Nyomi. If you ever need someone to have your back, just let me know, alright?"

She looks confused by his offer, but she nods again with a new smile. "Thanks, Dryden. I may need that in the near future."

I hope to all the gods that Ny doesn't get into enough trouble to have to call for dragon backup. I wouldn't be surprised if my father did something soon, though. The time might come where I need to fight him, and if I'm being totally honest with myself, I believe that time *will* come no matter what.

Nyomi

I'm walking, but I don't know where I am. All around me is darkness, though not like the dark of night. This is complete blackness with no stars and no distant flickering candlelight. My feet continue moving me forward, but when I look down, I can't even see my own body. The only indication that I even exist is the feel of my bare feet touching rough earth, and the chill that blows through my hair and across my skin.

I have no control over my legs. I can only let them take me to somewhere unknown. A smell touches my nose, like dirt and evergreen trees. All I hear is the sound of wings flapping above me and water rushing in the distance. Are my eyes even open?

I try to open my eyes, with no luck. I'm pretty sure they're closed, and maybe this is only a lucid dream. I'm probably lying down in my bed at Unidad Castle and dreaming of a midnight stroll through the surrounding forest. That has to be it. *Very logical, Ny.*

My feet stop moving, settling against a cold, grassy floor and a new sound reaches me. Muffled voices, talking about something I can't understand. The crunching of leaves and twigs registers in my ears and I spin toward it. I try to ask who is there, but my voice doesn't work for me.

Warm hands grab my shoulders and begin to shake my body back and forth. *What the hell is that?* "Fatis, Nyomi! You are sleepwalking. Wake up."

Alston?

Suddenly, my eyes fly open and I'm staring at the faerie healer. His wide green eyes are searching my face and he sighs when he realizes that I'm alert. "There you are, my fatis. You had quite a journey."

"Where am I? I don't understand how I got here." I look around at the tall green trees and the blooming flowers all over the ground. It's nighttime, actual nighttime with a moon and stars up above. The blackness is gone and I can finally see that I'm wearing my long nightgown and standing barefoot in front of at least a dozen faeries, including my so-called fated mate, Alston.

I jump back from Alston's hold on me and I throw my arms up in defense. I'm surrounded by strangers, and Fae strangers at that. Was I kidnapped from my bed?

"Who are all of you?" I shout at the wide-eyed faeries and none of them speak except for Alston.

"Nyomi, you seem to have walked all the way to us in your sleep. You are in the land of Fae, your rightful home. You must have felt our presence here."

Oh, dear Unity, I walked to Fae? I think back to my dream of walking through the woods and I realize he's right. "How could I have found you all in my sleep? That's impossible."

Alston laughs softly and I notice a few others behind him smiling as well. "You don't know much about the Fae, do you, fatis? We can feel each other, like a spiritual presence. We are all connected by magic, and that presence in you feels ours. Don't be afraid, alright? You are in no danger here."

I look from face to face of the pointed-eared faeries all smiling back at me and I know what Alston says is true. They don't mean me any harm, and it was I who reached out to them in the first place. I stand up tall again and dip my head to the others.

"I...uh. I'm sorry for interrupting your night. I'll return to the castle." I turn to leave, even though I don't fully know how I made it here without detection in the first place.

Alston reaches out to me, grabbing my hand in his. The feeling of his touch is pleasant and warm, but it doesn't draw me in. I turn to look up at his sharp features and he smiles down at me. "You do not have to go. Won't you stay with us?"

I get lost in his eyes for a moment, just imagining what it could be like to give in to our connection. I can't though. It's not the same as what I have with Caz.

I shake my head and turn to leave, but a melodic voice speaks behind me before I can take more than two steps back into the trees. "Nyomi Keene?"

I spin around. Keene was my father's last name, that I only just heard for the first time from Queen Freya. I search the faces watching me and find the owner of the voice, a woman maybe in her late thirties or early forties steps between the others. She has fair skin and curly red hair, where a black crown sits just atop her head. *The Fae queen?*

"That's not my name, your highness." I don't mean to sound so jilted, but my heart hurts just hearing who I could have been in another life.

The Fae queen raises her thin eyebrows and her lip quivers slightly as she studies me with piercing dark eyes. "Oh, goddess, you look just like him." A single tear slips from her eye and drops from her cheek.

I draw my chin back, suddenly unsure of how to talk to this crying woman. "I'm sorry, Queen…uh, your highness. I don't know what you're talking about."

She closes her eyes briefly and nods with a scoff. "Of course you don't, dear." She steps closer to me, her movements smooth. She's so elegant that I couldn't imagine ever moving that way even if I practiced for years. "My name is Ensley Mason and I am the queen of the Fae people. I was born Ensley Keene, and my brother was Theon Keene."

I gasp and step backward, feeling like I was just smacked across the face. "You're my aunt?"

She nods and new tears bubble up just below her eyes. "Yes, Nyomi. I believe I am your aunt."

So many emotions and questions flood my mind. What was my dad like as a kid? Why didn't he tell me about you? Do I have more family? Why did you start a war with the king?

Somehow, though, I don't ask any of them. I just say, "I have to go."

I turn back to the dark woods and take off at a full sprint. I don't make it too far though when thin arms wrap around me from behind and I'm pulled into a tight hug. I don't know how I know it's Ensley, but like Alston said, I can feel her spirit or power connected to my own. Her hold on me reminds me so much of my dad's hugs that I break down.

I turn in her arms and let her hold me while I cry harder than I have in years. She shushes me while rubbing soothing circles on my back as I cry like I did when Dad was killed. I never imagined I could have a family in the world, and now I finally found someone. My trainer, Everaux, is supposed to be my uncle but I haven't seen him in almost a week, and now I have an aunt.

Queen Ensley pulls back from me but doesn't release my shoulders as she looks at my tear-stained face. "I was so mad at Theon when he left our family. I couldn't understand why he would disappear without a word, but I get it now."

I sniffle and wipe my eyes. "What do you mean? Do you know why he left?"

She nods with a sad smile. "He left to protect you, Nyomi. You and your mother I imagine. I don't know who your mom was, but I know with all of my heart that Theon loved her, and I'm sure when he found out there was going to be a baby, he dropped everything to keep you safe." She raises a hand to sweep my hair from my face and the touch is so motherly that I nearly lose it all over again. "You don't have to go back, you know. You can stay here with us, your family."

My heart clenches tightly at the idea, but my mind wanders to the other family that I have made. Clio, Bastian, Dryden, Azra, Arnoux... Caz. I can't disappear in the night.

I shake my head. "I'm sorry, but I do have to go back. I know it doesn't make sense right now, but I have a family back there too, and I can't leave them to the mercies of King Alix."

She sighs and slowly lets me go. "I don't think you realize how much I do understand about that, my love."

CHAPTER 23

⊷ ⇥

Nyomi

I've spent 3 days watching the other initiates fight and suffer punishments for their losses. It seems like King Alix only found it in his heart - or whatever the pumping thing in his chest is - to whip Caz, but the others have mainly spent their evenings without nourishment in the castle dungeons. It's not as if I haven't gone without food and water many times before, but I think about spending a night in those cells again and every part of me hurts. Call it bad memories coming back or just fear, I don't really know.

I have been avoiding Caz, as well as pretty much everyone else. I've felt lost after meeting my aunt since thinking I was the only family I had left. I left her out in the land of Fae and trekked back home in the dark alone. So much for exploring whatever I could be feeling for Alston. I haven't seen him even once since that night.

Today, a new round of trials will begin, and I have heard talk that it is going to be more fighting. All that I've learned about the past trials, fighting wasn't the bulk of it. There were mazes to test the mind and assessments of cunning and strategy. It's no surprise though that King Alix wants to see even more bloodshed.

I pick up my speed as I enter Mutua Arena from the short tunnel below the stone stadium seating. I don't know what'll happen to me if I'm late and I don't plan to find out. The tunnel opens up to the large dirt floor of the arena where my opponents are beginning to form a line, facing something to the south.

I catch Caz's eyes and he nods to me with a sad smile. His signature long-sleeved button down shirt hugs his chest tightly. My mind wanders to that night in his bed and a clear picture of what's below that shirt forms in my head. So much strength and power hidden away by stupid clothes. Such a shame.

I make it to the center of the large circular field and wave to Dryden as I step to his side. He doesn't return my wave and I follow his eyes to the seats on the south end of the arena. I freeze, suddenly feeling very much like a small animal in a cage.

At least a hundred people are sitting in the stone seats, watching us initiates with curious faces and the hope of being entertained in their wide eyes. King Alix stands in front of the crowd, the elder mage by his side as usual. I thought I once liked her, but her allegiance to the wolf king has rottened her for me.

"It is a new day here in Unity!" King Alix spins in his spot above us, speaking to all in attendance. "Our initiates have fought across this land, but I think it is time they fight for the people they may some day rule over." He spins to the spectators. "What do you think?"

The crowd cheers and hoots loudly, making my skin crawl with unease. I don't like being put on show for a crowd, but I chose to stay here and complete these trials. There's no turning back now. I look over at the other initiates and of course the sirens bow for the crowd, big fat smiles on their faces. The trolls pound their chests, and Dryden simply waves at the cheering crowd.

Caz looks over at me with an apologetic grimace on his perfect face. He clenches his jaw with a tight grin and raises both of his hands as a presentation for the on-lookers while he flexes his biceps. I can't help the lightness in my chest at seeing him be so willing to go with the flow, and honestly, who really cares? I shrug and roll my eyes at the excitement from the crowd and I grip the hilt of my sword, sliding it from the sheath to present in the glimmering sunlight.

With a couple of showy spins and slices of the sword like my dad taught me, I quickly sheath Theo and curtsy for the roaring crowd. I catch Caz's surprised eyes again and wink at him before standing straight once more. If they want a show, I can give a damn good one.

The king lifts his hands, calling for silence, and I don't miss the dark glare that he throws my way. *Screw you too, King Asshole.* "Alright, the rules are a little different in today's trials. Our initiates will team up based on which kingdom they are from, wolf with wolf, troll with troll, siren with siren, vampire with vampire, and our lone dragon."

I turn to Dryden with a sorry smile. He just shrugs, accepting his lot in the trials. Even though he's on a team of one, he is still one of the better fighters here and has as good a chance as any to make it to the end.

The king grins as he looks at our eager faces. "Today, it is time for a game. The game will be Hide and Seek. A child's game as you may remember it, but with much higher stakes." He turns to the high mage at his right and waves a hand at her, a command. "Madam, let's show our initiates what they will be seeking."

A sickness twists in my gut at the change in the king's tone. I have a bad feeling, and I just know whatever he has planned will not go well.

The high mage raises her hands in the air and five images appear as a mirage above our heads. A few gasps pour from the watching crowd as everyone takes in what the mage is showing us. The first image is a young troll girl, maybe thirteen years old with gold-colored hair. She is bound by rope around her hands and feet, and a cloth is tied around her mouth so she can't speak. Fear stains her sweet features.

A roar from my left shakes the ground below my feet. Faxon's face is bright red with anger and beside him, Echo has a murderous look on his round face. This girl means something to them.

I look back up at the images and the second one is much like the first. A figure in black, bound and gagged in what looks to be a cave. He is a boy, maybe sixteen, and by the silver in his eyes, it's clear that he is a vampire.

The third image shows an older woman, mid-forties. She is tied up as well, but she struggles against the ropes. Her beautiful green eyes and bright red hair match Nyx perfectly. A siren.

In the fourth flickering image of light, a woman with dark brown skin, around the same age as the last, sits with tears in her eyes. Dryden blows out an angry breath beside me, actual steam leaving his nostrils.

"Dryden?" I speak his name softly, but he doesn't respond.

My eyes reluctantly take in the fifth image. The young woman is wrapped in rope so tightly that she can't move more than her head to turn and look around the dark space with wide green eyes. Her dark blonde hair is covered in dirt and she has a bruise above the cloth around her face. My chest tightens and a fury like I have never experienced rolls through me.

Clio.

"Father!" It's Caz who roars in the sad silence. He takes a step forward with claws growing from his fingers and fur rippling down his muscular neck. "What are you playing at?"

King Alix shrugs like it's any normal day. "It's the Kingdom Trials, son. As I said, the stakes in this game are higher than you are used to. It's time for passion and anger to fuel you forward." He looks from face to face as he speaks. "You have each seen a loved one in these images. Your task is to seek them out, and save them. They don't know where they are or what has happened to them. Each was taken from their home in the night, and all they need is for you to rescue them."

Murmurs from the crowd float on the air. They are seeing their beloved king in a new light, and I hate that none of this surprises me in the least. *I'm going to kill him.*

Azra steps forward, stopping beside Caz. "How will we find them?"

King Alix grins again, loving his little game. "My guards have left trails for you to follow based on your abilities. You will need to use your senses and your wit... if you have any." The pointed look in my direction has me growling in my throat. The sound is barely discernible but I catch Caz's eyes as they flick back to me. I can't be sure, but it looks as if the color in his angry eyes shifts to a shining silver momentarily before returning back to normal. *Strange.*

"Now," the king continues. "Enter the forest that runs south toward the gathering grounds. You will find your first clue there."

With that, he taps the high mage on her shoulder and the two of them vanish without even a word of luck or encouragement. They're just... gone.

CHAPTER 24

✦←→✦

Cazimir

Every inch of me is trembling with anger. Anger at my father and his complete disregard for his family. I knew from a young age that he was ruthless and often cruel, but to have his own daughter kidnapped... I should have known nothing was beneath him.

Each of the initiates charge forward together, desperate to find the clues that will lead us to our loved ones. Just knowing that Clio is scared and alone somewhere has my pulse pounding in my ears as I run from the large arena, leaving the crowd behind. I can only imagine that our movements will be broadcasted to the onlookers once we leave. The mage magic will track us during this... *performance*.

I turn to my right as the nine of us exit the tunnel that leads into the south woods. Nyomi is running beside me, desperation matching my own across her face. She cares for Clio, as if they were family, and I know Ny will do whatever it takes to help me rescue her.

"Do you see anything?" Ny dives into the bushes, ignoring the other searching initiates as she looks for any trace of Clio.

I open up my senses, sniffing the air from left to right. I can't smell anything other than the normal scents in the area. Vampire venom, blooming lilacs, pine, Ny. I shake my head, clearing Ny's mesmerizing scent from my mind. *Stay focused, Cazimir!*

"Here," Echo shouts as he pulls a wood-carved necklace of a flower hanging from the tree above him. "It's Lani's!" He flips the necklace around and reads something from the back. "South."

Faxon pats his cousin on the back and the two of them start running south. I growl as I watch them go. *Keep looking! Find something!*

Ny and I scan the dirt below us and my eye catches a glint of something half-buried at the base of a thick tree. I drop to my knees to dig up the thin blade. A wolf head is carved into the hilt of the knife. It's Clio's knife.

Nyomi drops beside me and her eyes spread wide as she stares at the knife. "Is that Clio's? Does it say anything?"

I flip the knife around and find one word carved into the wolf's neck, reading it aloud. "East."

Ny and I make eye contact and jump back to our feet in unison. Without another word, we run together, moving east to look for more clues as to where Clio could be hidden. *Oh, gods I hope she is okay.*

✦←→✦

Nyomi

Caz and I run east for at least a mile before he picks up a scent that has him skidding to a stop. "Wait, wait."

I stop beside him and watch as he raises his nose toward the sky, his eyes shifting to black as his wolf senses take over. "What is it? Can you smell Clio?"

He looks around and steps closer to me, his black eyes unchanging. "Ny, I smell her, but it's not her normal scent."

"What do you mean?"

He grimaces as he sniffs again and his lip curls up in disgust. "It smells like Clio, but mixed with the smell of blood as well."

I gasp and cover my mouth with my hand. "Is it her blood, Caz? The king wouldn't hurt her would he?" *Who am I kidding? Of course he would.*

Caz looks down at me with sad eyes and he shakes his head. "I don't know anymore, honestly. I never thought my father could kidnap his own child until today."

My heart breaks for him. I loved my dad with all of my heart, and I know he felt the same way about me... but Caz doesn't have that love. I reach up to stroke the stubble on Caz's handsome face, and his eyes close at my touch. He sighs but moves away so fast that the moment seems like it never happened.

He turns back to me, the black gone from his irises. "We have to keep going. Who knows if they have eyes on us right now."

I just nod back to him as I follow his lead. I want nothing more than to hold Caz in my arms again. A few days without him has felt like a year. I keep my eyes on Caz's back as he tracks Clio's scent. He prowls forward like an animal on the hunt, and I trust in his footsteps.

"This way," he says, shifting to the right and pushing through tall wild reed grass.

A small clearing opens up and I slam into Caz's back as he stops abruptly. I have to cling onto his shirt so I don't fall backward on my ass. "What's going on, Caz?" I step around him and my mouth drops open. "What in Unity is that doing there?"

The animal carcass on the ground is torn into pieces, skin peeled back from muscle and bone, with blood pooled all around it. I have skinned enough animals for food to know that this kill is hours old. Still, the stench hits me like a brick wall and my stomach turns upside down. Whoever killed this fawn left it without taking any meat from it.

"Why skin it and just leave it?" I don't understand.

Caz grumbles something beside me and I turn to him questioningly. He repeats the words louder for me to hear. "It's another clue. Just a wasted death to lead us toward Clio."

I scrunch up my nose in disgust. "So, the king just leaves dead baby animals in the woods as part of a game?" My blood boils beneath my skin as I stare down at the young deer.

I begin to shake as my anger rises in my throat and a blue glow surrounds me. I gasp as I look down at the blue lightning magic that wraps around my arms and legs. "Dammit!" I curse to the sky at the sudden faerie magic's appearance.

Caz steps in front of me, blocking my view of the blue sky. "Nyomi, if we are being watched, you cannot let them see this."

I shake my arms out with no luck. "I don't have any control over it. It's just..." My words stop when a familiar feeling fills my chest.

The worry on Caz's face is evident as he watches me. "What? Are you alright?"

"I'm fine. I think..." I focus on the warmth that fills me and I can almost see Clio's round green eyes in my mind. A feeling like a tug on my chest has me spinning toward the south. "I think I know where Clio is!"

Caz's eyes go wide and he looks around us. "Where? How?"

I shrug because I honestly don't even know how I know. I just grab Caz's hand and tug him along with me, trying to avoid looking at the dead animal again. The blue lightning around my skin still glows as Caz and I run hand-in-hand. I do nothing to try and stop it because I know it's the Fae magic that is helping me see Clio.

I follow the tug on my chest, climbing over fallen down trees and splashing through the noise creek that tries to make us turn east. I don't care about the cold that seeps into my clothes, and Caz doesn't seem to mind either as we continue south, drenched and now covered in mud from the dust that picks up around our footsteps.

A rocky cliffside that towers up above the trees finally stops us. I look along the wall that stretches to an unknown distance on both sides. "Do you know this place?"

Caz nods and looks in both directions, still holding my hand in his. His warmth against my palm is almost too distracting, but I can't help the lightness in my heart due to his touch. He closes his eyes for a moment and I can tell that he is listening and smelling the air. I can still feel the tug toward Clio but the blue magic is fading, taking the tug with it. Caz pauses and his eyes fly open, shifting to black as he stares down at me.

"I found her! She's *in* the wall. Hurry and search for a cave!"

I release Caz's hand and run to the left along the wall, separating from Caz who runs the opposite direction. I stop at a deep crevice along the rock that is wide enough to fit a grown person, even the trolls. I step into the darkness and my eyes fail to adjust to the change. *Come on, stupid wolf sight! Kick in!*

"Caz, I could use you over here!" I call behind me, and Caz appears in seconds.

He steps into the dark with me and I can feel his hands on my arms, but I'm still blind in the dark. "I'm here, Ny. Let me go in deeper and see if I can find her. Her scent is strong so she has to be here."

I nod, though I can't tell if he sees it or not. In the next instance, Caz's warm lips cover mine, moving softly. His hands slide to my neck and he kisses me deeper before releasing me and whispering against my ear. "Thank you."

Suddenly, his body leaves me standing cold and alone in the dark. I turn back to the opening of the cave and move to stand just outside once more, waiting for Caz to return with Clio. I can't stop the bouncing of my legs as I sit on a rock with my eyes glued to the cave.

After a few minutes, my eyes catch a glimpse of Caz's light brown hair as he exits the cave. He tows a dirt-covered Clio, untied and walking freely, behind him. My whole body sags at the sight of her. "Oh, thank the gods, Clio!"

I jump to my feet and run over to her, my mind for once not focused on her brother. Clio's smile glistens in the sunshine and her eyes fill with tears as she opens her arms for me. She lets me pull her into a tight hug and I even surprise myself at the familial gesture. Just a month ago I couldn't imagine hugging people so freely.

"Thank you for finding me, Ny." Clio's soft voice surprises me with it's timid tone.

I push her to arms length and scan her from head to toe. "Are you hurt, Clio? Are you okay? How long have you been in there?"

She shakes her head, her smile broadening. "I'm fine, Ny. I told the same to Caz." She looks over at Caz's worried eyes. "I have a few bruises from fighting the men who took me, but they didn't hurt me. It was dark out when I was brought here, but I don't know what time it was."

I brush her messy hair from her face. "I'm glad you're alright, but that damn…" I clench my teeth to stop myself before I start bad-mouthing her father.

Caz growls beside me and I turn my attention to him. "Don't hesitate, Ny. I know exactly what you want to say. The damn king needs to be stopped."

Clio scoffs and for the first time since I met her, she looks like a warrior and not a princess. "I know he's my father, but I agree. He won't be forgiven for this."

CHAPTER 25

⊶ ⊷

Nyomi

I sit beside Caz on his bedroom floor, crossing my legs awkwardly as all present eyes watch me curiously. Yesterday's so-called "game" of Hide and Seek is finally over, and the initiates are pissed. Our secret meeting has so far been a whole lot of staring at each other in an uncomfortable silence.

"Okay, somebody needs to say something. I'm about to lose my damn mind." Azra speaks up as he runs a hand through his black hair. Arnoux chuckles beside him and that sends the rest of us into a laughing fit.

There are nine of us in total. Caz, Clio, Bastian and I went around to the bedrooms after the castle quieted down for the night. We gathered the vampires, the trolls, and Dryden. The sirens were left out of the meeting for obvious reasons.

Caz clears his throat and looks around at our mixed-up crew. "I agree. I suppose that's my cue to speak. First of all, yesterday was shit." Grumbles of agreement mingle together in the room.

Dryden's nostrils flare as he nods. "They took my mother from her home, knocked her out and tied her up. She hasn't even had proper time to grieve since we lost Juno, and this is how they choose to test me?"

My heart aches at the pain in his eyes. "I'm so sorry, Dryden. This shouldn't have happened."

Faxon shifts his weight from foot to foot, his bulky frame causing a shadow to fall over the room from where he stands in front of the flickering candle. "My little sister is not yet thirteen and that bastard king had her thrown into a pit like a hog-tied animal." Spit leaves his lips as he talks, his anger laced through his words.

Clio's voice rises above the grunts of rage. "My father has never been a kind man. I won't pretend to respect him, or to defend him any longer. All I ask is that we can keep this meeting confidential."

I look around and each person nods in agreement. Bastian reaches a hand over to Clio and she places her hand in his. I can see the calm wash over her at his touch, and I know that feeling so well because of Caz. I look at Caz again as he stands in front of the others.

"Well, if we're all in agreement that the conversation here stays between the nine of us, there is something you all need to know. The Fae are back in Unity, and they're bringing a war to my father's doorstep."

Everyone looks at each other with wide eyes, but they remain quiet as I stand to talk. "I have spoken with the faeries and I think we should side with them.

I know it's not news that I'm tainted... half wolf, and half of something else. Well, that other half happens to be Fae. I know my existence is an abomination in the eyes of King Alix and many others, but all I want is peace in Unity. The way it should be."

I connect with each and every pair of eyes in the room, and not one person looks at me with hatred or disgust. I look into Caz's eyes last, and he smiles back at me. He turns to the others again.

"Nyomi is our connection to the Fae queen. Though it goes against our ancient laws, I would like to help the Fae queen dethrone my father, and have a vote for the next ruler of Unity."

Azra scoffs and shakes his head as if exasperated. "That's a whole lot of news in a few words, Cazimir. Are you sure you're capable of this task? I mean, Alix is *your* father."

Caz opens his mouth to speak but all of us jump when the bedroom door swings open and Queen Freya steps inside, quickly closing the door behind her. The whole room freezes, each person unsure if we've been caught in the act of treason and are about to be executed.

She throws her long fingers on her hips and raises a single eyebrow as she surveys the room. Her eyes fall on Caz and she sighs sadly. "Actually, Alix is not your father, Cazimir."

I spin toward Caz, chewing on my lip nervously. He looks at his mother and tilts his head in question. "I don't understand. Who is my father then?"

Everyone present just looks between Caz and Queen Freya, silent and waiting for something to happen. The queen's shoulders sag and she walks up to Caz. She takes his hands in hers and the look of motherly love on her face has my heart clenching tightly.

Clio clicks her tongue. "What about me?"

Queen Freya grimaces as she looks toward Clio. "I'm sorry, dear. Alix is still your father."

Clio's lips drop into a deep frown. "Gods, it's no fair!" The true look of childish disappointment makes her look younger than ever and I'd be smiling if it weren't for the bomb being dropped on Caz.

The queen looks into her son's eyes. "Cazimir, I never loved Alix. I was thrown into a marriage with him out of duty to Lupos and Unity. I loved another man at that time, with my whole heart. I thought about leaving with you, but after having Clio, I knew I would never do anything to risk her, so I stayed with Alix." Caz nods, and I know he agrees with his mother's choices. "But, your real father's name was Carro."

Azra and Arnoux's gasps of shock have us all spinning in their direction. Azra closes his eyes as if in pain as he says, "Well, shit."

Everyone watches the vampires with the same looks of confusion on their faces. Caz shrugs and his eyes look wildly between the twins and his mother. "What? What am I missing?"

Queen Freya glares at Azra before turning her attention back to her son. "Cazimir, your father, Carro… His last name was Ennui. He was a vampire prince… brother to the current king of Vampir… uncle to Azra and Arnoux."

Caz just looks down at his mother with a confused expression on his handsome face. He closes his eyes for a moment before looking around the queen at Azra and Arnoux. "So, I'm… tainted?" His eyes find me and he looks as if reality has finally knocked him on the head.

Azra breaks the silent tension with a long breathy whistle as he nudges Arnoux in the side. "Hey, bro. Looks like we have a new cousin."

And for some inexplicable reason, the last thing in Unity I expect happens. Caz's lips lift as he bursts into a full blown laugh.

PART 5

A TRIAL OF MATES

CHAPTER 26

✦←→✦

Nyomi

I stare into the criss-crossed blackish lines of the perfectly laid wooden floor. A task that no doubt took hours to complete nearly a thousand years ago. It's not often that I get time to really appreciate the intricate beauties of the castle's design. When I arrived, I couldn't help but associate the building with King Alix, leaving a dark stain on everything I saw. Now, though, it all feels a little bit brighter.

The door to my bedroom creeks open slowly and Clio's blonde head peers in at me. "Slumber party? I could really use some girl-time."

I sit up from the prone position on my bedroom floor that I have been in for ten minutes, half-dead from lack of sleep. "Yes, please," I groan out with a lazy smile.

The dark under Clio's blue eyes is a rare sight, but it shows just how much the night has drained the life from her. It has been a night of non-stop talking with the initiates in Caz's bedroom. I couldn't have imagined just a few hours ago that our little meeting would reveal so many long-hidden secrets.

My fated mate is half wolf-shifter and half vampire. Well, one of my fated mates. I still don't know what to do about Alston, my "fatis" healer. Honestly, a night of lost sleep is nothing compared to the overwhelming dramas of my life.

I yawn and climb up into my bed, patting the empty spot beside me for Clio to claim. "Come on. We can at least be comfortable while we talk."

Clio smiles and wiggles her small frame into the blankets. "What a night, huh?"

I scoff and throw my head back. "I don't have words to even describe the things running through my mind, Clio. How are we going to move forward with so much of the past dragging us back?"

She shrugs, but I can't mistake the hope in her eyes. "Hey, I'm the one with the psychopath father and half-vampire half brother... If I can leave that behind and still dream of a better world, then so can you."

My eyebrows shoot up at her words. "That sounds absolutely ridiculous, do you know that?"

She snorts as laughter pours from her. "Oh, goddess, we are a pair, aren't we?"

"I don't know much about friendships, Clio, but I'd like to think this is one of those friendships that lasts a lifetime."

Her wide grin brightens the dark room. "Well, we are a bit more than friends, right? You *are* my brother's fated mate after all."

I grimace. "So, I guess I should've told you this sooner, huh? It has been a little crazy."

Clio nods. "You mean how you are fated for Caz, but you also have a fated faerie mate who is also a healer in your long lost aunt's army?"

My eyes fly open so wide that they go dry momentarily. "How do you know all of that? I have only told one person about my Fae mate."

She looks almost guilty. "Well... Bastian told me, actually. Caz tells him everything, and Bast and I talk quite a lot." Her pink cheeks turn even pinker as she avoids my eyes.

I sit up and lean toward Clio, ready to get down to what I've heard called "boy-talk". "So, are we going to talk about *your* fated mate? A certain burly brunette guard?"

Clio rolls her eyes. "He's not my fated mate, Ny. I mean, I'm not eighteen for another month yet."

"Do you feel like he could be, though? You're not far from your birthday. Maybe the bond is coming a little early for you? I can tell Bastian is drawn to you."

Her blush deepens. "You think so? We have held hands a few times and we spend a lot of time together, just talking. He's almost three years older than me, and way more experienced..." Her words trail off, but I get the meaning well enough.

I chew on my bottom lip. I never had the sex talk when I was a kid. Everything I learned was from Bellona's niece, Bridget. She wasn't really friendly, but she was open to giving me all of the details of her own experiences. My dad only told me where babies came from, not how they were put there.

"Are you... I mean, have you..." I try to think of the best way to ask this extremely uncomfortable question. "Have you ever dated?" *Smooth, Ny.*

Clio chuckles like I told some great joke. "Do you really think my overprotective brother would have allowed me to date someone other than my fated mate? He would've skinned any guy alive for even trying to kiss me."

I can't stop the smile that graces my lips as I think about Caz taking care of his baby sister. As long as he doesn't tell *me* where to go and what to do, I like the idea of him looking after Clio and keeping the wolf boys at bay.

I nudge Clio's arm and snuggle into the covers deeper as I yawn. "I don't know a ton about Bastian, but if Caz is his friend, and he lets you two spend time alone, then he must be an honorable man. I don't think it matters what he has done in the past. If he's your mate, you will be the only thing he sees."

Clio lays her head back with a sigh. "You're right. I think I love him already, even though I haven't come of age yet. Is that crazy?"

I shake my head, but do I really know what that kind of love is like? My mind wanders to Caz and I smile sleepily again. Maybe I do know. Just as sleep threatens to pull me under, Clio suddenly sits up and reaches below the comforter to her long socks.

"I almost forgot!" She pulls one of the socks off of her delicate foot and a folded up piece of paper falls out onto the mattress. "This was given to me yesterday by the wall wreckage when I was helping clean up. A man in a hood snuck it into my hand and said to give it to you. It was before the whole crazy kidnapping and I didn't have a chance to give it to you until now."

I grab the paper and peel it open to see smudged ink scrawled across the wrinkled parchment: *Follow the magic at midnight. I am waiting. ~Your fatis*

+←→+

Nyomi

I draw the thick cloak tighter around my shoulders, hoping that the black cloth will keep me hidden in the shadow of the trees. After reading Alston's note at least a dozen times, Clio and I decided to sleep for the remaining hours of the morning and have another 'slumber party' the following night. Tonight.

Thankfully, the "understanding" king granted us initiates a day to rest from the last trial. I have spent the majority of the day between my bedroom and the dining hall, eating my feelings away and debating on whether I really want to venture into the woods to meet up with Alston at midnight.

Here I am, though, winding between the trees with Theo on my hip, still not totally sure I'm making the right decision. Alston's note said to follow the magic at midnight. No date was specified, so who even knows if he'll be out here? The only thing keeping me moving is the pull of our bond.

I've realized that this awareness of a magical connection between creatures is the thing that led me to Clio in that cave. It's a faerie ability that I am more grateful for than whatever that blue lightning is meant to accomplish. It's certainly easier to control than the freaky body electricity.

The pull of magic grows so strong that I know I have to be close to Alston. I am nearly to the gathering grounds, as far south as I can go before hitting the remainder of the king's wall, and the air is silent beneath the half moon. A squirrel runs past my feet and I jump back a step, running into something hard.

"You are afraid of squirrels, fatis?" I spin around and step away from Alston's arms. He is smiling down at me, his sharp jaw casting a shadow across his neck.

I shake my head. "Not normally. I guess I'm just a little jumpy lately."

Alston's smile falls and his eyebrows press together at the center of his forehead. "I wish you didn't have to be afraid of anything, Nyomi. You should be free and fearless."

I scoff. "I've never been free. I can't even imagine what that feels like."

He steps closer to me, his healer eyes scanning my body like he did the first time we met. The black of his pupils widens, bleeding into the forest green, nearly covering the color completely. He searches me completely, making me squirm.

"I really wish you wouldn't look at me like that, Alston." My voice is too quiet as I speak.

Alston's eyes meet mine, his pupils returning to a normal size. "I'm sorry, I didn't mean to make you uncomfortable. I only wanted to make sure you're un-injured."

I nod. "I know, but it's not like we're just *people* to one another. We're…"

His slow smile crawls back into place. "We are fated mates… meant to be."

Alston takes another step toward me and I'm mad at myself for not immediately retreating. "Alston, you need to understand something…" *Spit it out, Ny!* "You're not my only fated mate."

His smile doesn't leave his handsome face like I expect, but a smooth chuckle like liquid leaves his lips. "I know, Nyomi. Your wolf side is fated to the prince, Cazimir."

"How did you know that?"

"The Fae have been watching everything. This war isn't some spur of the moment act of vengeance. We have been doing our homework, and any faerie can see the magic that connects you and him." He reaches a hand out and grabs mine, stroking it gently with his thumb. "Just like the magic that flows between us."

I stare up into Alston's green eyes, letting myself imagine the possibilities for a minute. I can feel the pull, and the magic that swirls around us when we stand so close like this. It's thick and inviting.

"Alston, I don't know what I'm supposed to do. I feel… a lot for Cazimir." *Say you love Caz. Make it clear.*

Alston licks his lips and his eyes narrow slightly, in a dark and sexy way. "Why do you think I called you here? We can't know what you may feel for me if we don't try something."

I focus on the comforting feel of his hands as they move up my arms, beneath my cloak. "What...uh, what exactly should we be trying?"

His hands slip over my shoulders and stop on my back. Our chests are pressed together now, and I can feel the pounding of his heart. "Will you let me kiss you, Nyomi?"

My eyebrows shoot up and I want to say no, but Caz's words come back to me. *"I imagine you're the only one for him as well, and he's a damn lucky guy who likely deserves a chance."* Alston does deserve a chance, and I can't just let our connection go as if it means nothing.

I slowly nod, giving him my answer without words, and Alston leans into me. His lips hover just above mine, his breath hot against my skin as he hesitates. I close the gap, standing up on my toes to deepen the kiss.

Alston's hands slide down my back, resting low as he pulls me tighter to him. I wrap my arms around his neck and my cloak falls to the ground, temporarily forgotten as Alston's tongue dips in between my lips. There's no mistaking the heat and emotion that is shared through our kiss, but something still feels like it's missing. I allow Alston to press my back gently to the tree beside us, and his knee slips between my legs, bringing his body closer to mine. Our lips separate for a moment, but it's all I need to place my hands against his chest and push him back just slightly.

His forest green eyes stare down at my mouth and then travel to my gaze as he titles his head in question. He watches me as I watch him, and I can tell the moment he realizes the same thing that I do. Alston isn't the one I want. He takes a step back, running a hand through his black hair as he nods with a sad smile.

"You won't come back with me, will you?"

I blink back the tears that want to come as I shake my head. I can almost feel Alston's heart breaking and it physically hurts me. "I can't, Alston. I'm sorry."

He nods his head once more, and without another word, he disappears into the night.

CHAPTER 27

❧ ⤜ ⤛

Cazimir

"Cazimir. Will you stop walking so I can talk to you?" My mom trails behind me down the long dark corridor that leads to my old bedroom.

Nobody sleeps on this end of the castle anymore. Even Clio spends most of her nights sleeping in Nyomi's room. I had to smother myself under a pillow to block out their conversation last night, even though I desperately wanted to eavesdrop. Maybe I could've listened if it wasn't my little sister talking to my fated mate about guys.

When I heard Clio enter Ny's room tonight, I bailed, wanting just one night of peace and quiet. Of course my mother found me before I could escape.

I look back at the woman who gave me life. Her eyes, just a little bluer than mine, stare back at me, slightly slanted with sadness. She wants me to understand why she loved another man other than my… her husband, and why I never knew of this.

"Mom, I don't know if I really want to hear any more."

She stills and hurt crosses her face. "I thought you were relieved when I told you that Alix isn't your father. You seemed... happy."

I shake my head. "I'm thrilled to not be tied to that man, mom!" I look around at the dark hallway, lowering my voice. "The fact that you loved someone else, I get it, alright? But what I don't understand is that I was never told about it until now."

She starts to speak but I interrupt, even though I feel like an ass doing so. "I have lived my life in the shadow of the man whose blood was supposed to be my blood. I thought I was meant to follow in my father's footsteps, to rule like he has. It has been a strain on me for as long as I can remember because I was sure there was no way out of my destiny. But now," I scoff, a harsh breath leaving my throat. "I feel like I don't have an identity anymore."

Damn, I sound like such a baby.

My mom steps closer to me and her lips squeeze together tightly. "Cazimir, I am so sorry for making you feel that way. Can I tell you my side of the story, where it began twenty years ago?"

I nod, and she brushes her thin fingers through her waist-length hair, combing out any snarls. "Okay, well... I grew up with Alix, in Lupos. He was a decent child, willing to help others, and he always kept up with his studies." Her eyes look past me, focusing on the memory of her childhood. "When I turned eighteen, I shifted for the first time, and Alix was there to watch, along with both of our families. My mother and Alix's parents had a sort of agreement. They were sure that when my wolf side appeared, Alix and I would be fated mates. Alix's parents ruled Lupos, cousins to the king of Unity. My mother was a high-born single woman, since my father died when I was a young teenager. She needed the support of the Duras family, and my marriage to Alix was to be the ticket to ensure both of our futures."

I try to imagine my mom as that young vulnerable woman, and my heart breaks for her. I've never met my mom's mother, but I've been told about her incredible, hard-working spirit.

Mom continues, "Well, when my wolf side emerged, it was obvious that Alix and I weren't fated for one another. The connection wasn't there. So, we held off on marriage, and Alix was called to the Kingdom Trials." She pauses, leaning her back against the hallway wall. "I went to a few of the trials with my mother. We were invited to visit during some of the final battles. It was clear at the time that the wolf princess of Unity was well ahead and on track to winning it all. Her name was Rhae, Nyomi's mother."

I cross my arms and relax against the wall beside her, trying to understand the story. "Ny's mom was going to win the trials? But why didn't she?"

Mom looks at me like I should already know the answer. "She fell in love with a faerie. I met Rhae and Nyomi's father, Theon, while visiting for one of the big fights at Mutua Arena. They were supposed to fight one another, but it was clear that they had a deeper connection. Rhae won the fight and I spoke to her for a moment afterward. I asked if she liked the Fae prince and she told me that it didn't matter if she did or not. She said that love wasn't a freedom, it was a risk. I told her that if I could ever love someone, being with them would be worth the risk."

I turn my eyes to my mom in shock. "Are you saying that Nyomi is the result of your advice?" My mind spins as I try to comprehend that new information.

She laughs softly. "I don't think I'm so convincing that I shaped a stranger's life, son. But, that was the very moment that I met Carro." She says his name with a sigh. "He was listening in to our conversation and approached me afterward. It was my first ever interaction with a vampire. Carro was incredibly handsome with silver eyes and broad shoulders, just like yours." She pats my shoulder before continuing. "He asked me if I really believed that love was worth risking everything, even if that love was forbidden. I told him fervently that I absolutely believed it. His large smile made me feel like I was standing in the brightest sunshine. I wanted to see that smile every day for the rest of my life."

It's stupid how much I understand that feeling. I can't even imagine the hurt I'd feel never seeing Nyomi smile at me again.

"After that day, I didn't see Carro again until the trials ended. Rhae was doing so well that she was supposed to take the throne, but at the last minute, she suddenly dropped out, saying she was unable to complete the trials. This left Alix as the winner, and he was crowned king of Unity."

"Why did Rhae do that? She could have won and changed the rules so she could be with Theon."

My mom's eyebrows press together as she shrugs. "There was never a real explanation, but I believe it had something to do with Alix. After he won, Rhae and Theon went back to their homes. I think they began a relationship and eventually ran off together, disappearing completely. I did the same thing with Carro. He came looking for me at my home, and he asked if I could meet him at the border between Lupos and Vampir. We met there every night, and we fell in love. After a few months, I was called before Alix at Unidad Castle. He proposed to me, saying he still wanted to marry me since neither of us had fated mates. I couldn't tell him about Carro, and I had just found out that morning that I was pregnant. We would have been killed for creating a tainted child, so I was forced to accept his proposal."

I shake my head, trying to wrap my mind around it all. Could I have been born like Nyomi? Always on the run with two parents who loved me? Then where would I be? Clio never would have existed.

"Mom, what makes you think Alix had anything to do with Rhae dropping out of the trials?"

She clicks her tongue. "Well, after marrying Alix, I didn't end my relationship with Carro. I saw him regularly and even brought you to meet him when you were a baby. Carro loved you, Cazimir. He was amazed by you." She pauses as I take in those words. "One night, Alix had me followed. He had suspected that you weren't his son once he noticed that you looked nothing like him. He found out about my relationship with Carro, and he threatened to expose us and even you, which would name you as a tainted child and have you executed. He said to me, 'I didn't become king of Unity by being an accepting man.

Tainted relationships and tainted children are not welcome in this kingdom.' Then he told me that the only way to move forward would be if I gave myself to him completely, loving nobody else, and if I gave him a child of his own."

Her eyes fall to the floor as a look of shame comes over her. My mom's freckled cheeks look pale with grief, and my heart hurts for that young mother all those years ago. She sacrificed her freedom for me, breaking her own belief in the power of love, just so I could live.

I reach out to my mom, pulling her into my arms. "I'm so sorry, mom. You deserved a better life than this. I understand why you did what you did, and why you didn't tell me." I pull back so I can look at her teary eyes. "I owe everything to you, you know?"

She sniffles and rubs at her eyes before patting my scruffy cheek. "All I ever wanted was happiness for you and Clio, Cazimir. I still believe that you both can have the life that I couldn't. Just don't stop fighting."

I nod, but another question claws at me. "What happened to Carro... my father?"

Her eyes are lost again as she thinks back. "He was killed only a month after Alix made his threat. They said he was attacked while hunting, but nobody knew what did it. Nobody except me."

My whole body goes rigid with anger. I bite down, talking between my clenched teeth. "It was Alix, wasn't it." It's not a question, because I already know.

Alix took the throne from Nyomi's mother. He made my mate grow up in hiding, scared and alone.

He threatened my mother, causing her to sacrifice her life, and he killed my real father.

I look down the hall and find a set of gray eyes watching me from the dark. Nyomi heard the whole story, and it's for her that I'll kill the man who raised me.

CHAPTER 28

+←→+

Nyomi

I stand with my back against the wall, hidden from sight in the dark corner of the long hallway. I listen to each word that Queen Freya tells Caz. The details of what happened with my parents in the Kingdom Trials, the tragic love story between Freya and Carro, and the truth of every pain that Alix Duras has caused.

When Caz's haunted eyes find me in the shadows, the hurt coming from him is like a magnet dragging me forward. I have to fight to stay put and not interrupt his conversation with his mother. After leaving Alston in the woods, I went straight for Caz's bedroom, only to find it empty. I was able to tap into that feeling of magic that connects each of us, and I ended up here.

"Cazimir," Queen Freya grabs Caz's hand in hers. "I am going to bed. Make sure you and Nyomi are not discovered, alright? I won't be able to stop

Alix's wrath." She turns and her eyes find me instantly. "Good night, Nyomi."

I blanch as I step into the dim light. "Good night. I'm… I'm sorry… about everything."

She leaves Caz and comes to me, touching my cheek gently. "You should not be sorry for anything. Just be careful."

With that, she leaves Caz and I alone in the quiet hall. I turn to Cazimir and I'm at a loss for words. What does one say to their fated mate after they learn that the man who raised them killed their actual father out of spite? *I should just leave.*

I make up my mind to turn and run like a coward, but Caz is by my side, grabbing my hand before I can go anywhere. "Ny, can we talk?"

I nod slowly and Caz pulls me behind him, into his old bedroom. We enter the dark room, barely illuminated by the bits of moonlight streaming through a large window. Caz releases my hand and steps back into the hall.

I spin around to him. "Where are you going?"

He smiles down at me. "Do you have wolf sight, Ny?"

I shake my head. "No, I don't."

"Well," he disappears into the hall and returns in seconds with a lit candle in his hands. He reaches the flame up to the sconce on his bedroom wall and lights the unused candle in the holder. He places the first candle on a table beside his bed and returns to me with a cocky grin.

"I didn't want you to think I was dragging you into my dark room to suggest something or take advantage of your shortcomings."

My mouth falls open. "My shortcomings? So, you think you're better than me?"

Caz's warm chuckle is like sweet melting honey on my senses. "I never said that. I'm just trying not to be too... I don't want you to think I'm expecting..."

I hold my hand up to stop his rambling. I look around at the warm candlelight making the shadows of the bedroom dance to the rhythm of our heartbeats. "And you don't think shutting us alone in a candlelit bedroom is suggestive?" I raise a single eyebrow at him.

Caz rolls his eyes as he turns away from me. From behind, I can see him run a hand along his face in frustration. "Ny, we need to talk."

I move around to the front of him. "I know that. That's why I'm here."

"So, how much of my conversation with my mom did you hear?" He chews on the inside of his mouth as he watches me with worried eyes.

"I think I heard most of it. I heard your mom telling the story of how she met your father, and my parents. About why she stayed with Alix and... Caz, I'm so sorry about Carro. I know you probably had hopes of meeting him."

He shakes his head. "I didn't really. I don't think I've had time to even imagine what it would be like to have a vampire father. Up until recently, I didn't have much respect for Arnoux and Azra." He scoffs, almost a laugh. "My cousins I guess." He looks deep into my eyes and takes in my outfit. "Why did you come looking for me, Ny? I thought you and Clio were having a sleepover."

I play with the hilt of my sword, avoiding Caz's gaze. "I returned to the castle to try and find you, but you weren't in your room. I heard you and your mom talking and didn't want to interrupt. It seemed important, and I guess I was right."

Caz closes his eyes as he nods, but then he suddenly looks at me with his eyebrows dipped in confusion. "Wait, you returned to the castle? From where?"

My body stills and then I shuffle my feet nervously. "I received a note… from Alston, my uh… that Fae healer. He asked me to meet him in the forest, so I did."

Caz's face is emotionless. "Your fated mate?" I nod. "What did he want to meet you for?" He steps away from me to sit on the edge of his bed, looking down at the floor instead of at me.

"Do you want me to be honest, even if it might hurt you?"

He looks up at me. "I always want you to tell me the truth, Ny."

I try to ignore the hurt in his eyes as I continue. "Alston wanted me to give him a chance. He… kissed me, and I let him."

Caz stands abruptly and he stalks toward the window at the far end of the room. In the glow of the candles, I can see the muscles of his forearms flex against his rolled-up sleeves. His breath comes out harsh as he avoids looking back at me, leaving me staring silently at his broad back.

"So, that's why you came here… to tell me that you chose the faerie." It's not a question, but an angry statement.

I open my mouth to speak but Caz turns and glares at me. "Well, thanks for your honesty, Nyomi." *Nyomi?* "You can go ahead and run off with the faeries."

My eyes fly open and a completely childish fury rolls through me at his attitude. "Seriously? You'd be just fine with me leaving and never looking back?"

He shrugs with a deep frown warping his plump lips. "I don't really care. Your life isn't mine to control. I told you to explore your feelings for the healer and you did. Congratulations."

I blow out an angry breath. "Gods, Caz! Do you realize how damn idiotic you can be at times?"

He throws his arms out. "Good thing you don't have to worry about me anymore, then."

I spin around, too mad to look at him, and my shoulders sag. How in Unity did we get to this point? Right, because my fated mate is a jealous hothead.

I cross my arms and mutter under my breath. "All I wanted was to tell you that I love you, asshole."

The words are barely spoken as I whisper them through clenched teeth. I look toward the bedroom door, ready to leave, but large hands grab my waist and spin me around. Caz holds onto my hips as he leans his head toward me, desperation in his nearly black eyes.

"What did you just say?" His voice is tight and needy.

I try to push at his hands but he doesn't release me. "It doesn't matter, Caz. You told me to leave, so I'll go."

He growls and lets go of my hips to grab me by the sides of my head. "Nyomi, please say it again."

"Say what? That you're an asshole?"

"For the love of the gods, Ny! The part before that!" His voice lowers to a gentle plea as his eyes close and his thumbs rub along my cheeks. "I'm begging you to give me hope, Nyomi. Please say the words again, so I can know that I didn't dream them."

His turquoise eyes open slowly to drink me in as I lay my hands on his chest. "Caz, I came back here to tell you that I love you. I understand that fate gave me choices, and I choose you, okay? I don't want to leave. I want *you*."

Caz's hands remain on the sides of my head and his eyes study me, as if he's trying to figure out if I'm lying to him. He licks his lips and I groan in frustration, feeling like I should have just kept my mouth shut.

"Aren't you going to say something? At least start yelling at me again so I don't have to stand here like a loser in silence."

Caz's lips lift at the corners and he shakes his head. "I love you too, Ny."

My heart flutters and the insecure girl inside of me cries out. "Are you sure? I've been so difficult." *Great, Ny. Now he's going to take it back!*

Caz lets out a breathy laugh. His hands slip into my hair and tug gently on the strands so I have to look up into his eyes. "You are a difficult and fierce woman with a stubborn head and a huge heart. I love you for everything you are, so yes, I am *completely* sure." His smile falls as his eyes lock onto my lips.

"I'm trying so hard not to lose control now that I know you love me too."

I smile back at him. "Oh, for Unity's sake, *please* lose control."

The command barely leaves my mouth before Caz has me in his arms and his lips crash into mine. I throw my arms around his neck and suck his bottom lip in between my teeth, biting it gently. Caz growls deep and the sound rumbles against my chest.

I swing my legs around his hips, clinging onto him for dear life, and my sword smacks him in the thigh. He grunts, but doesn't separate from me as he reaches a hand between us and unhooks the leather belt from my waist. Theo hits the floor with a thud, and Caz leaves it behind, carrying me back to his large bed.

Caz drops me onto the bed and immediately covers me with his body. His mouth returns to mine and he kisses me achingly slowly, his tongue sweeping across my lips as he tastes me. I reach for the buttons of his white shirt and begin undoing one at a time, letting my fingers brush his skin along the way.

"Too slow," he groans out. Claws stretch from his fingertips as he leans back and he cuts through the last few buttons before tugging his shirt off entirely.

My eyes widen as I take in his bare chest and sharp claws. He's every bit the wolf as he is the man, and his wildness excites me in the most primal of ways. Caz starts to lower himself back to me but I hold my hands out to stop him. I take a few more seconds to drink in the hills and canyons that his muscles create across his skin, and I run my fingers along the warmth.

"Are you going to stare at me all night, Ny?" His smirk is teasing as he watches me ogle him.

I blush and shake my head. "I can't deny that I'd like that very much, but I think I would like something else even more." *Goddess, when did I become so daring?*

Caz growls as his eyes darken and he pounces on me, making the girliest giggle leave my lips. He wraps his arms around my waist and pulls me tightly against his bare torso before flipping onto his back so that I'm sitting on top of him.

"Your turn," he says with his voice so gravelly that I'm sure his wolf side took control of his vocal chords.

Caz's large hands slide up my legs, claws gone, and his fingers dip below my black tunic. His hands splay across my bare stomach, stroking my skin and causing my breath to hitch. I grip the bottom of the fabric and drag the tunic over my head, shivering at the cool air that hits my skin.

Caz's eyes slowly leave mine and his gaze is like a caress against my naked skin as he studies me. "You are so beautiful, Ny."

I smile as I repeat his words. "Are you going to stare at me all night, Cazimir?"

The soft chuckle that leaves him makes me grin so wide that my cheeks hurt. He sits up with me straddling him and our bare chests collide. Caz's mouth covers mine as his hands cling onto the skin of my back and he presses me harder against him.

His lips kiss the corner of my mouth, then my cheek, and across my jaw before stopping at my ear as he whispers my words back to me. "There is something I'd like even more."

Caz nibbles softly on my earlobe and the sound that leaves me is a cross between a squeal and a moan. I wrap myself completely around him as he stands with me in his arms, and I let him lower me to my feet. We both reach for our pants simultaneously and remove the last bits of our clothing until there is nothing left between us.

I don't even realize that I'm trembling until Caz covers my hands with his and places gentle kisses on my sweaty palms. "I love you, Ny, and I am yours no matter what." He steps closer to me, not breaking eye contact as he speaks. "I'll do whatever it takes to have a million more nights with you, just like this. We don't need to hurry."

I sigh and I look from one of his eyes to the other and back. "I think I'm terrified, Caz. I've never been as happy as I am at this moment, and I don't want it to end."

He kisses me so softly that I could have imagined it. "You're terrified? Gods, I am scared out of my damn mind." He laughs. "I've never done this before, Ny. I knew that I'd find my fate someday, but I couldn't have imagined someone like you in my most incredible dreams. Like I said, I am yours. Right now, tomorrow, next week, until Unity ends, and whatever comes after. Okay?"

I smile and shake my head. "Sheesh, Caz. If I didn't already love you, you would have me with those words alone." I press myself up against his body and wrap my arms around his neck. "I choose right now, *my* mate. And every day after."

Caz growls again in that way that I love. He hoists me up into his arms before flipping me back onto his bed and covering me with his warmth. Our lips crash together in a heat like nothing I've ever experienced and every nerve of my body feels like lightning coursing through me. I can faintly see the blue glow of my Fae magic spark to life as Caz moves against me, rhythmic and powerful.

I cling onto his back, magic pouring from me as we claim one another and let the rest of Unity disappear.

CHAPTER 29

⊷← →⊶

Nyomi

"Do not fight it, Nyomi. It is your destiny. Stay alive, push through, and use your strengths. This is all I can tell you, now wake up and protect your mate."

"Ny," Caz whispers to me.

I gasp and sit up in bed as a *thump thump thump* rattles my mind. I look around at Caz's bedroom and the stream of morning light pouring in through the tall, narrow window. Another *thump thump thump* from the bedroom door makes me jump.

Caz is standing beside the bed, getting dressed so quickly that his movements are a blur. "Ny, get dressed right now." His voice is so quiet that I have to strain to hear his words. "My father's guards are at the door."

I throw a hand over my mouth as my eyes widen, and I drag my naked body out of Caz's bed. He doesn't wait for me to dress myself and instead, he quickly tugs my discarded tunic over my head before I can even blink. The fabric falls halfway down my thighs, but I still hurry to cover myself as Caz's door breaks from its hinges.

A large black wolf steps into the bedroom with broken slivers of wood in his fur. Clearly the one who busted the door down. He moves to the side to let two men with swords enter behind him.

The tallest man with shoulder-length hair and skin as dark as night looks at Caz. "Cazimir Duras, this seductress is tainted and has tricked you into her bed. She is to be arrested immediately."

I scoff. "Seductress? Really?"

Caz steps in front of me with his shoulders tense as his torn shirt hangs from his body. "You will not be taking her, Dom."

The big guard, Dom, looks apologetic as he steps further into the room. "It's the king's wish for the girl to be locked up. I'm sorry, Cazimir."

Fur sprouts across Caz's arms and I can see his claws break free of his skin at the ends of his fingers. Before he can lunge for the guard, King Alix steps into the room.

"Son, there's no need to fight my men. You know the laws. Initiates who break the rules of the trials will be disqualified. I'm protecting you so that you may have a chance to rule."

I take a step backward and my foot brushes against something. *My sword!* I stay on top of the weapon, ready to fight if I need to.

Caz growls at the king. "If Nyomi is to be disqualified, then it's deserved for both of us. Disqualification isn't the same as imprisonment, *father*. We'll leave and not come back."

Alix shakes his head and laughs evilly. "Cazimir, come on. You can't leave. This…" he gestures between Caz and I. "Infatuation was just a game gone wrong. It's time to finish playing and get rid of the girl." He looks back at me, his eyes traveling up and down my body. "If you aren't playing with her, and you actually have a relationship, then you both will be executed. Is that what you want, *son*?"

My heart sinks at the thought of Caz dying for me. The king doesn't know that we are mates, or if he does, he wants to cover it up and get rid of me so Caz can rule Unity without a tainted mate. I can't let this happen.

Caz begins to speak but the voice from my dream fills my ears. *"Protect your mate."* I make a sudden and hopefully not stupid decision as I shove Caz in the back. He stumbles forward only slightly and his eyes whip back to me with confusion.

"Ny?"

I force myself to glare at him as I square my shoulders. "A game? Really, Cazimir? That's all this was to you?" His eyes go wide as he looks back at me, and I continue yelling. "I can't believe you let me think you cared about me!"

I pray to the gods that Caz gets the hint and plays along. If not, then we both die. He watches me in silence for an achingly long minute before he stands up tall and throws his arms to the side in frustration.

"Come on, Nyomi. You had to know."

I huff and bend to pick up my sword. I pull out the blade and aim it at Caz. "How could someone do something like that? I won't go with your crooked guards! I'll fight to the death!"

Alix laughs behind Caz. "That can be arranged. What do you think, Cazimir? I think it would be much more satisfying for her to have a reunion with the place where her father was killed."

My body begins to shake with anger, but I keep my eyes on Caz. He looks back at Alix and then to me. "I agree, father. I think it would do her some good to rot for a while. I've had my fun."

Caz's words may have hurt me once, but the magic that connects us now that we are bonded holds strong, like a wave of light giving me a sense of peace and hope. I step toward Caz with my sword and I swing it in the air, narrowly missing his neck. He moves so fast that the air is knocked out of me when he grabs my wrist and slams my back to his chest. I drop my sword to the ground and struggle in Caz's grip, forcing tears into my eyes.

"Let me go!" I kick and scream.

"Happily," Caz says as he shoves me into Dom's arms. "Enjoy your time, Nyomi. I'll see you again really soon." His voice sounds taunting and malicious but I have hope that his words are the truth.

Dom's hand clamps around my mouth and I breathe in a powdery substance that makes me cough and gag. Caz's jaw clenches tight and his eyes look wild as he watches me fight whatever drug the guard has given me. I look deep into his eyes as a drowsiness flows through my body and weakens my limbs.

"You're an asshole," I say to him like I did last night when I told him I loved him.

My eyes flutter closed, but I can faintly hear Caz's voice as I fall into darkness. "You too."

←→

Cazimir

"Damn it, Bastian! Where are you?" I yell as I search the edge of the forest where Bastian should be on duty.

It's so early in the morning that the birds are still chirping happily at the new sunshine. I'm desperate to find Bastian and get Ny out of those dungeons. I hated talking to Nyomi like she was nothing to me. She is my world, and pretending she isn't goes against the bond we have, like a knife digging into my heart. It felt... wrong. Especially after spending the best night of my life drowning in her.

Of course, my girl chose to use her mind against my father and his men when I would've fought to the death to protect her. I'll still fight to the death if it means freeing her from that cage. She deserves a throne and all of Unity at her feet, not a dark cell alone.

"Caz?" Bastian steps out of the trees a few yards down the line, confusion pressing down on his thick brows. "What's up, man?"

I run to his side and grip him by his armored shoulders. "Nyomi has been taken to a cell in the dungeons. We need to get her out."

His eyes open as wide as saucers. "Gods. I'll do whatever I can to help, but where will she go once she's freed? Alix won't stop looking for her."

"I know he won't. That's why we need to join the Fae now. Ny's aunt will protect her, I'm sure of it." *Gods, I hope it's true.*

Caz rubs a large hand down his bearded face, releasing a rough sigh. "Okay. We'll need to tell the others as soon as possible."

I nod and glance around for any eavesdroppers. Our voices are whispered enough to not be overheard, but my paranoia is at its peak. "I'll need *you* for that, Bast. You can go tell everyone that the time to leave is tonight, and we'll need a meeting place. The damaged wall will make travel through the border easier, and you know the watch rotations, right?" He nods. "Good. Then I'll just need to figure out the hard part. Getting Ny past the prison guards."

"I can do that." Clio's voice drifts to us as she skips our way like it's any other day. "Caz, you can't be the one to get Nyomi. I don't know what Dad... *my* dad... has planned for Ny, but I can guarantee he won't let *you* anywhere near those dungeons."

I can't stop the low growl in my throat. "I'm not going to let her stay in that place any longer than she has to, Clio. I'm going in there."

Clio rolls her eyes at me. "Come on, Caz. You think I want Nyomi to·have to relive the torture she went through all over again?" Her eyes grow cold and strong. "She's my best friend, and she has probably told me more about her past than she has told you, so don't act like you're the only person allowed to care."

I'm taken aback by the ferocity in my little sister's voice and I look over at Bastian who stares at Clio in awe. "Well," I say, meeting Clio's eyes. "Are you absolutely sure you can get in there without getting caught?"

She nods sharply, her blonde hair bobbing with the movement. "I know I can, and Mom is going to help me."

Bastian laughs. "Your mom is already in on this rescue mission? It's barely after sunrise."

"She came to me first," Clio says matter-of-factly. "Just a few minutes before I came to find you guys. She told me that Nyomi was arrested and locked up. She said she would distract the king tonight so I can get her out."

I shake my head, amazed at my mother. The woman I have always known as sweet and even simple, has secrets and tricks up her sleeve that I never would have imagined. I think about Clio's plan, and I feel absolutely useless.

"What about me, sis? I just leave and wait for you to meet up?"

Clio shakes her head. "Don't you have a trial today?"

I scoff and throw my hands up. "I'm not going to go do some stupid task for the king while my mate rots in a damned cell!"

Bastian lays a heavy hand on my shoulder, stifling my anger as Clio speaks much quieter than myself. "Caz, you have to go to the trial. Just think for a minute instead of letting your tiny wolf brain take over. If you go and pretend like Ny's capture doesn't affect you, then you can tell the other initiates about tonight, without suspicion. That way Bast doesn't have to run around looking for them, and he can focus on planning our exit."

I grind my teeth together as I try to clearly think about this plan. It makes sense, and I hate everything about it. I sigh and nod, afraid that if I talk again I'll only yell at her.

Clio claps her hands around mine, her fingers unable to reach all the way around. "This will work, Caz. I know I'm just the little princess, but I see everything. I see the desperation in the king's eyes when he thinks about losing his throne. I see the love you have for Ny, and I see the possibility for a better future. We only need to play our parts for one more day… and then we can be free."

I look from Bastian to Clio and back again. Clio is right. We need to use our brains, and then when we join the Fae army, we can use force to end the king's reign.

CHAPTER 30

◂← →▸

Nyomi

I'm nine years old and Dad left me again. "It's just a supply run," he says... just like he said last time. It's not that I don't like staying with Bellona. She is a wonderful cook and the little bed in her attic is so comfortable and warm. Her home feels like my home when I'm here, but I hate being without Dad.

He only leaves me twice a year. Each time it's the same thing. I stay with Bellona for a few days and then Dad comes back looking refreshed and almost glowing, like magic surrounds him. I've never seen actual magic before, but I imagine it looks a lot like that. And every time, I ask him to tell me about his trip, but he doesn't give me any details.

"Nyomi, dear. Come play inside with Gordon. Staring at the trees isn't going to bring your father back any quicker."

I grumble under my breath and stomp toward the moss-covered house. Bellona stands in the doorway with her large hands on her rounded hips. Her violet eyes follow my movements and she grunts, disappointed in my attitude.

"Now, you stop that moping, child. Is it really so bad having to spend a few days with an old troll?"

I roll my eyes. "Bell, it's not about you. I don't like Dad leaving." I shrug and my head falls forward. "Every time he leaves, I'm afraid he won't be coming back."

Bellona lifts my skinny body into her arms and squeezes me tight, but not near as tight as she could. "Your father loves you with his whole heart. He will always come back to you."

I lay my head on her chest and sigh, choosing to trust that she's right. I don't know what I'd do without my dad.

I jump, my eyes flying open as a gasp leaves my lips. The movement makes me groan against the crick in my neck from sleeping on the hard stone floor. Living in a castle has spoiled me this past month. It's impossible to know how long I've been sleeping because the dungeons stay pitch black at all hours.

I squint against the dark and can only make out odd shadows in the corners of the square cell. The shadows feel like beings watching me, and I shiver at the thought. "Goddess, I need to get out of here."

I rub at my sore neck and think back to my hazy dream. Not every memory is as clear as the ones when Dad walked away from me to do his "supply runs". I hated not knowing where he was, or if I would ever see him again.

It was years of the same routine before we were taken by King Alix's men. Now, *that* memory is like a frozen image in my mind, more permanent than the others. Dad and I had been hunting, as far east as we could before hitting the sea. The animals that lived near the water were usually more active and easier to pin down.

I didn't have my sword with me then. Just a bow and some arrows on my back as I stalked the woods beside my father. He was a skilled hunter, and I tried to do everything exactly as he had.

I sidestepped a jagged boulder when my eyes saw the large buck on the hillside. I couldn't help my excitement and I gasped at the thought of having so much meat to fill my belly. The deer should have heard me, but its focus was entirely on something off to my left. Dad and I turned at the same time, but not fast enough to stop the knockout punches that the beefy guards threw at us.

I awoke hours later, my head foggy and my body stripped of any weapons. Just like now, I was surrounded by darkness and only the shadows to keep me company.

"Dad," I called out softly over and over again, but I got no response.

It was another bunch of hours before two large men with torches dragged my bloodied father into my cell and dropped him at my feet. The man with the shaved head and evil eyes laughed at the tears I cried for my broken father.

"Don't cry for him, tainted girl. Cry for your own fate."

That was all the man said to me before kicking me in my side and leaving me in a ball on the floor beside my unconscious father. It felt like a day at least before Dad awoke, and he was able to embrace me.

I cried in his arms. "What's going on, Dad? Are we going to die?"

"No, sweetheart. We'll both be back home in no time." His gray eyes focused on mine and I felt hope in his gaze.

"How do you know that? There's no way out of here."

Dad smiled sadly back at me. "You are a fighter, Nyomi. I know that you have a future out in this world. With my whole soul I know it."

I didn't mention the fact that he knew I had a future, but he didn't say the same for himself. I didn't get to say many more words to him at all before the guards came back and slit his throat.

After Dad was gone, it was just me, alone and vulnerable. The two guards took their time taunting me. They'd take turns slicing me with their claws so I'd bleed, or kicking me over and over until I passed out. Or they would leave me in the dark without food or water, just the thoughts of my father's death in my head, replaying on a loop.

I would never have made it out of their clutches if the bald guard hadn't decided to move me outside. The second my bare feet touched the soil and he turned his head, I ran with all of the strength I could muster.

Sitting here in this dark room now, the memories of my past cover me like a thick blanket of fear and pain. But the thoughts of Caz help bring a little light to the darkness.

I climb to my feet and slowly move around the cell. My legs are chilly from being thrown in here without any pants, or even underwear. All I have for a covering is this flimsy tunic. I find bars at one end of the room, but just slats of stone on the remaining three walls.

Locked in like an animal, with no escape.

Hours pass while I pace back and forth, and my breath catches in my throat when a glow appears down a dark stretch of hallway. I back all the way away from the bars, fear choking me as I imagine the ghosts of Zaros and his partner coming to inflict a new kind of pain.

My heart pounds and my legs begin to shake as the candle's glow moves closer to me.

"Nyomi?" Clio's voice is like a twinkling bell that echoes off of the low ceilings of the dungeon.

"Clio?" I blink through the fear that held me against the wall and I run back to the bars. Clio's blonde head pokes around a corner and her whole body sags when she spots me.

She quickly looks me up and down. "Are you okay? Have you been hurt?"

I shake my head. "No, I've been sleeping and pacing mostly. I haven't seen another person down here but you."

Clio nods and I can see the relief in her blue eyes. "Thank the Gods. My brother would have lost his mind if I brought you to him bruised and broken."

My heart hitches. "Is Caz okay? Is he here?" I look around her, but all I see is a dark tunnel.

"He and the others are waiting for us outside the wall. I came to get you by myself, though Caz's head nearly exploded at the idea."

Even after everything, I laugh at my sweet friend. "I can imagine."

Clio sets the lantern on the stone floor beside her and digs around in a hidden pocket at the front of her dress. She pulls out a large key like nothing I've ever seen before. She sticks the key in the rusted lock, turning it once, and the cell door creaks open.

I blow out a long breath and run into Clio's small arms. She hugs me tightly before pulling away and nodding. "Okay, we have to go, like now. The dummy guarding the door won't be out for long."

I follow Clio's footsteps in the dark tunnel, just the small lantern lighting our way. "How did you knock out a guard, Clio? You haven't shifted yet, have you?"

She giggles. "No. I used the same trick that they used on you in Caz's room. Sleeping powder. It's made by the mages, and can only be obtained by the king and queen of Unity. The big oaf on duty tonight thought he was getting a kiss from the princess, but he got a nap instead."

My jaw drops open as I stare at the back of Clio's head. "How in Unity did you learn to be so cunning?"

"Bastian and Caz have taught me a lot. I don't think they ever realized how much information I truly retained, but I'm really glad I sat through all of their lectures."

"Me too." Where would I be without Clio? I don't even want to think about it.

I follow her out of the tunnel and onto the dirt path outside. I pull in a delicious breath of fresh air and shiver against the cold that wraps around my bare legs. It seems to be well into the night and the nearly full moon glows above our heads. Clio side-steps a very large man who lay passed out against a rock beside the dungeon entrance and I hurry past him before he wakes up.

"Do you know where we're going," I ask her, wrapping my arms around myself to stay warm.

"You're going back inside." The masculine voice behind me causes Clio and I to jump.

The large guard who knocked me out with the sleeping powder, Dom, stands in the shadows of a tall evergreen tree. He steps closer to me with his sword drawn and his eyes panicked.

"Dom!" Clio whisper-shouts at him. "Go inside and forget we were here."

Dom's shoulders sag and he groans as he takes another step forward. He's young, incredibly dark skinned, with kind eyes. "Princess, this woman is a prisoner. You can't take her. Your father…"

Clio steps forward, in between me and Dom. "My father has destroyed this kingdom. I know you, Dom. We grew up together. You can't possibly believe that the king of Unity deserves your loyalty."

He runs a hand along his face and sheaths his long sword on his hip. His eyes dart around, and back toward the castle. "Fine."

He lets out a long frustrated breath before unhooking the leather belt around his waist that holds the sword. "Take this. It's the least I can do for drugging you." He tosses the heavy weapon at me and I catch it easily.

I look up, wide-eyed, at the young guard. "Thank you, Dom. I won't forget your kindness."

He nods once before looking back at Clio. "Stay safe, princess. Please. I'll tell no one of your escape." Clio nods back at him, and he takes off on a run toward the castle.

Clio turns to me as I buckle the sword around my dirty tunic. "It's about time we get away from this place, don't you think?"

I turn my head back to the castle that towers above the trees like a dark monster. "Yes, I really do."

CHAPTER 31

◂←→▸

Cazimir

I'm pacing. I can't stop moving back and forth across the cliff side, looking down at the valley below that leads into the kingdom of Fae. My ears and nose have been on high alert, hoping to hear Nyomi's light footsteps or smell her summer scent. My stomach could grumble with the hunger that I feel for that woman.

I tug at my hair for the thousandth time, wanting to rip the damn strands out. "I'm going back," I growl the words out.

Dryden steps in front of me before I can turn back into the woods between us and the king's land. "Woah, man. They'll be here, okay? Don't you have any faith in your sister?"

I throw my hands up. "Just because you broke a few of Echo's bones in the trial today, that doesn't mean you can stop *me*."

"Hey!" Echo shouts from where he stands near the cliff's edge.

Dryden doesn't flinch, so I groan. "What if they got caught, Dryden? What if my mom wasn't successful in her distraction? What if…"

Azra cuts me off, the only other person in our band of allies who seems as worried as myself. "Stop saying those things, cuz! I'm freaking out over here!"

"You're freaking out? Ny is *my* damn mate, Azra!" *Childish ass.*

Azra's eyes narrow as he steps toward me, his narrow nose nearly touching mine. "I don't give a shit that she's your mate! I love her too, you know? We all care about Nyomi."

If steam could come out of my nostrils, it would. I don't like hearing Azra claim that he loves Ny, but it's also no surprise. And honestly, I'm glad that she is loved. It's why we're all here…for her. Still, I want to kick his ass so bad.

I clench my fists and take a step back. "I know," I say, trying to calm myself down as I look around at the initiates and Bastian. The only ones I didn't recruit were the sirens. "I'm grateful that you are all here. I just… I want her back."

"Well, that's good to hear." Ny's lilting voice reaches my ears and I whip my head toward her where she steps through the trees.

I can't believe I didn't hear her coming, but I was too wrapped up in my temporary anger toward Azra. Everyone exhales at the same time and they rush to Nyomi and Clio, embracing them both. Bastian lifts my sister into his large arms and in one swift motion he kisses her lips like it's his lifeline. My eyes go wide and Ny laughs as she watches the kiss with happiness.

Nyomi's laughter floats to me in the night air and my heart feels lighter than ever as I stare at her. She meets my gaze and steps out of the group of happy voices.

"Did you miss me, Caz?" She stalks slowly toward me and I work very hard to stay put.

I know this woman now. I know every curve of her body and every noise she makes when I kiss her bare skin. I know the gray in her eyes, as if the almost crystal-like color is forever burned into my brain.

Ny stops a few inches in front of me, her eyes never leaving mine. "Aren't you going to kiss me?"

I close my eyes briefly and my voice is animalistic as I respond to her question. "Ny, we are surrounded by people that would not like to see what happens if I kiss you now."

Her lips lift into a perfect smile. She turns to the group that's still chattering along together about our next plans. "Hey guys, Cazimir and I will be right back."

A few of the men snicker and wink at us before returning to their conversation. Clio rolls her eyes and holds a hand up. "Just go kiss each other so we can get a move on. No details please."

I don't hesitate another second as I lift Ny into my arms and take off at a speed that I didn't even know I was capable of. Ny gasps, clinging onto my shirt for dear life until I stop at the spot on the cliff edge that I took her to after killing the prison guards. Ny opens her eyes and looks around at the spot before meeting my gaze again.

I tuck her messy hair behind one of her ears and stroke my fingers down the trail of dirt along her neck. "Are you okay, Ny? Did anyone... were you harmed?"

She presses her lips into a thin line as she shakes her head. "Nobody hurt me. I was left in a cell, completely alone with my stupid thoughts until Clio came." She looks down at her dirty shirt. "The dungeon isn't the cleanest of places, but luckily, I didn't have to stay long. I probably look like hell."

I continue to slide my fingers over her collarbone and between her breasts. My hands want to explore her everywhere, dirt or no dirt. I press my palm against Ny's stomach and reach for the buckle of the belt around her waist, tugging it so that she is pressed against me.

"I'm sorry," I say, needing her to know how horrible I feel for letting her get taken. "I should have fought harder. We could have run."

Her eyes narrow on me and one of her small hands dips into my tortured hair. "Don't, Caz. Don't be sorry. I let myself get taken so that we could be together again. If you fought them alone, we wouldn't have gotten here."

I nod. She's always right. "I have been in so much pain since you were taken from my bedroom. I can't survive without you, Ny."

Her hand in my hair tugs softly and she raises up on her toes. "You have me now, Caz. I'm yours..."

I cut her off with my lips, swallowing her words like a delicious wine. She moans against my mouth and opens her lips for me to press deeper, rougher. This kiss isn't tender like the ones in my bedroom. It's hard and desperate.

My wolf side roars at me, craving his mate like a drug. Ny practically crawls up the front of my body and I help her the rest of the way with my hands under her backside, hoisting her against me. Her arms tighten around my neck, making our kisses almost painful and intoxicating.

I step forward until Ny's back is against the smooth trunk of an aspen tree. She growls as her hips move against me and our lips separate momentarily. Ny's gray eyes are darker than normal as she looks into mine.

Her lips move to my ear and her voice is a warm, breathy whisper. "I'm not sure if you're aware of this, but I'm not wearing any underwear."

My entire body stiffens at her words and I move my hands to the bare skin of her thighs, stroking up to the naked curve of her pelvis. *Holy Unity, she's right.*

Ny looks into my eyes again and a small smile creeps across her face. "Well, what are you waiting for?"

A deep and feral growl leaves my throat and I'm a hundred percent sure it was the wolf that made the sound. What *am* I waiting for? Nyomi is mine, and I am hers.

Our lips crash together again, softer this time, but just as hungry. Our movements are fast as we take everything from one another, clinging to the other, sharing every breath, desperate and selfish. *And achingly perfect.*

Nyomi

Thankfully, Bastian had packed me a few changes of clothes while I was locked away. After returning back to the group with Caz, I was able to change into a clean pair of pants and a fresh tunic before we set off toward Fae.

It has been incredibly hard to make eye contact with anyone since losing myself in my mate on that cliffside. Most of these guys have heightened senses of hearing and smell. It doesn't take a genius to know what we had been up to.

Thankfully, it seems like the others don't care enough to comment, and I'm grateful for that. I feel like a naughty teenager in love for the first time, unable to keep her hands to herself, but it's not like it's that far off. The only difference is that this love is permanent.

Caz and I walk hand-in-hand for the majority of our hike to the Fae camp. The navigation falls on me and my gift to be able to find the faeries with my magic. They have moved since my last trip to the Fae camp, but finding them is just as easy as it was then.

"Is this the place," Echo asks, his heavy feet stomping around for any sign of the Fae.

"It should be. I can feel them here." I close my eyes and focus on the pull I have toward my aunt and Alston. "Queen Ensley? Alston? Are you here?"

The nine of us wait in silence, and a small sound has us turning to the right. A tall brunette faerie steps out of the blossoming trees that are beginning to shine in the light that comes just before sunrise. His green eyes scan our party and he smiles at each of us.

"Welcome, friends of Nyomi's. We were hoping you would come."

I step in front of the others and extend my hand to the faerie. "Hello. I hope it's alright that we're here. I'm Nyomi Mailo... Uh, Keene. Nyomi Keene."

"Yes, I know that, Nyomi. I am your uncle Oren Mason. I'm mated to Ensley." His smile crinkles the skin around his green eyes as he looks down at me.

"Oh," I say, surprised, and I bow my head to him. "Well, it's nice to meet you, King Oren, your highness. Is the queen here?"

He nods with a warm chuckle. *Was it because I bowed?* "Yes. Come with me." He looks back at the other initiates, Clio, and Bastian. "The rest of you may come as well."

I glance over at Caz's warm eyes and he takes my hand in his as we follow my uncle through the blossom trees. The forest opens up to a large clearing at the center. Canvas tents of all sizes are sitting in the circle, and the sound of early morning chatter floats around the camp. The air is light and inviting, giving me a sense of... peace. The sun is nearly risen now, though large clouds block the light and the scent of a distant rain fills my nose. Even in the gloomy morning, being here still feels so comforting.

Oren stops in front of a bigger tent at the center of the others. Before he can even step inside, my aunt pulls back the canvas door and grins widely at me. "Oh, my sweet Nyomi! I knew I felt your presence!"

The Fae queen wraps me in her arms, breaking my contact with Caz. I giggle in her hold and hug her back as Oren laughs beside us. He surprises me by grumbling something and joining in on our hug, squeezing the both of us in his long arms.

The three of us separate and Oren gives me an apologetic look. "I'm sorry if that was weird. Ensy and I have waited so long to get to know you. You're like a lost daughter to us both."

Ensy? That's so cute.

I shake my head. "No, of course not. I've grown accustomed to affection lately thanks to these two." I point to Caz and Clio who both smile back at me, looking more alike than ever.

My aunt looks at the prince and princess of Unity and she holds a hand out to each of them, which they shake. "It's nice to meet you both." She looks from Caz to me and back again, her eyebrows raising. "You two are mated?"

I blush and nod. "Uh... yes. This is Prince Cazimir Duras, and his sister, Princess Clio Duras."

Ensley's eyes widen as she stares between the two. "Oh, you're..."

Caz grimaces. "Yes, our father is Alix Duras."

Ensley's face twists in shock and anger, but Oren grabs her hand and she instantly calms down. "I'm sorry," she apologizes. "I have no love for your father. I guess I expected his children to align with him."

Clio shakes her head. "Technically, Alix is my father only. But I can assure you, your highness, we are *not* on his side in this war."

My aunt nods and she seems to calm down. "Well, I do want to hear more of *that* particular story, but my people are waking up for the day and we need to do introductions. I have talked of my beautiful niece so often, and I'm certain many of them don't believe she truly exists."

We all laugh, and I turn to the rest of the people in our group. "I'd like to introduce my friends." I point to the trolls first. "Faxon and Echo of Trog. Azra and Arnoux of Vampir. Dryden of Dracon, and Bastian of Lupos."

My aunt and uncle nod to each of them and everyone shakes hands. "You are all initiates in the Kingdom Trials," Ensley asks with curiosity.

Azra nods with the others. "Yeah, we're an interesting bunch."

"I'll say." Oren laughs and his eyes fall on Dryden.

I follow his gaze to the dragon prince, and I'm taken aback by Dryden's harsh scowl. "Are you okay, Dryden?"

He shakes his head and crosses his arms as he stares at Ensley. "Are you responsible for the fire at the castle? The fire that killed my sister."

I cover my mouth with my hand. I forgot about the fire that was blamed on the Fae. Juno had faerie magic scars on her body. It makes sense why he'd blame them.

My aunt tilts her head in confusion. "Your sister was the girl in the fire?" Dryden nods with his jaw clenched tight. Ensley lifts her head high and she calls out above the camp. "Lucas? Lucas Craven!"

It's silent for a long minute before a young man around my age runs up to us. His eyes go wide when he sees the crowd of us gathered before his king and queen.

The boy bows to Ensley before standing tall like a soldier with his hands behind his back. "Yes, madam? You called?"

She nods. "Lucas, you were scouting Unidad Castle the night that a fire started, correct?" He nods. "Will you please tell us what happened that night?"

Lucas looks shy as he scans our faces. "Um… well, I was cloaked, invisible. I was searching the perimeter, looking for weaknesses and ways into the castle. I had been able to enter the kitchen from an unlocked door when a woman's cry got my attention."

He pauses, lost in the memory. "I stayed along the shadows of the kitchen, worried my cloaking spell would fade. Then I saw this young woman enter. She was beautiful, but she was crying as an older mage woman followed her inside. The mage was using some sort of magic to keep the girl from moving. She said to the girl, 'what did you hear while you were eavesdropping?'. The girl said she heard nothing, but the mage didn't believe her."

Another pause as he looks around nervously. "Anyways, I figured the girl must've overheard something bad because the mage grabbed her around the throat. Then, the girl breathed out this breath of fire that lit the whole room up. I was stunned, and I jumped out to try and save her because the mage wasn't letting go, but the mage saw me and shoved me aside with her magic. She thanked me for showing up at just the right time, and I didn't understand what she meant at first."

"Why'd the mage thank you," I ask, my breathing heavy as I listen to his story.

Lucas' eyes are sad. "Well, she siphoned my magic and then used it to shock the girl. The shock killed the girl and left marks on her. Fae marks."

Dryden's voice is strained as he steps toward the boy. "A mage killed my sister?"

Lucas looks up at Dryden, shrinking under his fierce gaze. "I'm sorry. I couldn't stop her. I wasn't a match for the mage's magic. She left me sitting there, and then the fire got bad so I ran."

Dryden closes his eyes and I can see tears pool up at the base of his eyelashes. He shakes the sadness away before opening his eyes again and nodding to Lucas. "Thank you for trying to help her."

My aunt dismisses Lucas and she steps toward Dryden, laying a hand on his shoulder. "I am so sorry for your loss. My people aren't after the blood of innocents. We just want a better kingdom for everyone. I understand if you wish to not join us, but we would be grateful to have you."

Dryden watches Ensley for a moment. "I was wrong for blaming the Fae. It looks like the mages are just as corrupt as the king. I'll do whatever it takes to stop them all."

CHAPTER 32

◆←→◆

Nyomi

I feel like royalty, and I guess I sort of am. All of the Fae people have greeted me with so much kindness and joy, welcoming me and my allies to their fight. I've learned that the attack on the castle is supposed to happen in only a day, so our timing seems to be impeccable. The idea of storming Unidad Castle after making it my home for the past month is overwhelming.

Caz has remained by my side, keeping me grounded as we meet the army. It's not just an army, though. We've met families. Men and women with their children, camping out to prepare for a battle that should have happened seventeen years ago. I've caught glimpses of Alston as he has watched us from a distance, but he hasn't come to say hello to me. I can't blame him for being distant after I rejected him. I'm sure he can see the bond between Caz and I.

Just when I'm sure I've had enough stimulation for one day, a familiar voice stops me in my tracks. "Well, finally you kids made it to the party."

Caz and I both spin around to see Everaux grinning back at us. Seeing him now, knowing that he was my mother's brother, I feel like an idiot for not knowing we were related. My eyes match his perfectly, and our hair color is the same shade.

Caz and Everaux embrace before they both look at me expectantly. I fiddle with my fingers. "Uh... I'm not sure what to do in this situation."

Everaux chuckles. "Well, I'll start. Hello, Nyomi. I am your uncle, and I never knew you existed until about a week ago."

I scoff and rub my temple. "Is this really my life?"

Caz places a kiss on my cheek. "Yes, Ny. This is your life."

Everaux looks between Caz and I and his eyebrows raise high. "I see you two are done with all of the arguing? Seems like a drastic change from when we were studying in the library."

I blush. "Yeah, we found out that we're actually fated mates. Unexpected huh?"

He nods. "*Very* unexpected."

I shift from foot to foot. "So, why did you leave? Was it to join the faeries?"

He shakes his head. "Not at first. You see, I have a family. A mate and a daughter nearly your age. Your cousin I guess." He laughs softly. "Alix was threatening my family if I didn't steer you off course in your training."

My mouth drops open. "What an ass!"

"I agree with that statement," Everaux says. "I left in the night to go home to Lupos. I knew the Fae were hanging around, after the rumors, so I took my family and went looking for them. We arrived a week ago, and that's when Ensley told me about you and your parents. I knew then that you were my niece."

My mind spins as I try to take in the major changes in my life. I have two uncles, two aunts, and a cousin even? I thought I lost my family when Dad died, but I was so wrong. Caz wraps me in his arms and drags me away from the others, saying goodbye to Everaux for us both.

I look up into my mate's eyes and sigh. "Caz, who am I? I was an orphan only a month ago. I feel like my identity is at war with itself."

Caz strokes my cheek gently, his touch warm and comforting. "You are Nyomi." He kisses my cheek. "My mate, loved by so many." He kisses my nose. "You are a warrior, strong and fierce." His lips brush my forehead. "You are a niece and royalty in two kingdoms." He kisses the corner of my mouth. "You are a marvel, Ny, and the incredible thing is, you have the potential to be anything else you could ever want." His lips find mine, hot and slow.

Caz pulls away from me and I lay my head against his chest. The sounds from the camp float to us where we stand just outside the circle. I choose to believe he's right, that I am not done finding who I really am. If only I could see a future past this war.

◆←→◆

Nyomi

My aunt set us visitors up in four canvas tents. I don't know who had to give up their rooms, but nobody seemed to mind. Tomorrow, we are supposed to go to war. I'm grateful for a place to sleep other than that dark prison cell where I slept last. It seems wild to me that it was only a day ago that I laid in that dungeon, alone and scared.

Everything is happening so fast, and I've barely had time to process it all. I don't even have my sword to back me up in the fight that's coming. I feel wholly unprepared, even with Caz holding me tightly as he sleeps beside me.

I listen to the wind blowing around our tent, and soft voices float to me in the breeze. I guess I'm not the only one awake. I climb out of bed, careful not to wake my handsome snoring mate, and I venture barefoot out into the dark camp. A small campfire is lit a few tents down from mine, and I find Azra, Arnoux and Alston sitting together beside it.

Oh, goddess.

I walk up to the men and take a seat on a log beside them. "Hey guys. Shouldn't you all be sleeping?"

Azra grins at me with that sexy smile that once made me weak in the knees. "We could say the same about you, little warrior. Having bad dreams?"

I shake my head, trying to avoid Alston's warm gaze on me. "I haven't even been able to doze off long enough to dream."

Arnoux nods, but remains silent as usual. Alston stands beside him and lays a hand on his shoulder. "Would you both mind if I spoke to Nyomi alone?" I swear Alston's hand glows where he touches Arnoux, but it fades so fast that I second guess my eyes.

Azra stands and tugs his brother up with him. "We need sleep anyways, right bro?" He turns toward Alston. "Thanks for the chat, man. See you at the front lines."

Alston nods to the vampires and I wish them a goodnight before they scurry off toward their tent. Now it's only me and my rejected mate, sitting silently beside the flames.

Alston and I both try to speak at the same time, and then we apologize in synchronicity as well. I shake my head with a laugh and Alston makes a motion like he's zipping his lips up and throwing away the key.

His green eyes bore into me, reflecting the fire in them as I speak. "What were you guys talking about out here?"

He shrugs. "Just getting to know each other. They seem like really good guys."

I think about the glow I saw when he touched Arnoux. "With your healing magic, can you see emotional damage in a person, like you do with physical injuries?"

Alston shrugs, suddenly looking guilty. "Sometimes I can't, but when it runs deep enough to have a physical effect, like... causing someone to be mute for instance... then I can see it."

My mouth drops open. "I knew I saw your hand glow!" I lower my voice to a whisper but it still comes out like a shout. "Did you heal Arnoux?"

"I don't normally heal others without their permission, I just… the damage was clear inside him. I couldn't just leave it alone." He sounds sorry for what he has done.

"Alston, that's amazing of you to do something like that for a total stranger."

Alston's eyes light up at my praise and I instantly feel bad for putting that look on his face. That look of love.

I chew on my bottom lip. "Alston, listen…"

He holds a hand up to stop me. "Don't. I already know what you're going to say. It's why I wanted to speak with you alone. You've completed the mate bond with Prince Cazimir."

My cheeks have got to be redder than ever as he looks at me knowingly. "I'm so sorry, Alston. I don't know what to say other than that. You deserve the world, and I feel like I just keep disappointing you."

Alston shrugs and he sighs sadly. "I didn't want to talk to you so you could apologize for loving someone, Nyomi. I understand, okay? I know what that pull on your heart feels like. I felt it for you from the moment I saw you. *But*, what I wanted to say was that when you completed your bond, no details please." *Oh, gods.* "Since then, that pull toward you became tolerable. You made your choice, and you chose to love him. It was as if, in that moment, you also gave me the freedom to move on."

I look between him and I, at the glow in the air that connects us, and I can finally see it too. The glow isn't as strong as it was before I chose Caz. The bond isn't broken, but it is significantly less potent.

"So, you're going to be alright, then?"

He nods with a small smile. "I am going to be alright, Nyomi. I promise you that."

I sigh and feel like I can breathe deeply for the first time all night. This day has been taxing, though wonderfully so. Maybe my future can be happy.

Alston laughs softly. "You know, your aunt is crazy about you, Nyomi. She's so happy that you came here today."

I smile. "I'm glad too. I can't believe my dad just left his family and raised me without telling anyone, though. I understand why he did it, but I can't imagine it was easy."

Alston's chin jerks back as he watches me with an eyebrow raised. "Your dad didn't keep you a secret. Queen Ensley has known about you since you were a toddler."

For the second time in just a few minutes, my jaw drops. "What? How is that even possible? You guys have been in the human realm for almost my whole life."

Alston sits up straight, the fire light dancing on his sharp jaw. "Nyomi, didn't anyone tell you about the messages your dad sent through the portal twice a year?"

"They absolutely did not."

"Well, about every six months, a message came through the portal to Queen Ensley from Unity. I don't know how exactly he did it, but it couldn't have been easy. Your father would update the queen about the politics in the kingdoms, about the herbs he took to keep him looking more human, about the king's wall and his guards. He would also tell her about your life, and how you were growing up. I never got to see the messages, but the queen would tell us all stories about the happenings in Unity and her niece. She loved you even then."

Tears spring to my eyes as his words sink in. That's where Dad would disappear to? Not to have one-night-stands with random women. Not to go on supply runs. He was preparing the kingdom of Fae for this fight. He was sharing his pride for his daughter. My dad never stopped fighting for Unity, and there is no way in hell I'm going to let him down now.

CHAPTER 33

≪←→≫

Cazimir

The large gray castle towers over me as the only home I've ever known. I could draw the place from memory, including every crack and layer of moss from centuries of standing tall. Clio stands on my right, and Nyomi is pressed close to my left. I'm flanked by our small army, mixed with vampires, trolls, wolves, dragons and faeries, and those of us in between. Behind them is a large army of Fae warriors.

The Fae have been preparing for this day for nearly eighteen years. They have been cast out, stripped of their homes, and left to survive in a world that doesn't accept them. Now is their chance for vengeance, and my chance for bettering the future of Unity. So much rides on this moment.

"Mom is in there. Why'd we let her stay behind? It was stupid." I grumble to Clio.

She shrugs. "I tried to convince her to come with us, but she wanted to stay. She said she was needed on the inside, whatever that means."

Ny lays a hand on my arm. "She will be okay, Caz. I'm pretty sure she's smarter than all of us combined. She can handle herself."

I nod in agreement. Ahead of us, the fae king and queen return from scouting the castle grounds. Their faces are grim, but not hopeless.

Queen Ensley sighs. "So, my guess is that the mages gave Alix a little insight into the future. He has gathered nearly as many men as we have here. He's prepared for a big fight."

"All wolves?" I ask, my nose picking up the musky scent of wolf in the air.

She shrugs. "As far as I can tell, they are mostly wolves, but I did see some sirens and a few trolls. I don't know how many."

King Oren lays a hand on his mate's back. "We can handle them. They don't have the numbers or the magic that we have. Even if the castle is filled on the inside with fighters, they can't match us."

Everyone takes a tentative breath together. I look from face to face, knowing that this could be the end of any of them. "Well, let's take back our kingdom. I say we fight until the gods come back to smite us."

Ny smiles back at me, her gray eyes sparkling with excitement as she grips the borrowed sword on her hip. "I love you, Caz."

I lean into her and steal a searing kiss from her perfect lips. "I love you, Ny."

← →

Nyomi

"Fight well, Nyomi. Stop the mage. Her power can wipe them all out. Just get to the mage."

The voice from my dream two nights ago fills my head. I'm wide awake, but I still hear the gentle female tone. I look around, but everyone is staring forward at Ensley.

My aunt stands tall in front of her people, ever the adored queen. She raises both of her hands high in the air and blue lightning wraps around her skin. The magic lifts from her and swirls like a tornado above her head. It's a signal for the army to attack, and that's exactly what they do.

As one massive hoard of warriors, we all run toward the king's land, shouting and drawing weapons. Some Fae have the same blue lightning shooting from their fingers, while others fly forward, using the wind to launch them into the air. It's a rainbow of blues, purples and reds as each faerie has a unique gift of magic, and I almost stop running just to marvel at the sight.

We break through the treeline and the king's army circles the castle like a wide moat of wolves and shifters on two feet. I turn toward Caz and he nods once before leaping forward and shifting into his wolf form in the blink of an eye. The first sound of impact is like a shockwave all around. Swords, teeth and massive bodies slam together in a frenzy of battle.

Clio is small and swift, easily moving through the crowd without being touched while she slices whatever she can as she goes. A true born fighter. Behind her, Bastian's hulking wolf body protects her, tearing into the flesh of the wolves that dare come close to Clio.

Azra and Arnoux fight with long knives, cutting through the army with unmatched speed and precision, taking bites out of the enemy and paralyzing them. The massive Echo and Faxon ram into the crowd head-on, knocking a few of them out with one blow.

A screech above my head has me looking up at the red dragon that blows deadly flames onto the wolves closest to the castle walls. Dracon. He is fierce and swift as he slices through the air with his wide wings.

The Fae throw magic, shocking the enemy and burning them from the inside out. Some create shields around their people, helping to isolate some of the battles within the grounds. It's all complete and utter chaos.

I tear my eyes away from my warriors as a wolf charges toward me. Drawing my blade, I slice it through the air, nicking the wolf on his large snout. He howls at me before swiping a paw at my waist. I dodge the sharp claws and call upon my Fae magic. Blue lightning circles my wrists and stretches past my hands to fill the long blade with blue sparkling magic. I stare in awe at my own magic and the wolf growls at me.

"Come at me, wolfy," I say, excited to see what my magic blade can do.

The wolf obeys and lunges at my face. I swing the blade, cutting through the wolf's chest. The lightning grabs hold of his furry body and the wolf drops to the ground, writhing in pain and shaking from the shock.

"Holy, Unity," I gasp as I watch the dying body.

Shouts of battle surround me and I look up to see some of the wolves have joined our side, fighting against their own kind. I'm amazed at the sight. At the top of the castle stairs, a familiar face watches the battle below. The high mage, Mora. That voice of warning told me to find the mage and stop her. I don't know why I feel like I have to listen, but I do.

I push through the fight as I climb the steps. Most of the creatures fighting around me steer clear of my glowing blade as I pass. I can't find the turquoise eyes of my mate anywhere along the way, but I try not to think about it. *He's okay, Ny. He's strong. Stop the mage.*

I reach the top step and stop a few yards away from Mora. She smiles wickedly at me, confident and unfazed by the carnage surrounding us. "Hello, Nyomi. Welcome to the finale."

I shake my head, holding my sword high. "This isn't the finale. Unity still has a future, as long as Alix is killed."

Mora laughs harshly, her gray hair bobbing. "Oh, sweet thing. The king isn't going to die here. You and your entire army of outcasts will be the ones to burn."

I scoff and scrunch my nose up. "Okay, freak. Let's just fight."

She narrows her gaze on me and flashes sharp teeth I never knew she had. Her hands raise in front of her, and a blast of golden light shoots from her, knocking me back onto the stone ground. I climb back up, running toward her, but she throws her hands up and I slam into a hard invisible wall.

I jump up again, growling this time. I don't try to get close to her. Instead, I pull out the dagger hidden in my boot and I flick it at Mora. The blade slices just past her cheek, but the long strip of dripping red tells me that I cut her. The satisfaction is short lived, though. Mora roars and a hot air hits me from the breath she throws out. Rotten breath that makes me gag.

I hold strong, thankfully not landing on my ass this time, and I fight through the mini hurricane. I'm not far from the mage now, and I swing my blade at her. Bits of blue magic leave the tip of the blade and touch her chest, but she only jolts once and flashes her teeth, angrier now.

I shout over the sounds of battle from behind me. "Why are the mages doing this, Mora? Do you all truly believe that Alix is worthy of the throne? Do you think so little of Unity?"

She growls. "Not all of the mages are on my side. My sisters don't see the potential for our kind. This kingdom should not be ruled by children who cry and let their people walk all over them. It needs power, true power."

I scoff. "Seriously? You think Alix has that power? He's a coward and a cheater."

Mora smiles wickedly again, her teeth glistening against the sun. "Little tainted girl. You know nothing. Alix isn't the power, I am. He is my puppet. I should have ruled this kingdom, but my kind are not welcomed on the throne. Trials after trials, we watch and grant our wishes, but never are appreciated. With that king, though, I can finally show Unity what it needs."

I stand frozen. "You want to rule Unity by controlling its king? What about speaking up? What about finding a ruler that will listen to your needs? Is that so impossible?"

Mora grimaces. "Oh, but dear, where is the fun in that?"

I take a step back as the mage begins to grow, her shoulders becoming broad and her teeth stretching past her bottom lip. I swing my sword, again and again, missing each time as she fades in and out of focus, in and out of existence before my eyes.

I move to swing my blade as hard as I can, raising my arms high above my head, and I realize my mistake as soon as a knife materializes in Mora's hand. She thrusts forward, aiming the sharp blade at my chest, but my vision of the knife is blocked by a mess of black hair.

The cracking sound of steel against bone pierces my ears, but it's not my bone. I stare wide-eyed at Alston's back as blood pools from the hole at the center of him. My sword is still in the air above my head, and I drop it behind me.

"Alston!" I shout and move around to his front.

Mora stares at him, her dark eyes wide and unblinking, and it's then that I notice the long sword sticking out of her neck, Alston's sword. I spin toward the Fae healer and he is staring down at his chest where the mage's knife sits, impaled deep into him.

Alston blinks at me. The dead Mora drops to his feet and he stumbles backward, clutching the hilt of the mage's knife. "Nyomi, I'm sorry. Don't be mad at me."

I reach for Alston, grabbing his shoulders as he slowly sits down on the stone steps. I follow after him and brush the hair back from his face. "No, Alston. Don't be sorry. I could never be mad at you."

He tries to smile up at me, but his eyes look pained and he grimaces instead. "I lied to you, though. I... I said I could... move on from you." He chokes on the pain gripping him as he speaks.

"That was a lie?" My voice cracks as a small sob escapes my lips.

Alston makes a shrugging motion and then grunts. "I could never... love someone else." His eyes stare into mine. "This is... better. Now I d... don't have to try to live without you."

I shake my head. "It's not better, Alston. I don't want to lose you."

"I love you," he says softly, and he doesn't say another word, just stares at me as he lets out a long and final breath. Tears drip from my cheeks, mixing with the blood on Alston's shirt. I look up as feet approach me, and I find Caz's hooded gaze staring down at me.

My body begins to shake, the connection with Alston snaps like a cord pulled too tightly, and a growl rumbles from my throat. I drop onto all fours as claws rip from my fingers, and fur sprouts along my forearms. My head snaps back to Caz who stares wide-eyed at my sudden transformation.

A woman materializes from the air beside Caz, her hair bright white, blending into the white robe handing off of her. Caz doesn't seem to notice her beside him, but I stare into her black eyes. She kneels on the ground in front of me while I struggle to fight the change coming over me.

"Nyomi, let the shift happen. You have done well, and your wolf side is ready for this world." Her voice is melodic, and I instantly recognize it as the female voice that has guided me over the past few days.

"Why are you helping me? You're a mage… just like her." I look over at Mora's dead body.

The woman in front of me smiles and shakes her head. "Mora isn't like the rest of us. We saw your future, Nyomi. And we accept it."

I taste blood in my mouth as my own fangs lengthen and dig into my tongue. I try to keep my eyes on the mage woman but she disappears. I meet Caz's gaze again as he bends down and speaks soothing words to me, telling me that it will all be okay. Every part of me cracks and rips until I am no longer myself. Until I am the wolf.

CHAPTER 34

Cazimir

"Ny! Nyomi, can you hear me?" I look into her blackened eyes but it's as if she doesn't see me through them.

I never thought that her connection with Alston was the thing keeping her wolf side back, but it's clear now that it was. I should be jumping for joy that Ny is finally all mine, but a piece of her heart broke with Alston's death, and my heart felt the pain.

I run my hands through Ny's black fur, soft and warm. She almost purs against my touch and recognition comes back to her eyes. "Ny? Hey, it's okay. I'm here with you."

Ny's wolf eyes blink a few times and then she searches my face before jutting her long tongue out and licking my face. I almost laugh, but the day has been too much for laughter. I press my forehead to Ny's and I breathe in her familiar scent.

"We need to go to the throne room, Ny. We need to find Alix."

She stares for a second before her large head bobs up and down like a nod. I nod back to her and jump to my feet. "Follow me. You might as well stay in that form. It could help you."

Nyomi and I run through the halls of my home. Her claws clink against the tile floors as she keeps an easy pace by my side. The castle is silent, as if it were any other day, not the day that war was brought to our doorstep. Ny and I round the sharp corner that turns into large double doors. The throne room.

I push the doors open and see him. Alix is sitting in his throne that was made special for him. The tall wooden back towers above his head, carved into a wolf's head that looks down on any who wish to have an audience with the king. Beside Alix, my mother sits in her usual place, but she is bound by something that slithers along her arms. *Tentacles?*

"Welcome, son. I'm glad you made it through all of that mess outside." He looks unfazed by my appearance, but I can see the small tick of his jaw as he speaks.

"I'm not your son, Alix. Get off the throne and fight me."

He raises an eyebrow and holds a hand to his chest as if my words hurt him. "Really? After I raised you for twenty years, trained you to be a warrior, taught you how to be just like me. Now you're suddenly not my son?" Beside me, Ny growls low and menacing with every word Alix speaks. He looks down at her. "And who is this? A new friend?"

"It's my mate, Alix. Don't you remember the girl you locked away in your dungeons?"

His eyes actually widen as he takes another look at Ny. He wasn't expecting her to be able to shift, which means we have the upper hand. "My mage told me Nyomi didn't have the shifting ability. I guess she was wrong."

I stand taller. "She's also dead, on your doorstep."

Alix's eyes become flames as he shoots up from his seat. "That's impossible!"

I shake my head. "Apparently it's not. The high mage is dead. Now release my mother and fight me. Your reign is over."

He takes a step down, but only one. "I don't feel much like fighting. Why don't you put on a show for me, just like the trials. I have a very skilled opponent."

Alix whistles and the sound echoes off of the high ceiling. The tentacles holding my mother in place begin to unwrap and Nyx steps around her throne. "Hey, Cazimir. Long time no see."

I growl at the siren. "What in the gods' names are you doing here, Nyx?"

She glares at me. "You left Iris and I behind. Where else were we supposed to be?"

"Would you really have come with us? We couldn't trust you." I look around the large room. "Where is she? Hiding so she can attack us from behind?"

Nyx's face falls and I can see worry etched in her eyes. "She was taken from me. All I have to do to get her back is kill you and your mate."

I look from Nyx to Alix. "You're holding Iris hostage? Just so you can get someone else to fight your battles? You damned coward!"

Alix flinches at my words, but he remains standing with his head held high. "Just kill the bastard, Nyx. Then you'll get your cousin back."

Nyx looks back to me, her eyes narrowing again as she stalks forward. Nyomi growls in response to her movements, and Nyx flicks a long tentacle at her. Ny yelps when the appendage whips her in the snout, but it doesn't stop Ny from lunging at the siren. I place my trust in Nyomi to hold her own against Nyx, and I run for Alix. His eyes go wide momentarily before he flashes fangs at me and dodges my attack.

Alix spins around, his claws grabbing onto the back of my leg, but I ignore the pain and dripping blood. I leap onto his chest and throw my fist into his face repeatedly. His whole body shifts beneath me until he is in wolf form and I'm sitting on his back. I jump off of him and he gnashes his teeth, reaching for my neck.

"I don't want to kill you, Alix."

He doesn't respond to my words, he only lunges at me again and again, making me dodge each attempt. His large body flies past me and I extend my claws to dig them into his back as he passes. Alix howls against the pain and his black eyes flick back to me, angry and ferocious.

His bones crack and shift as he becomes human-like again, fully dressed, just like he taught me. "Give up, Cazimir. I taught you everything you know. You cannot beat me."

I glance over at Nyomi and Nyx going head to head, evenly matched. My eyes turn back to Alix. "You may have taught me skill, but you know nothing about bravery or honor. You are a scared man, afraid of losing your throne, and afraid of becoming nothing."

He laughs. "You think I'm afraid? You know who was afraid of me, Cazimir? Carro was afraid when I hunted him down and slit his throat." My blood boils as he speaks. "You know who else was afraid, son? That faerie-lover, Rhae. She cried out when my men held her down while I stabbed her through the heart."

Nyomi and Nyx both stop fighting as Ny's howl pierces the room. Nyx doesn't make a move toward Ny, and it's clear why when I see the blue lightning sparking off the ends of her black fur. She is Fae and wolf in one, the ultimate weapon.

Alix's eyes stretch wide as Nyomi stalks toward him. "Kill her, siren! Now!"

Nyx just watches on, not willing to touch Ny. She shakes her head. "You know what, your highness? I think I'd like to see what happens when you're faced with fear."

Ny inches across the marble floor, each step cracking with electricity as she stares into Alix's eyes. Alix shouts again. "Nyx! You will never see Iris again if you don't kill the girl!"

Nyx scoffs and crosses her arms. "And how will you keep her from me once you're burning from the inside out? I think I'll take my chances."

I keep my eyes on Nyomi, her eyes focused and each of her slow steps slow and teasing as she moves. She is a beast, a marvel, and absolutely incredible. Alix is backed into his throne, his hands trembling with fear as he watches Ny approach his feet.

"You'll regret this, Nyomi. It's treason to kill your king."

Ny's lip lifts in a snarl. Her body flexes as she prepares to pounce onto Alix, but my mother steps between them, her back to Nyomi. "You're not her damn king, Alix."

She holds Nyomi's lost sword above Alix's body, and she plunges it deep into his heart with a single thrust. Alix coughs and gasps as he stares up at his queen for a long moment. And then the room goes silent.

Nyomi

The Gathering Grounds are packed, citizens from the six kingdoms all blended together in crowds of chatter and laughter. My new hearing can pick up individual conversations among the gathered groups. Some faeries and trolls joke together about their homes, teasing the others in a light manner. A young vampire girl and a dragon boy flirt as they chase one another around the grounds, their giggles like tinkling bells.

I stand above the rest, my long royal-blue dress flowing well past my feet, resting against the dirt. A few of the visiting royals pass me, shaking my hand or bowing low with grateful smiles. I give each of them the same courtesy, though my heart pounds from all of the attention, the admiration.

I try to keep a smile on my face, but my nerves are running wild. It was only months ago that I was hunting bunnies for my first meal in a week. Only months ago when I was alone, unnoticed, an orphan, a fugitive. Now, wide eyes of various colors look upon me as if I am a goddess to behold. If only they could see the little girl that hides deep within me.

I begin twiddling my fingers together and chewing on my bottom lip, but warm arms wrap around my waist from behind. Every part of me melts into him, my mate, my king. His lips kiss the sensitive spot just below my ear as he whispers to me.

"Stop chewing on that lip, Ny. You have me for that."

A true grin stretches my lips. "Don't give me any ideas, Caz. I'm supposed to be representing Unity, not ravishing my mate in the shadows."

I turn to Caz, taking in his bright turquoise eyes that glow brighter against the black suit that hugs his body. His hair is too perfectly brushed to the side, and I can't resist reaching up to ruffle the strands a bit. His smile is intoxicating as he searches my face the way I do his.

"I love you so damn much, Nyomi." His hands squeeze my waist, comforting and warm. "Don't be nervous about all of the eyes on you. They're not mocking or judging. The people of Unity chose you as their queen for a reason. They love you, and they believe in your kind heart, just as I do."

I sigh and nod, a bright light filling the dark hole that I keep wanting to sink into within myself. "You're right. But they chose you too, as I choose you every day. I couldn't stand here like this without you by my side, you know?"

He shrugs. "I think you could, but I'm grateful I get to have the honor." He smiles, broad and perfectly happy.

"Okay, you two. We're all waiting for some words from the King and Queen of Unity. Are you just going to stare at each other all night?"

Caz and I both look over at Clio's teasing smile, hand-in-hand with her mate, Bastian. Behind them, the large crowd is silent as they stare up at the two of us. *Oh, holy Unity.*

A blush stains my cheeks and I'm met with smiles and snickers from each of the kingdoms. "I'm so sorry, I didn't realize."

Caz laughs, a sound like warm, dark chocolate. "Thank you all for coming! I'm sure you can't blame me for being distracted by your queen." He glances over at me, his eyes roaming my body.

A few more laughs and whispers fill the entertained crowd. I have to tear my gaze from Caz once more to address our people. "Okay, okay. We are all here today for one singular purpose. We are a kingdom. Yes, our lands are separated by borders. Our individual talents and abilities make each of us unique and different. But, whether you are a wolf, a vampire, a troll, a siren, a dragon, or a faerie." I look out at each of them. "You are all a part of one kingdom, our kingdom, Unity."

A few people shout their agreements into the night air. Caz smiles out at them, but his face takes on a seriousness. "One month ago, the reign of Alix Duras ended." He flicks his eyes to Clio, but she only smiles softly back at him. "Alix never deserved his title as King of Unity. He was selfish and cruel. There was a woman who should have been our queen twenty years ago, Rhae Wolfe. Rhae was a wolf shifter who fell in love with a faerie, Theon Keene. This was a mate bond, one that could not be broken. And the laws made it so that Rhae and Theon had to run." He looks over at me, his eyes loving. "But their love produced the woman standing beside me. A woman that we once called 'tainted' or 'mixed'. A woman whose power far outshines any that I have ever seen, your queen."

Crowd members cheer and clap their hands together, a show of acceptance for everything that I am, everything that my blood is made of. Caz continues after the cheers die down. "So, tonight is a celebration. Nyomi and I wish to thank each of you for choosing us to rule this kingdom. The laws that once separated mates of all kinds are no more, for as long as we shall reign. Now, dance, eat, and celebrate together!"

Cheers echo on the high pavilions above us, and Clio runs to wrap me and Caz in hugs. "I love you guys."

"We love you too, Clio. None of this would be possible without you two." I look between her and Bastian.

Bastian leans down to kiss his mate sweetly on the lips and Caz makes a gagging noise beside me, ever the high ruler of an entire kingdom.

Bast punches Caz in the arm. "Hey! I can't help that I love your little sister. Get used to it."

I laugh at the two of them as they wander into the crowd of chattering people. Azra and Arnoux run up to us, their smiles wide on their handsome faces. Azra hugs me first, holding me tight and close to his chest. Caz clears his throat beside us, and Azra drops me back to my feet.

"Sorry, cuz. I figure it's the last time I'll get to hug the little warrior before you go off and start having little pups." Azra winks at me.

Caz glares at him teasingly and throws an arm around the vampire. "We're family, Azra. I expect we'll still see plenty of one another, especially when you start ruling Vampir."

Azra shrugs. "Yeah, we'll see."

Arnoux hugs me next, much gentler and less touchy-feely. "Congratulations, your highness," he says in my ear, and I can't help but jump at the sound.

"Gods, Arnoux. Everytime you speak, I feel like a stranger is sneaking up behind me."

He laughs, the sound very much like his brother's warm chuckle. "Sorry, Nyomi. Shall I go back to silence?"

I grab his arm and shake my head wildly. "Absolutely not! Alston didn't heal you for nothing, and when I see you so happy, I feel like he's still here with us."

Caz grabs my hand, squeezing me for comfort. "He is, Ny. You're here because of him. That makes him everyone's hero."

I think back to the moment Alston died in my arms, telling me he loved me with his last breath, but I don't cry. I smile at his memory, and I think of the marble statue of him that is in the works on the front steps of Unidad Castle.

The vamps return to the dance floor, taking a couple siren women into their arms for a slow dance. The music floating through the air is inviting, but another familiar face keeps me from dragging Caz out there.

Dryden and his mother stop in front of Caz and I, bowing at the waist. "Amazing speech, your highnesses," Dryden says with a grin.

"Thanks, Dryden," I say. "You don't need to bow to us, though. None of you do."

Dryden's mother steps toward me, but pauses. "Is it alright if I hug you, Queen Nyomi?"

"Of course!" I wrap my arms around her neck and she squeezes me back tightly.

Her eyes are wet when she steps back and dips her head to Caz. "Thank you, both of you, for finding out the truth about my Juno. And for avenging her."

Caz nods. "Don't thank us, madam. Dryden did everything he could to make sure the truth was found. The high mage is gone, and the rest of the mages have been nothing but sorry for not stopping her sooner. They send their love to your family."

She nods with a soft smile, and Dryden hugs both of us. "I'm excited to see Unity in twenty years with you two on the throne. Let me know if you ever need another guard on the grounds."

With that, the two of them disappear back into the throng of dancers. Caz turns to me and takes my hands in his. "Will you dance with me, my queen?"

I smile back at him with a nod. "Do you really have to ask, *my* king?"

He drags me behind him until we reach the center of the dance floor. The music lowers to a slow and sensual rhythm as Caz pulls me against his body, his hands dropping to rest on the small of my back.

I move against my mate, heat filling the space between us, not that there's much space to fill. I look around us at the other dancers, a mix of races and species blending as one under the same stars. My aunt Ensley and uncle Oren dance close together, both of them smiling when our eyes meet. Beside them, Everaux and his beautiful wife whisper words of love to one another.

Everything feels right at this very moment. For the first time in my life, a flare of pure hope spreads inside my chest, but even more than that. It's a surety that the future of Unity is a great one. I look back up into Caz's eyes, and I dip my fingers into the hair on the back of his neck.

I breathe in his scent, the smell of home. "So, about those pups we need to run off and make together. How do you feel about that, King Cazimir?"

His lips curl up into a wicked smile. "I can't tell you my thoughts on that with so many ears listening in. It wouldn't be… appropriate."

I shake my head at him while we move as one to the music. "Will you tell me later, then?"

He thinks for a moment before lowering his lips to mine, but not yet touching my skin. His words whisper against my waiting lips. "I'd rather show you if that's alright."

My wolf side growls softly at his words. "Yes please."

Caz closes the small distance, his mouth covering mine in a slow kiss that matches the rhythm of the music. I savor the taste of my mate, and my heart leaps at the idea of our future as King and Queen of Unity.

THE END

Review This Book

It means so much to me that you bought my book! Writing is such a passion of mine and I look forward to your feedback.

So, if you liked this book, whether it be the characters, settings or adventures, I'd like to ask you a small favor. Hop on over to Amazon and leave a review with your thoughts. It'd be so great to read what YOU have to say!

From your friend, Abigail Grant

Other Books by This Author

Exclusive Freebies:

A Vision in Thessaly: The Intended Series Prequel

Shifter Cure: Hidden Cure Series Prequel

A Trial of Vengeance: The Kingdom Trials Prequel

Complete Series:

The Intended Series

The Rescued Series

Hidden Cure Series

The Kingdom Trials Series

Printed in Great Britain
by Amazon